After being turned down by eight different establishments, Charlotte realized they were never going to hire a woman, so she'd have to be a man...

It was well after dinner time. Charlotte hadn't had a decent meal since dinner the previous day. She felt faint, and it was difficult to stay in the conversation. She couldn't help staring at the table. Sugar and salt were not unusual, but to have a cloth on the table was reserved for special times and those times did not usually include the young girls at the orphanage.

"Son? Son, what do I call you?"

Charlotte looked into his face blankly. Growls emanated from her belly and seemingly echoed like a canon.

"Have you eaten? Would you like a bite to eat?"

Charlotte nodded, her spirits perking up at the prospects of nourishment. The man excused himself and stepped into the next room. When he came back, a woman followed him and began preparing food.

"My wife, Emmaline, will get you fixed up. It's probably hard to answer a lot of pesky questions when you are hungry."

Charlotte jumped on the plate of food like a lynx on a brook trout.

"Whoa, slow down there, boy. Don't you want to take your gloves off and wash up?"

Curbing her hunger was the only thing in her mind, and she didn't realize that she was sporting Bartholomew's leather gloves.

Considering her dainty hands, she shook her head to removing the gloves.

After Charlotte ate her fill, the room stopped spinning, and she was able to think better.

"You should tell me your name. It will be a lot friendlier than calling you 'boy.'"

To this, she slowed her chewing and swallowed. A cool sip of water rinsed her mouth before she said, "Livery. Charles John Livery is my name, sir."

Through three generations in Colonial America, the women of the LeSage family show a rare strength and courage. Anne, a wild spirit, plots treason against the Crown, constructs secret passageways, and leads an adulterous life.

After her husband, Anne's son John, is killed, Emma turns to prostitution and drugs, abandoning her daughter, Charlotte, to an orphanage near Concord, New Hampshire.

Charlotte grows up in the orphanage where she is raped by the hired hand. She runs away from danger and becomes Charles, pretending to be a man so that she can find work and safety. She falls in love with her workmate, Jack, who is also in love with Charles but cannot admit it. Jack hopes to save himself by marrying Elizabeth, Charlotte's long-lost best friend. As Charles becomes mentally unhinged, only one person knows all of the pieces of the puzzle and how to untangle the deceit, laying bare the truth that can rescue Charlotte, reunite the best friends, and let love be unfettered.

KUDOS for *Broken Rider*

In *Broken Rider* by K K Willey, Charlotte LeSage is abandoned by her mother after her father dies. She grows up in an orphanage. When she is repeatedly raped at age thirteen by the hired hand, she flees to safety in Concord, the nearest town, where she pretends to be a male, Charles, in order to get a job and survive. But living as a man is not easy, and Charles faces many challenges, including falling in love with her work mate, Jack. Jack, who see her as his best friend, has no clue she is a woman, and his physical attraction to Charles terrifies him to the point that he decides to marry a woman he doesn't love just to prove he is a "normal" man. With excellent character development and well-researched facts, the book has a refreshing ring of truth. For historical romance fans, this one is a must. ~ *Taylor Jones, The Review Team of Taylor Jones & Regan Murphy*

Broken Rider by K K Willey is the story of three women in Colonial America. Anne marries John LeSage, a sea captain, and travels with him by ship to the new world where she becomes an influential part of the New England community. Anne raises three boys, and the story continues with her oldest son, John Junior. John marries Emma, and they have a young daughter, Charlotte. Emma is a good wife and mother, but when John dies in an accident, she is left destitute and turns to prostitution to support herself and her daughter. But realizing that it is no life for a child and that it could be dangerous as well, she takes Charlotte to an orphanage. When Charlotte is thirteen, she is raped by the hired hand and has a baby. The sisters at the orphanage take the baby away and give her up for adoption. Charlotte is again raped by the same hired hand, and she decides she will never be safe as long as she remains at the orphanage. So she leaves her best friend, Elizabeth, and flees to Concord, where she tried to find work. No one wants to hire a young girl, so when Charlotte is mistaken for a boy, due to her short hair—a standard for girls at the orphanage—she goes with the flow, changes her name to Charles, and gets a job as an assistant driver for a dry goods merchant. Things go well for her for eight years, and she excels at her job, until she makes the mistake of falling in love with her coworker, Jack. Then her best friend from the orphanage, Elizabeth comes to Concord to teach, and Charles fears she will be unmasked. *Broken Rider* is well written, well researched, and is told with an authentic voice, that takes you back in time to when women had almost no say over their own lives and it was truly a man's world. A story of courage, love, self-sacrifice, and determination to survive no matter what, this is one historical romance fans should love. ~ *Regan Murphy, The Review Team of Taylor Jones & Regan Murphy*

ACKNOWLEDGMENTS

Katelyn, Mikayla, and Shane are my source of strength and happiness. Thank you for your talents and love (and for pushing me to complete a project).

And to my oldest and dearest friend, Shelly, who accompanied me on countless grand adventures in the forested and rock intrused wilds of our imaginations, where goodness always prevailed and hot stew and a clean table awaited our return.

Broken Rider

K K Willey

A Black Opal Books Publication

Part 1

Chapter 1

The storm tossed the fluyt deftly as if in punishment for its deeds. The captain's new wife, Anne, held tightly to the bedding in agony, rearing up only briefly to vomit into a chamber pot that she clutched to the berth for fear of losing it. Sudden lurching of the ship from the turbulent swells had all unsecured items rolling about the floor and shelves. The noise of the items and the storm was unnerving, but Anne only noticed the din if her grip loosened on the putrid smelling pot—the unsavory thought of being covered in the vomitus made her heave again.

The anger of the sea seemingly lasted a lifetime. The men above deck struggled with the rigging and held tight to the ropes. It was a dangerous trip in which a less skilled crew might have washed overboard and perished. This stolid crew worked as one and guided the small vessel with only brief lapses in duty from each sailor's nausea.

Safely restrained inside the ship, Anne's energy was entirely spent from the taxing voyage, and, finally, she managed to fall asleep. The fluyt rocked less violently several hours into the lass's slumber, as the ship had traversed the worst of the storm. Anne dreamed peaceful dreams of her home in England, her sisters and brothers and other relations that she knew she would never see again unless they elected to make the journey to the New World. Anne had the mind of an independent woman of nineteen years and was not prone to sentimental concerns. She lived in a time that afforded one's mind to think and ponder about such philosophy, but the age also yielded the reality of much death from disease, poverty, and malnutrition. A child grew up with death as a part of life: elders died, parents and children died. It was not anticipated, but it was expected. Still, Anne dreamed of happy times, soothing and optimistic visions of what her life might hold.

The fluyt was now gently rocking on its voyage, and Anne was beginning to awake. She heard the creaking of the timbers and an occasional thump from above deck as the sailors tended the rigging and had time to start on repairs. Anne felt a cool and pleasant draft across her face. She was too groggy to open her eyes and wished to return to the peaceful, sound sleep of the dead she had been summoned from. Her body felt paralyzed as she sensed the tangible world. Her thoughts tried to skulk back into that peaceful, dark other world, and she would gladly relax her thoughts and abide with a defiant laugh if the Angel of Death beckoned her soul.

It was a strange position our minds could put us in to allow our bodies to heal. The air that entered the quarters was damp and cold but gently encouraged Anne's sluggish mind into a more cognizant state. Moist and salty.

Tangible but gentle was the sea air as it brushed across Anne's face, bringing her an awareness of her existence and the simple senses of touch and smell. The salubrious air had banished most of the stale stench from the small cabin. It followed that Anne was at peace and light in her heart.

Captain LeSage entered his quarters. He had worked long shifts at the helm to keep the fluyt on course. Anne smelled his pungent, masculine odor as he entered, and she wished to rouse herself from her groggy state and greet her husband. She watched as he removed the heavy, oil-coated rain coat that reeked of fish oil and the warm woolen sea overcoat that most sailors wore. John removed his shirt and poured himself a bit of port wine. Anne watched his bearded face as he drank. Even in the flickering lantern light, she noticed his tired eyes and the dark, weathered skin on his cheeks. The hair on his chest was pressed and compacted against his skin from his perspiration. This rugged look of the sea sent chills of excitement through her veins and took her breath away. She loved him and had no regrets about leaving with him to make a life together in the Colonies. As she woke, she noticed light coming in from the deck besides from the lantern John had brought with him. Anne was disoriented as to whether it was early morning or late afternoon. Her mind was mainly blank, as if aroused from an induced sleep. She would lay subservient to Death as easily as she would for pleasing her husband.

John set his empty glass on the rimmed and balanced table, removed his boots and trousers, blew out his lantern, and crawled into bed with his lovely wife. His fatigue was great, and he settled into the bunk as easily as a corpse into the grave. Anne was now fully aware of her surroundings and greeted him by lazily running her hands up his bare legs and caressing his bottom. His skin was cold from being on deck, so Anne cozied closer. John moaned, a tired but happy sigh, as she fondled him gently and tenderly.

With effort, he turned over to face her. He did not wish to seem ungrateful, for his wife was a sacred gift given to him by the Supreme Deity—he felt the matrimonial prize he had earned could as easily be taken from him at the least sign of insolent behavior on his part. He reached toward her delicate face and moved her long, dark hair aside in a caring gesture. "You are well?"

"I am well. You are worn unto fatigue."

"*Oui, hors de combat*. You have worked nearly as hard as I—and done so all abed!"

"*Oui*, my love, but I am strong, and I shall work just a bit more." Anne's seasickness had subsided, and she was happy to see John. He was a middle-aged man of thirty-one, but very strong and virulent. He thought his young wife a delicacy even when he was so fatigued. Her willingness for him boosted his energy to the savage male model, but John, innately gentle, made love to Anne with mild clemency, making sure of her pleasure along with his own.

Chapter 2

John's fluyt made port three weeks later at Hampton in the Chesapeake Bay, where they were to unload cargo and go north to Tappahannock. His ship had made many journeys to Virginia, and he had spent much time in her ports. He particularly liked the port and the people around Mishipeshu. After a few days at Tappahannock, the crew went south again, toward Jamestown and Mishipeshu. John showed Anne the port and introduced her to the people he knew. Most of the people spoke English, which was a relief to Anne since her French was minimal, at best, and she knew nothing of Dutch or Spanish.

John purchased a medium-sized brick home in the Mishipeshu area. Original settlers began with hovels of wood, taking several seasons to plant, reap, and transpose the wooden-framed homes to brick or stone. "This should be fine to start with, Anne, but we can commission for additional rooms to be built, as well as a servant house."

"John, this is a huge house already!" Anne rubbed her slightly bulging middle, their first child growing within.

"We shall be blessed with many children, Anne, of

this I am sure. My brothers, Georges and René, wish to return with me on my next voyage. They will be in your service, and until then, Stéphane Timothé of the crew has voiced his desire to stay with you as a servant. He is old for staying aboard ship. His wife is here, too, and she will be grateful to keep him ashore. She will cook and clean for you."

෨෧෨

Anne and John were content for all their years with the homestead. Cows were milked, vegetables planted and children were raised. The family made due with what they had, be it a year of bounty or a year of slim return. Anne was happy and had no regrets about the transatlantic move. She dearly missed John while he was at sea, however, and tried not to worry about his safety. Their reunions were treasured. John would stay in port for extended stays during less temperate times when the Atlantic was rough or politics made it dangerous. He would take shorter journeys to the Caribbean and West Indies, where the climate was balmy, and trade was abundant. John missed Anne, too, and enjoyed seeing his children, who seemed nearly grown each time he returned.

Ten years galloped by in the blink of an eye. Anne bore her first two children within the first two years—strong, healthy babies who seemed to withstand all ailments and harsh weather. Anne tended the house and servants with the finesse of an older woman. She appreciated the help of Martha, the wife of Stéphane Timothé. He succumbed to pneumonia after about thirteen months of being landed, which was a sad event, but Martha was happy to have had him home even for such a short time. Her grief was directed at caring for

Anne and the two young baby boys, John, Jr. and Jo-ëlle, which seemed to work well for all.

John's brothers proved to be useful for several years in the brick home. Georges was a tall, quiet man who was devout to the church. He always tried to improve himself in a humble Puritan way, striving for perfection of himself and chastising his inadequacies. René had a more rogue demeanor. He worked hard at what he did and could get any chore completed sooner than seemingly possible, which enabled him to relax and "play" for the rest of the day. René had a lot of energy and a strong animal magnetism.

At half past three in the afternoon, René had completed his day's work and was on the prowl. Sometimes he would go into the local tavern and drink. Sometimes he would spend some time with John's sons, but this wasn't usually the case. Small children were women's work. René, like most men of the time, did not wish to be bothered by children until they grew to the age when their schooling should be taken over by the men folk, at about ten years of age. Like John, and probably all LeSage men, René had a distinct desire to fill—women and sex. Anne knew this to be true of any man, but with the brother of her husband, she felt it was a sin not surpassed by any other. René was good looking, strong, and had allure. He was hard to say no to.

One afternoon, the house was quiet, and Anne worked on needlepoint by the fire. It was a cold spring day, reminiscent of late winter. Standing water outside began to freeze over, and most residents took the livestock into the barns. René approached Anne in the great room by the warm hearth.

"René, are you done with your tasks for the day?"

"Yes." René came close to Anne and touched her soft cheek that was warmly lit by the flickering fire.

She ignored his advances. "Have you seen the new puppet show the Mayberry's have?" she asked.

"I am not interested in puppets, Anne."

She continued sewing. René touched her chin and rubbed his hand down her neck. Anne closed her eyes and took a deep sigh. She was five months pregnant with John's third child and tired, but very much aroused by René's pass. She didn't consider the sanctity of René's wish. A larger consideration for Anne was that of physical endurance in this time of immense fatigue. Mentally, Anne was ready to abandon the day and lose herself in hedonistic pleasure. She smiled to herself.

René knew Anne would consent. Wheedling his way to his desires was a natural gift. Patience mixed with his charming demeanor enabled him to achieve anything he set his mind to. Besides, being his brother's wife made her his property, too—at least it enabled him to enjoy the betrothed family benefits.

She looked up into René's dark eyes, and he took her hand to lead her to the bedroom. She stood and put the sewing in her seat then turned to face the paragon of masculinity. He took her in his arms as they kissed. The woman was lifted with ease, and he kissed her passionately as he made his way to the master's room. Anne ran her fingers through his long hair and held his face to hers as she returned his primal advance with as much zest as her aggressor.

They entered the bedroom, and René set Anne slowly and gently onto the bed. He slithered under her skirts. His warmth invited her and stirred her blood into a froth. Anne helped to remove garments, but her lust, in full form and raging savagely, made her clumsy and dizzy. She lay still, allowing René to continue. As he disrobed her, he slowed to match her befuddled mood and then paused, marveling at her protruding abdomen.

He caressed it softly. "Is he kicking you?"

"Of course. If you put your face right here, you shall feel him, or her."

"You have two boys already, do you think this is a girl?"

"I think it is God's secret. These are joys that He keeps from us for a short time, but they are just hijinks of His. All families are happy with a new baby and do not care if it is a girl or a boy."

"Do you hope for one or the other?"

"I do not care. I will love this child like I do my boys. It is John's baby, and I will do my best, with God's blessing, to have it born a healthy child." The thought of John made Anne lust for him, so she tended René's needs with fervor.

When René was sated, Anne asked him, "Do you not have a woman of your own? Will you not marry soon?"

"There is no one I particularly fancy. The maidens in town are rather common, and I do not care for the daughters of most of the shop keepers. I shall remain alone for a time, I am afraid."

"Perhaps you should consider something else."

"What do you mean, Anne?"

"Perhaps another town would suit you. Something more exciting, new people."

"I have thought of moving to the western frontier of Virginia. My skills are varied, I would do well in a young community. I have learned some Algonquin. I think I would do fine with the different tribes on the frontier. Most of the Indians are peaceful, anyway. Do you worry for me?"

"Of course, I would worry for your safety, but I think you would do handsomely on the frontier, as well. Where do you think you will go? What will you do?"

René ran his hand up Anne's leg and halted to stroke her hips. "Would you miss me?"

Anne grabbed René's head and brought it to her face. She kissed him and placed her hands on him gently.

"You would miss me," he stated.

Anne pushed away from him and smiled seductively. "I want you to be happy, like John is."

She thought good thoughts of all people and was subservient to happiness and peace. She truly loved René as she did John—as a replacement for John, because his absence ran for the better part of each year. Her loyalty to her husband was paramount to any other relationship: John ubiquitously occupied her every thought. When René eventually opted to take his leave to find his own way, Anne would wish him Godspeed and great success.

Chapter 3

The ground crunched in the shaded parts of the path. Sunshine bathed most of the landscape, though it was still early in the morning. Agriculture, livestock and leveled forests had had a positive effect on the settled areas near Mishipeshu for any cold blooded creature. The defaced natural aspect allowed much more direct light, which warmed the earth to its vibrant, jolly spring glow earlier in the day than in years past.

Anne stepped carefully as she wound her way through town, in hopes of preserving some dignity for her boots that endured a perennial crust of mud, and also because haste could lead to careless capsizing, resulting in harm to her or her unborn baby.

She marched toward her destination with a healthy smile and greeted everyone she met with equal respect, whether the person was a lady, businessman, or slave. She was a happy and content individual, had much luxury, and was part of a dedicated group of women that aided and assisted each other with true, sisterly fellowship. Her careful stride was quick through the streets.

"Good morrow, sister!" Anne said.

Her friend Margot Ellen emerged from a side

street, a little winded from trying to catch up to Anne. Margot Ellen's face beamed with the warm smile she was known for. "And good day to you, dear friend! We can enjoy the stroll at a leisurely stride, no need to hurry."

Margot Ellen was close to Anne's age, but plump and suffers pain in her joints. She was as sweet as could be and well respected by the other women. Anne slowed her gait and enjoyed walking with Margot Ellen.

The women ambled through the small settlement together and, little by little, Margot Ellen's breath slowed to a normal rate. She began to make small talk but was interrupted by the pounding of feet nearing them from behind.

"Hello, Mother! Hello, Goody Smithy!" was gaily shouted to them as John, Jr. zipped by the women. Comments were stifled quickly as another small sprite, in pursuit of the first, echoed the same greetings mid-flight.

This time Anne shouted, "Joëlle! John! Where are your manners?" But was is too late. Lickety-split, the brothers ducked down another street at full speed. "Oh, those boys of mine! Only God knows the mischief they may be up to!"

"Boys will be boys! Anne, I am so happy to see you well! Your time will be here soon. So exciting!"

"Well, Margot Ellen, I think you are putting the cart before the horse…"

Margot Ellen's cheeks were rosy as her perky excitement rendered physically as well as emotionally.

"I know, I know. Several months to go, but it is such a lovely thing to look forward to! A new little babe! Look yonder, Beth Ramsey is just stepping out. I can't wait to show her these new stitches I've embroidered."

"Margot Ellen! How devilish you are!"

"I am not. I just think Beth Ramsey should be aware that others have just as much talent as she. She gloats so!"

"Perhaps, but we all know that you are just as able as she with stitchery. Come, now, let's be pleasant. Good morning, Beth, how are the twins?"

"Ornery as the rooster when he knows he is headed to the chopping block. Bucky went to milk them today and nearly lost an eye. It may be time for meat come Sunday supper. I told my husband no good would come of a two-headed goat, and we should have slaughtered it when it was young and tender. The problem, of course, is that the servants won't eat it because they are sure it is an omen from the devil."

"Ask them why they think the devil would send that goat as a calling card," Anne said evenly without provocation. "I think Lucifer would have more productive tasks than trifling with a goat."

All three ladies laughed at the absurdity as they entered the yard of their friend, Abigail Trenton.

The servants John provided allowed Anne a certain place in society. Like so many girls growing up in England, Anne was not educated formally. She did not come from affluence, but she was not ignorant. Many of the household's chores were tended to by her staff, granting Anne time to follow her own pursuits and to spend time with elite wives of the village. Women would congregate to spin thread, sew, or just chat amongst themselves for pleasure. Anne absorbed their behaviors and means, assimilating and integrating into their ranks.

As political iniquities grew in the early 1760s,

wives' conversations grew increasingly international. Women became divided, as distinct and dangerous lines were drawn between Loyalists, Tories, and Patriots. Most of the women were married to men who partici-pated in the local government and were proud of their community and trade. Over the next fifteen years, friendships would grow and be lost as citizens sided for and against the Crown.

Chapter 4

The Pig Beast Inn was an anomaly of architectural wonder. There was a great room and dining room that formed the heart of the goliath structure. Staircases mirrored each other on opposite sides of the house and led either to the family's rooms or the lodging rooms. A large fireplace speared the center of the great room with its rock hearth and heated the entire structure adequately.

The building was unlike any in Virginia, and built rather like a fortress rather than a home or place of business. The outside was rock with a distinctly Gothic flavor, arched and pointed windows elevate toward a turret-like roof. Not only did the grand fireplace serve for warmth and cooking, but it was a cleverly crafted flying buttress supporting a high ceiling and the adjoining walls to the two separate second floor wings. The inn's castle-like structure ended at these qualities. It was as if the builder forgot to finish a medieval masterpiece after the stone was set. It did not contain monsters, gargoyles, or carved animals. In fact, it was devoid of decoration entirely, ornate or plain. Since the roof was rather flat, it did have sloped drain holes but was without pipes or ornate chutes of any kind.

Martha always watched the boys back at the brick house and kept domestic matters under control while Anne trekked the familiar path to meet with the local group of women at her neighbor's home. The hostess was always her dear friend, Abigail Trenton. The Trenton's lived in the back part of the Pig Beast Inn—the heart and soul of the Mishipeshu area. The Trenton family's generosity to the community, and particular knack for running a business, made them financially strong and well respected.

Anne entered the Pig Beast Inn and the maid, Sally Betty, led her to the room where the other women had congregated. Anne had heard the women's raised voices since crossing the threshold. She listened carefully to catch up to what the deep and heated argument pertained to.

"...*yes*, but Beulah, most villagers do not *have* cash to spend."

"Nora is right, Beulah, how could anyone possibly purchase...well, *anything* needed?"

"Cash flow. Umm...You are perfectly right, ladies. The Colonies are going to continue to struggle because of that! Nora, you hit the nail on the head. So, what to do about it—"

"Anne, we were just tossing ideas around about how we could make the center of town more distinct. Here is a cup of tea for you," Margot Ellen attempted delicately.

"Fine, thank you. What do you mean by 'distinct,' Margot Ellen?"

"Anne, a town needs to be known," Beth Ramsey chimed in loudly with an air of the experienced, finer, and more cultured circles.

Abigail sat next to Anne as the others discussed the topic.

"How do you feel, Anne?" she whispered.

"Wonderful, Abigail, but I am still not sure what the group is discussing. I can bet, however, that since Beth Ramsey seems keen to promote the conversation..."

"That it is a trifle and unnecessary?" Abigail finished Anne's thought, and the two laughed privately. "Yes, but I think Beulah is concocting something over by the hearth. She got pretty excited about what Nora pointed out and then backed away."

Beulah Kebob-Flynn, of the well-known staunch family of Kebob-Flynns in Pynrighthfordshire on Gabalrith Fen in the North Country of England, was a slender, handsome woman, revered for being the epitome of matronly honor but could be downright pushy at times. She always seemed to come straight to the point of an issue and sum it up succinctly in three or four words after someone had spent an hour attempting to convey the same thought in a lengthy speech. She was jovial and well accepted in the community and a strong leader of the womenfolk.

After a time the heated and passionate discussion Anne entered upon cooled. The women had sewn and socialized amicably for several hours when it was time to return to their own homes. Abigail, Anne, and Beulah lingered after the others left. Abigail saw that Anne was tired. True to her trade of making guests comfortable, Abigail sought light and entertaining chat that would be pleasing to Anne. "So, the girls' names are Odette Océan and Rachael Anne, and boys are Sean and...what was the other name you said?"

"Oh, I don't know. I can't seem to remember anything. Samuel, I think. Maybe it was Abraham. I am so glad to fellowship with the ladies, even if it does make me tired. Being in the family way is such a blessing."

"It's a lot of hard work, Anne, don't fool yourself. While the wee lads sap most of your energy, the one on the way takes the balance. Martha helps you, and it allows you to keep your wits," Beulah retorted, candidly and accurately summing up pregnancy.

"Aye, if not for Martha, I would probably run through the wood in idiocy and be shot through the heart by a native. I should conserve my strength in the evenings and go to bed."

"Poppycock! Or, as my husband would say, *baliverne*! You are strong as an ox, and we need you more than ever."

"I do what I can. What else need be done? Will we need the captain to bring anything new on the list?"

"The servants are good commodity, especially with their skills. Manufactured materials are the biggest need since they are not created *en masse* in the Colonies. When is his ship due next, Anne?"

"Another three months. I hope he can dock until the baby is born. Georges and René have been working diligently on the project, but I'm afraid René is anxious and will leave us soon to pursue another adventure."

"Has he been courting a lass? He is so handsome, I am surprised that Beth Ramsey hasn't sunk her claws into him for her daughter."

"Abigail, her daughter is spoken for already and too young for René, anyway."

Beulah shook her head. "Too young or not, that brother-in-law of yours has spirit and drive. He is only a wee bit older than yourself." Silence filled the room and Beulah continued. "I'm surprised he is still here."

"He is needed on our farm, Beulah, he will not shirk responsibility." Anne blushed as she supported René's character. She knew what Beulah said was true—he was wild, young, and craved excitement. As

Anne thought of René, she tried to hold a stony expression so as to not betray the secrets she held with him. As she thought of his strong hands and gentle nature he showed with her, her face glazed over into a stare. She thought of being in her warm bed and being tended by him…

"Anne! Where is your mind?" Abigail shouted at her. "Beulah said she would like to walk you home. Are you agreeable with that?"

Anne jolted to her senses and agreed that company on the journey would be appreciated. The two ladies bid *adieu* to Abigail and began the walk through the wet streets.

"Anne, I would like to take a look at the work the boys have done in your cellar."

Arriving at the LeSage property, Anne and Beulah walked to the out building in the north of the lot. They entered the root cellar and found Georges still working, bringing up buckets of earth.

"Georges, it is time to rest and clean up! You work long, hard hours. René quit hours ago, I am sure."

"Aye, that he did, Anne, he did. Good afternoon, Mrs. Kebob-Flynn. I believe we have pushed through another two hundred feet in the past few days."

"My, my, Georges! At this rate, you could be in Massachusetts by Easter!"

Georges blushed and remained silent. Anne and Beulah walked through the tunnel to see how deep the hole had become. "Not only is it deep, but you could drive a team of oxen through it! Will the soil hold safely, Georges?"

"It should. I will reinforce it with timbers like they do in the mines, just for added safety."

Anne and Beulah left the cellar and walked to the main house.

"You do well in his absence, Anne," Beulah said.

Anne's mind was still on Georges.

"The captain, Anne," Beulah continued. "He is away so much of the year. I know you pine for him."

"I miss him dearly, Beulah, it seems an age since he was last here. I love him so much, I ache for him."

"No one doubts it, Anne. You are tired and should go inside and rest to collect your scruples. Let Martha take care of you so that you stay strong."

René greeted the ladies at the door. He gnawed a piece of dried venison and had a handful of nuts. "You examined the cellar, Anne? It is coming along fine." He was excited about the work he and his brother toiled at. "The earth is peculiarly soft down below, not a hard crust like what is tilled. We shall have ample space to stow roots and vegetables, salted meats, and nuts come winter."

"Aye, René, but as you speak of these delights, a pang in your stomach will lead you to another evening meal! You shall eat us out of house and home!" Anne teased.

He smiled, leaned down to kiss Anne on the cheek, reached for his tricorn hat, and walked out of the house, happily munching as he went.

Beulah had concern in her voice as she said, "Anne, people talk of René…and you."

"I'm sure they do. Tongues will wag whether the topic is virtuous or not." Anne kept from looking into Beulah's eyes. "René is the captain's brother, we are very close." She took no offense at Beulah's insinuation but did not wish to reveal anything from her expression, which was a sly smile. Anne's heart did not belong to René. She considered René leaving to pursue his dreams, and knew it was for the best. *I still have Georges and the other servants. Besides, René won't stray so far that he cannot return for visits,* she thought.

"I will show you the developments of the farm to-morrow, if it pleases you, Beulah. It is early for tilling, so the ground is still fallow from winter, but René and Georges have marked out the fields. I think we shall have diverse crops this year."

"I will come by first thing on the morrow, then."

"That will be splendid. Martha will have a small tea for when we return to the house, too. It will be an enjoyable time together."

Chapter 5

Beulah left the LeSage home until the next morning. When she walked up to the brick house on her return, Anne was sitting in the yard in a warm, sunny spot, listening to the sounds of the new day. Birds chirped and flitted about, gleaning tasty bugs, yard birds strutted around hunting the last, elusive seeds spread out at daybreak. Squirrels scurried up the few trees in the yard, chasing one another across branches and over the roof to other tree tops. Anne's baby kicked harder today, giving her peace that it was healthy. Beulah perched in the seat next to Anne for a while, and they chatted lightly before rising to walk the property.

Beulah assisted Anne to her feet.

"I am fine, Beulah. No worries yet."

"Wouldn't like for you to capsize!"

"Oh, don't bring up the sea, please!"

The door to the root cellar opened and spewed two urchins with very dirty faces. Joëlle froze in his tracks upon sighting the ladies. Big brother, Johnny, grabbed his arm and began pulling him away from the porch of the brick house. Anne rolled her eyes and ignored the two.

"A bit of nausea is healthy, Anne. This one will be as strong as your boys."

They strolled up to the brick outbuilding and looked across the land. To their left was the large Berkeley plantation, and to the right was Shirley and Daniel Plinthe's farm. Everyone, regardless of trade, planted vegetables and tobacco on the land. All farms were self-sufficient for survival, and tobacco really was money one harvested. The Crown limited many developments in the Colonies, such as large scale manufacturing, but encouraged tobacco crops. Tobacco required a lot of processing from planting to harvest, so many families had indentured servants or slaves. Hiring workers would not prove cost effective and, besides that, workers were not readily available to hire anyway. Captain LeSage's enterprise of bringing a motley crew to the colonies was sanctioned by the Crown and a sound investment for his estate.

Anne had spent her first few years away from England with ample hands to organize their new home. The LeSage family did not have the large plantation that the Berkeley's had, but the LeSage family goals were different. Captain LeSage sailed and traded goods. He did not traffic human lives, *per se*, but he did assist fellow countrymen and relatives when they desired to make a new start, contracted by a strong handshake. Passage brought these people to the Colonies and guaranteed a strong work force for the LeSage farm.

Anne was proud of her husband. John, Sr. was a humanitarian at heart, and he would deliver new servants to his wife every couple of years. Some would seek him out in hopes of passage on his ship, and others he stumbled upon on the wharf, down on their luck but with a beautiful story to tell of the greatness that would befall them with a new start. Once these travelers ar-

rived at the LeSage home, they began offering their
skills to the family. Skills brought home were that of
weavers, farmers, farriers, coopers, tailors, cobblers,
domestic staff, and blacksmiths.

Anne and Beulah walked across the acreage in the
serene morning air. A footpath across the land was an-
cient, and even though the soil had been plowed for
many years, it remained visible. Animals had trod the
path for generations and had no intention of changing
their ways because a silly farmer deemed a certain area
for crops. Georges had decided to accommodate the
animal highway after having his crops trampled in the
first season of planting. He often wondered if that was
why the original owners left. If they were too stubborn
and would not compromise their field layout, then they
were surely frustrated from tracks cut though the crop.
This made him laugh to himself to think that some people could not understand simple animal ways.

The path was fairly direct across the field toward
the Plinthe's, and then it veered north again and skewed
toward the Trentons' land and the Pig Beast Inn. The
path on the LeSage land had four stone markers along
it. Each was about three foot across by three feet in
width and nearly five feet in height. On the top of the
stone was a decorative pointed cap. The six sides of the
cap curved downward from the point.

"This looks as though it was brought straight to the
colonies from England or Scotland. And, is that glass at
the base of the crown?"

"Yes, Beulah, the top rests on a glass base. The
markers where here when we arrived. We can only
guess why they were put here. Georges thinks they reinforce the animal path."

"The design looks more akin to the Pig Beast Inn
than to your brick house."

"They are older than our home, too. Abigail thinks they were designed by the builder of the inn, and that owner used our land and the Plinthe's, too. The architect of the inn was indeed brilliant at his job. Abigail said there are many Gothic nuances and secrets in the design of the inn."

"Intriguing. But glass? A dear commodity to bring to the Colonies for bird houses."

Anne laughed. "Georges thinks the builder loved animals. That's why he marked the path. The markers show above snow level, even in the heaviest season. A hunter wouldn't need to stray far from home, nor would he lose his way back. The glass is a mystery. Maybe it is simply decorative."

"And yet, for an animal lover—to enjoy or eat— there are no animal statues incorporated into the design of the building, such as fawns, rabbits, or gargoyles, for that fact."

"True." Anne considered the architecture and agreed with Beulah's statement. "I don't know much about buildings, but I like the markers. Somehow they make me think of history here in Mishipeshu, even if we haven't been here for centuries like our families in England."

Beulah's mind was focused on greater things than pondering architecture. "By the way Georges is making progress, our task shall be able to forge ahead earlier than planned. The war between Briton and France will be over within months, by the way the men talk and from information from the Continent. We will be ready to set the plan afoot. Unrest in the area—indeed, the whole of the Colonies from above Philadelphia to below the Virginia settlements—is aching to bust out."

"You are an amazing woman, Beulah. How do you know such things?"

"I am older than you, Anne. My husband, Armand Hercule Flynn, is a gentleman farmer, and he has his thumb on the developments of the Colonies. Our relatives in Europe hear the other side of events and make us privy to the political temperatures. It is a game much like chess—each side makes their moves for advancement. The player who plans well ahead is usually the victor."

Chapter 6

Summer greeted the villagers with warmth through the day and banished freezing temperatures. Anne gave birth to a healthy baby girl and named her Odette Océan, after John's maternal aunt in Brest. John had made it to port later than expected because of bad weather at sea from *La guerre de la Conquête*. It placed his time with Anne at a better time for the birth of their daughter and helped Anne heal physically and emotionally. John spent most of each day with Anne and the new baby and afforded much time with their two, rambunctious sons. The time passed quickly and, soon, Captain John was at sea again, heading toward Europe.

Life was difficult for people to earn a living and raise their families. Oppression pressed its heel down on the less fortunate and got a foothold that boosted it, and empowered it, to just above the many that eked out their living.

John LeSage, Sr., knew of the struggles his own family had as he grew up in Brest, and it was his determination and hard work that allowed him to break from shipbuilding and turn to navigation. John was of a new generation. He, and like-minded individuals, were determined to improve life from that of toiling at hard labor without much gain. John was highly intelligent and had had elaborate dreams of what life could be if you gambled on the right facets of it. Family traditions were important, but, to John, there were many more exciting traditions to begin rather than to be steeped in the established ways.

John cared little for the cutting of timbers and assembling them into sailing vessels as his father did and his grandfather had done before him. John liked to use his mind, imagining new places and things to see and working out the math in a kind of map that could take him there. As a small boy, John would dream of voyaging to faraway places and learning new ways. As he grew, his father understood that this son was not made for ship *building*, but for ship *sailing*. John was encouraged by his father to learn about sailing and the seas. He studied lessons and apprenticed with master sailors available to him because of the family's connections.

John learned much more than sailing a ship from the captains and crews he worked with. He learned how to barter in the ports he visited and turned a pretty penny with the know-how. His shrewd and cunning skills helped him amass enough wealth to purchase the small fluyt that he sailed.

One October, ten years into his marriage, John returned home with gifts for his family and brought with him a man named Pierre Rideau. Pierre was trained as a blacksmith in France by his father and uncles. He was an adventurous young man of twenty-two years who desired to see more of the world rather than settle for the family business. John understood the penchant Pierre had for adventure and offered Pierre passage to Virginia in return for indentured servitude of five years at his home.

This was an honorable gamble, but a gamble just

the same. Restless men on an adventure could bolt once the ship docked, to pursue another path, leaving their debt behind, never to be seen again. John was a good judge of character and had only a few passengers welch on the accords struck. He could only take them at their word, but the passage provided much time to get to know the travelers.

On the voyage, a formal contract was drawn and signed by each person involved. Personalities that did not seem honest were soon flushed out by the crew. Rough weather had strength for getting all parties to sign. The captain would insure the reticent client be stowed below decks, preferably in the rankest, most cramped location. Heaving would cease long enough for the stricken to hold the quill and sign their "X," making all documents valid and ready for disembarking at the new port.

Pierre Rideau thought the price a bargain. He had heard the stories of Virginia from sailors and wished mightily to witness the natives and their heathen ways. He also wished to support the Colonists and thought that the King of England needed a good pummeling for his restrictions on production of goods in the New World. Pierre was a brilliant artisan and craftsman and was fervent in his opinions, but he was honest. He signed the agreement willingly and had the chance to ride out queasy times in the fresh air.

The fluyt unloaded cargo at the pier at Mishipeshu. The crew enjoyed a hearty meal at Turtle Tavern, just off of the *embarcadero*. Captain John sat with his first mate, Paul; the wharf and shipping master, Solomon Vos; and Pierre.

"We had a mighty gale here about a week and a half ago. It was all we could do to keep the moorings in place. The missus was sure she was going to wash out to sea, what with all the driving rain and the surf licking at the homes along the water's edge. Must have been hell for ships asea."

"No, we had smooth waters crossing." John took another swig of ale after crunching a couple more pecans from his plate. "That storm must have come down from a nor'easter."

"Aye," agreed Paul. "Wrong time of year to be of trouble to our ship."

"Well, it nearly blew Mishipeshu five and a half feet south. Had it lasted another day, you would have had to dock at Sint Maarten to deliver our shipment!"

The men were jolly and laughed at Solomon's joke. Paul ordered another ale as he mopped his plate with a bit of bread. "You know, John, if we could work things just right with the trade winds, we could pick up several hogs of rum in Trinidad before we are blown into Mishipeshu. We might even land a week before we sail, by the way Vos tells it."

Roars of laughter filled the tavern and, when John had composed himself and wiped the tears of laughter from his face, he leaned over to Pierre and translated, "*Vos dit leur dernière tempête assez forte pour passer* Mishipeshu *sud de pieds cinq ans et demi. Paul a dit, nous devons utiliser la force des alizés, afin que les terres de notre bateau à la Trinité, nous prenons.*"

Pierre laughed at the story, and Solomon asked John if Pierre knew any English. "He has studied much on the crossing, and the crew helped him daily. He has a long way to go, though."

"Yes, I...understand a little," Pierre ventured. "...but I will not be the words craftsman. Not yet."

The men laughed again and patted Pierre on the back with encouragement for his attempt.

John, Paul, and Pierre left the tavern to sail the

fluyt up the St. James, closer to the LeSage home. They landed late in the night and unloaded cargo to the root cellar quietly. Pierre opted to stay aboard with the crew until morning. John quietly entered the house and prepared for bed.

He was tired but happy to be back with his family. He slipped into bed next to Anne as she slept. He watched her for some time before he felt his hands were warm enough to gently stroke her soft face without startling her. Anne had worked extra hard that day. She and Martha were still cleaning up the house from the "storm that moved Mishipeshu," and they knew John's ship was due any day. Martha's age was slowing her down, so Anne tried to help as much as she could with heavy chores.

John caressed her face. He reached under the covers and rubbed his hand across her abdomen and her hips. She did not stir. John was tired and heavy from the meal and ale he had at the tavern and resolved to just snuggle in and go to sleep.

"*Deuet mat.*"

"Anne, are you awake?"

"*Deuet mat.*" She reached up to John's face, stroking his thick beard with her small hand. "Welcome." The words Anne spoke were not uttered skillfully.

"Ah, you have learned some Breton from Georges?"

"That is the extent of it, John. I am afraid I do not make a good pupil for language. I am so happy you are home!" Anne, awake now, held his face between both of her hands as she kissed him. He held her tightly and kissed her passionately.

"It is an old language that separates people for silly reasons. Work on your French if you have much time to spare for study."

Chapter 7

Pierre worked in servitude for the LeSage family, and he proved to be a wonderful asset for them. His English improved daily as he worked around the farm. John, Jr. and his brother, Joëlle, shadowed Pierre. Pierre was only a few years older than John, Jr. but was already a master at the forge. He taught the boys how to heat the fire and what to look for when selecting a rod of iron, how to hit it properly from the fire on the anvil and how to form certain shapes for normal repairs about a farm. Pierre taught them practical farrier techniques, and the boys taught him English and how to act like a savage young boy. Pierre's life had been a lot of work from a young age, which forced him to grow up fast and cast away puerile behavior. Johnny and Joëlle were spirited and a little impish when together. Their rearing was more conducive to having fun.

One morning, Pierre stoked his fire up to the proper temperature and laid irons to begin heating. He reached for his large tongs which he held the hot metal with, but they were not on the peg. Looking around the shop with no success led him out the door—the boys had taken the tongs, he was sure. He stepped outside and saw his tongs suspended in the air on a rope in the tree. Angry that the boys had played with his tools, he reached up for the tongs while on tip toe but still needed to jump a little to reach them. He grabbed the tongs and landed on his feet. The tension against the rope pulled over a bucket that had been balanced up in the branches. A cascading ballistic of fish entrails poured over Pierre's head.

Screams of laughter were heard as the two young boys ran from the side of the shop out to the fields. "I told you it would work! Run or he will catch us!"

⋰⋱⋰⋱

At supper that evening, Anne gave instructions for the men for the next day. The meal was a hearty spread, consisting of roast pheasant, scrapple, and pease porridge. Claret was had for the elders, and everyone supped together. Anne insisted that all partook of meals as a single household, with children included. Anne could not leave all traditions from childhood, even with her elevated status as a matron in the Colonies. She desired to hear of each person's day from Martha, being the eldest in the home, even though a servant, to the youngest that could contribute to the conversation. Ulrich Tristan was the youngest of the LeSage boys and was six years old. When he had the dais, Ulrich informed his mother, Anne, "I did my chores today."

"Is that all you did today, Ulrich? It took you the length of the day to accomplish your chores?"

Ulrich reached for more scrapple, his large blue eyes cast far from his mother's.

"Did you play today?"

"I played plenty, which is why I was whipped for not 'completing chores in a prudent tempo.'"

"I see. So apple pie is out of the question?"

"Yes, Mama. I will strive to do better tomorrow."
Ulrich ran from the table in tears.

"We've had better days, ma'am," Martha replied,
regarding the boy's behavior.

"And the two of you, Johnny, Joëlle?"

"Nothing but work, today, Mother," Johnny said.

Joëlle's eyes grew large at his older brother's in-
sistence of normalcy in their day. He looked from
Johnny to Pierre to his mother but did not utter a word.

"Yes, ma'am," Pierre offered, "the two young lads
did a man's day of work. They should watch themselves—strong men are needed for labor on all of the
farms. It would be a terrible loss to the LeSage farm if
they were mistaken for laboring men and captured and
smuggled aboard a ship headed for the Orient. But I
wouldn't worry too much, Joëlle—"

Joëlle's jaw slacked as every molecule of his being
focused on Pierre's words. He didn't even feel Johnny's sharp kick under the table.

"—only Johnny would be enslaved to carry loads
along the Silk Road."

Joëlle was hypnotized by the tale, while Johnny
reached for more pheasant and elbowed Joëlle a little as
he filled his plate. "What would happen to me, Pierre?"

"Oh, the Chinese wouldn't need you. You are too
small. They would roast you and eat you."

"Enough, Pierre." Anne ended the yarn with a grin.
"Pierre is pulling your leg, Joëlle."

Horrified at the outcome, Joëlle was relieved to see
Johnny sniggering. He was glad it was merely a mean
story, and he would not end up as hors d'oeuvres in a
foreign land. It didn't occur to him that Pierre was cov-
ertly warning the boys that he would get them back for
the bucket of guts.

Anne sighed. "Georges, I need you to organize the

cellar tomorrow. When the captain returns, he could have quite a lot for storage. Martha, you can bring in the pies now, while the men and boys clear their plates. I am going to sneak a tiny slice in to Ulrich."

"Spare the rod, spoil the child, ma'am."

"Oh, I think he will not spoil from a little treat. After I speak with Ulrich, I am going to the Trenton's to meet with Abigail and Beulah. I will be back late. No need to wait up for me."

Chapter 8

The trials for many families in the Colonies were different than Captain John's family in France had endured. Life, for most, was generally better in New England than it was for the LeSage family in Brest. Food was plentiful, and the Crown, being across the expansive ocean, did not administrate over every bit of minutia like governments could in Europe. Immigrants came to New England for many reasons, so all classes of people were represented. Most did not sail over to make fortunes, and the bourgeoisie that did come over represented a good percentage of the population, just not *une forte présence*. Everyone, from slaves and indentured servants up through the very wealthy, worked laboriously to live through each year. The prosperity each felt from their labors in the Colonies was worth tenfold to that in Europe. Added in was the empowering feeling they got while voicing their opinions as to what their communities needed from the labor.

Colonists were content in the New World. A very long arm did, however, stretch the span of the Atlantic, whereby the Crown seemingly managed to offer new roadblocks every time prosperity flourished. Still, many people were happy that they were British. The British Empire circled the globe, and its military offered great security to the sparsely populated New World.

"Anne, I will sail to Barbados in three days to pick up goods."

"For the Canadians?"

"Aye. I will sail them to a harbor near Nova Scotia, where the *Diane* will receive the cargo. The French are with them now, so the war could be ending soon."

"It seems so dangerous. Will your fluyt be fired upon? Will you make it home safely?"

"Do not worry, Anne, my love. My ship does not sail under English, French, or Canadian colors. I am a merchant with a ship considerably smaller than the frigates of war. I am not a threat and go mostly unnoticed in the northern ports. British and French captains, alike, greet me cordially up there because they know that my family in Brest probably built their ships! It should only take three weeks at the longest, my love. I will return and make ready for another run to Europe. I would like to take Johnny with me on this short jaunt. He is nearly ten years of age and could learn a lot aboard ship."

Anne looked at him sullenly.

"He will learn to be a sailor. He shall become a man, Anne."

❧❧❧

Anne was strong and Johnny mute as they said goodbye to John and the crew. She was worried for her son. He was still such a wee thing, and her first born. She reminded herself that illness rarely settled on the boy, and he was very strong. Still, she had this sense that fate would cut him down—as if this voyage would tempt Death just a little too much. John's plea to his wife was met with such reluctant and fearful discord that he decided to drop his request of Johnny accompanying aboard ship. Another day would come for his son to learn the ropes. As he shook Johnny's hand before boarding, he could feel sticky heat of anger surrounding his son, directly opposing the boy's icy mien from being denied passage to maturity. John smiled at his son and hoped he understood that this was only the first battle with Mother, and another adventure would arise.

Anne was visibly sad, and she felt alone. She worried for Johnny. She managed to keep him on land this time, in direct defiance of her husband, but she knew John had every right to take him when he chose. She tried valiantly to remember that God would take care of everything, and she should have faith in Him. To doubt meant that you turned your back to God.

Martha saw Anne sitting and staring, not reading or stitching. "Madam, you need to keep yourself occupied while the master is away. Women *are* blue after a baby is born, 'tis true! So you, too, must keep in step, or you will be available for Darkness to take a grip on you."

"You are right, of course, Martha. I just feel limp like greens that are picked and left on the drain board then not used." Anne was relieved that Martha had no inkling of her disagreement with John. She did not wish to be chided for being headstrong.

The door to the house opened, and Georges entered. "It is warm today, isn't it?"

"Aye, that it is, madam," replied Martha.

"May I bring you cool water, Anne?" Georges had cleaned up after laboring all day, and his combed hair and shaved face made him look like a young boy.

"Yes, Georges, that would be nice."

"Georges can entertain you and keep your mind

busy, madam. I need to do my evening chores. Georges, keep her mind occupied, read to her, help her with thread. It is difficult for her in the weeks after our new Odette's arrival."

Martha zoomed off to complete her next chore, and Georges sat with Anne. "Anne, I've broken through the tunnel. Everything is set." Anne was distant and seemed not to take notice of his words. Georges tried to assuage her worried humor. "John will be home soon, Anne, and Johnny knows the love of his mother endures to keep him safe. They will be fine."

"Yes," Anne answered mechanically. Georges could almost see Anne's thoughts return from the distant realm they had occupied, and, in a controlled, almost pleading voice, she said, "I would like to go to bed, Georges. Will you help me?"

Georges rose and helped Anne up, and the two walked into the master bedroom. Anne began removing her clothing and laid the garments neatly over a maple rocking chair. She poured water into the basin and splashed her face, dried it on a soft, small towel and removed the pretty, silver barrette that was holding her hair back. She ran her fingers through her long brown hair to liberate it from the tidy bun it had been pulled into all day.

Georges brought her dressing gown from the bureau and waited behind her. She turned to him and placed her hands on his upper arms. She felt his strong arm muscles flex through the broadcloth shirt. Georges gently lowered the gown over her head and guided it down her form, feeling the bulge of her waist resulting from the baby. "You are thinner now."

Anne took his hands and gently rubbed them against her abdomen. "Georges, I am so lost this time. Odette Ocean is so beautiful. So beautiful, and so healthy, and yet I don't seem to care like I did with the boys."

"Life will resume as it always has. You must be patient and heal in body and spirit."

Anne stood with a melancholy stare. She seemed like a sad, small child waiting to be held by her mother, knowing that would make everything all right from just the gentle pats, assurance, and caresses. He ran his strong hand against her face and moved her untamed hair back.

"You need to be loved," he whispered. Looking into her sad eyes, he cupped her face with his broad hands. She looked at him longingly, invitingly. He kissed her tenderly on the forehead. "I will love you."

Anne looked at him with hope. "Georges, make me feel again, please. Bring me to my senses."

Chapter 9

The agrarian society focused happily on crops, weather, and the raising of their families. Cries of injustices were elicited from the quiet communities as actions levied against the Colonies— such as additional taxes and quartering military units— spurred the people to rancor. The flow of political and radical events would eventually propel a miniscule rural civilization into combating the expansive British Empire in the quest for independence and the chance to govern themselves.

"Beulah, how *can* we help? Whatever our contributions, steeped with the grandest of public benevolence, they will only amount to a mole hill," implored Abigail Trenton.

"Ladies, you must be vigilant. Every small gesture from each and every one of us womenfolk will compound into insurmountable monoliths of strength, echoing throughout the Colonies with reverberations of a giant Persian gong," Beulah iterated once more to her friends for at least the thousandth time.

"Keep an even keel," Anne added softly, her expression laden with deep thought. She was excited about Beulah's plan to help and support Virginia's political views, though not entirely confident herself of what the tide of political fervor was, exactly.

"Definitely, Anne. I know we do little on our own, but put it all together, and it will make a difference to all of the Colonies."

"Well, I shall continue, Beulah," Abigail expressed with exhaustion.

"What is it, Abigail? Is there something wrong? Has Mr. Trenton had a turn of heart?" Anne believed in Beulah but considered Abigail her dearest friend. She did not wish for any wedges between her friends.

"Oh, no, nothing but trifles, Anne. It's just this whole 'shirt campaign.' My fingers have become so calloused and rough from sewing the heavy fabric, I am afraid Mr. Trenton will think he has climbed astride a grist stone one night!"

"I am sure, my dear, with a little effort on your part, the thought will never cross his mind," Beulah said with point blank aim and accuracy. She had a sly twinkle in her eye and tossed her head, as if crossing romantic overtures from a prince at a dinner party.

The women laughed at such spoken scandal and nearly dissolved with mirth each time the moment was alluded to during their evening together. Well into the evening tide, the group disbanded and made for their own hearths.

Beulah reflected on the time with her friends and smiled to herself. She knew the scope of what was to befall the good people of the Colonies.

She knew the destruction and carnage that it would leave behind, the sadness from loss, the irreparable scars from family to family, merchant to shopkeeper.

It is a good investment we shall all make, she thought, *it is the inevitable strength we possess*. Beulah sat, sleepily, in the back of the carriage as the driver swiftly returned his mistress safely to her estate.

Chapter 10

Joëlle pushed his little brother. "Go on, Ulrich, don't be a feather-head!"

"It will be easy, little pup. Besides, Uncle Georges wouldn't think we cared about him if we didn't do things like this."

Ulrich considered his big brother, Johnny. The little boy thought his two brothers were the best and was excited that they were playing with him today. He didn't wish to make them angry and have one of their fists smite him. Fear was always present when he was with the bigger boys, but he wanted to do what they did and carry the same smug look older boys had.

He decided that it was all in fun and reached deep within himself for the courage to do what the brothers told him to do. Besides, he loved Uncle Georges and did not wish anyone to think otherwise.

Johnny and Joëlle encouraged him forward toward his task. Ulrich bit his bottom lip, closed his eyes, and headed to the root cellar. Once Ulrich opened the door and stepped inside the dark cavern, Johnny and Joëlle slammed the door shut and braced it closed with a stick of wood, laughing as they ran.

A tiny voice cried in terror from being locked inside the dank, scary hole in the ground. The boys ran to the back field and hid behind the farthest marker.

"Did you see me jump that goose in the yard as we ran? I thought I was going to go headlong into the ground when I landed. I must have jumped three yards!" Joëlle was amazed at his skill.

"You jumped about a foot and half, if it was a hand!"

"It was two yards and maybe three, Johnny, you saw me! And if I couldn't have jumped that *high,* I would have knocked that bird's head clean off!"

"Yeah, and you could have rode the goose's body around the yard, 'Look at me, the Great Condé!'"

Johnny leaped away from Joëlle to avoid the younger boy's fists. Joëlle was a hot head, and Johnny always knew how to antagonize him. Joëlle swung at the air, his target deftly dodging each strike as the two danced around the field comically as they argued. Johnny was taller and much stronger than Joëlle but didn't want to fight him. It was just so much fun getting his goat!

"Drive the herd to the south! We will surprise the enemy with the speed of our steeds! Oh, no! Not until after I lay this egg! Oh, look at the size of that one— that egg alone could stop the enemy's army from over—" Johnny stepped in a vermin hole, and as he toppled over,

Joëlle's fist flew upward and smashed Johnny's face. Johnny's momentum pitched him into the firmly mortared rock of the old marker before he landed face down in the dirt. Johnny didn't move but moaned a little. His hands grabbed at clumps of grass to steady himself as he tried to slowly pull himself back to his feet. "Johnny! Are you okay? I—I didn't mean to hit you so hard!

As Johnny gained his footing and straightened out to his proper height, muddy and chunky blood ran down his face and oozed from his nose. "I will knock you all the way to Breton, so you and your amazing skills can enlist in the cavalry. You just better hope they take boys with no teeth!"

Joëlle sprinted away from the accident as fast as his legs could move. His brother's voice carried more wrath than Joëlle had ever heard. Johnny's threat coming from his blood-drenched face filled Joëlle with enough terror that it felt as though he was not running at all and could not escape. Anger, fear, and guilt filled Joëlle, but certain death nipped at his heels from Johnny's eminent retaliation.

Martha heard Joëlle stampeding back to the brick house and was ready for him. She thought filleting the two boys alive was appropriate for mistreating little Ulrich. "Joëlle, you should be ashamed of yourself! Idle hands are the tools of the devil."

"I didn't mean to—he asked for it—oh, Martha, the blood! I thought I killed him," Joëlle cried hysterically.

"Whoa, slow down, what blood? You speak the devil's talk. Anne! Come in here, quickly. Blood. What blood? What's got into you, laddie?"

Anne stepped in from the kitchen to see what the hullaballoo was about. After a few moments of Joëlle's dizzying and nonsensical testimonial, Johnny made it to the house and stood at the door, looking like he had escaped brutal slaughter.

"John Junior, what has happened? Is that your own blood or some poor animal's blood worn as costume to push little Ulrich to have nightmares into adulthood?"

"It's my own blood, Mother. Please don't punish Joëlle."

Martha was fit to be tied. The whole fabric of life was unravelling before her eyes. "God will punish you both for your evil antics! Joëlle, you go stand in that corner. I don't want to hear a peep, do you understand? Isaiah said it best. 'There is no peace unto the wicked!'"

"Yes, ma'am." Joëlle said, head hanging in disgrace.

"Johnny, go outside and get a bucket of water. I will find a rag to get you cleaned up. Anne, go to Ulrich and see how he fairs. He is by the root cellar with Georges," Martha shouted to the family as she looked for a rag and poultice in the kitchen.

The family obeyed her firm commands.

Martha managed to rein in the chaos of the day and prepare supper. She wasn't sure what evils she had committed to bring on such a punishment to her old, tired bones.

Chapter 11

S upper was light, but filling, as the day's events prevented anything elaborate to be prepared. Only a few crusts of bread from the previous day were left and given to the men. René and Georges caught several sturgeon from the river early in the morning and salted them to store. Two large fish had been reserved for the day's meal and roasted nicely. Greens and mushrooms rounded out the feast, washed down with rum the captain brought back from his last journey to the Caribbean. The children had goat's milk and water infused with herbs to wash down their meal.

"Once you have cleaned your plate, Johnny, put that poultice back on that cut," Martha insisted.

She had done an expert job of stitching John's head back together and did not wish healing be delayed, turning her handiwork into an ugly scar.

Anne had her fill of food and wished for the family "round table" to begin. Georges and Pierre were still eating and cleaning the serving platters of remaining morsels, so she started with René. "What has happened in your day, René?"

René swallowed a draught of rum. "I spent much of the day with Daniel Plinthe. We reinforced some fencing that had loosed. His mare, Ikwe, will foal any day now. She seems well."

"Will Mr. Plinthe need help with the birthing?" Anne inquired.

"Nay, he has Clement and Rataman to help. They are wise in the way of horses."

"Why didn't Mr. Plinthe have his slaves mend the fence? Helping one's neighbor is always prudent, René, but failing to complete tasks on our farm would not be."

"I finished my chores and tasks here, not to worry, good Anne. Daniel came by, and we shot the breeze a while. We had a pint at the inn and noticed the rails down when our venture padded to see his riding horses." René turned to address Pierre. "One of his plow horses needs a new shoe. Daniel will send her over in the morning."

Pierre nodded as Anne turned to Johnny.

Joëlle looked ashamed without any spoken words. Ulrich donned that smug look that he yearned for and waited for his brothers' trial to begin.

Johnny applied the poultice to his wound and tried to look as innocent as he could in light of the condemning facts. Anne breathed calmly and sipped her rum as she considered the information. After a moment of silence, she turned to Georges with a sweet smile. "Georges, will you tell the story of Gwennagwir? I think the children would enjoy it."

"*Oui, d'accord.* Listen carefully, boys, you may learn a good lesson." Georges took a hearty swig of rum and settled comfortably in his chair. Clearing his throat, he began. "The story of the Benevolent Gwennagwirs is a story from Breton. Your father, Uncle René, and I heard it told by our grandmother, who would entertain the family with the old stories while we sat together, stuffed from a large evening meal, much like tonight." Georges took another swig of rum. "Grandmère would drink wine while she orated. I wonder if she would have liked this drink from the islands."

The older boys try to settle comfortably into their seats for the story. The crimes they committed weigh heavily on their minds. Pierre filled Georges's flagon with more rum, and said with arrogance, "I would be most happy to tell the little ones the story, Georges. That way they will get the most accurate telling."

Georges waved Pierre aside and began his favorite yarn. "A long, long time ago, before our grandmothers and great grandmothers, and before their grandmothers and great grandmothers, tribes made endless war. The most fearsome tribe that overpowered all warring tribes was called the Keeper Tribe. They ruled the land and were granted the Timid Tribe for slave labor. There was never peace in the land, as all tribal leaders were vain and desired to be the ruling tribe.

"The Timid Tribe was a weak, non-warring tribe. Timids would not take arms against another tribe and were thought ignorant and crazy for their ways— cowardly for not fighting against other tribes, but crazy because they talked to birds. In spite of this, the Timid Tribe was a grand feather in the cap of the leader of the tribe that earned the Keeper Tribe title.

"If the strongest tribe were fishers, then the Timid Tribe would trawl the waters for the Keeper Tribe. If the strongest tribe were hunters and gatherers, then the Timid Tribe would carry out these tasks. If the strongest tribe were agrarian, the Timid Tribe would plow the fields, plant the crops, harvest, and process the bounty. Even without warring, the Timid Tribe would work long and difficult days that would last into the dark hours. All Timid people—children, women and men—

combined efforts to feed, clothe, and house the current governing tribe. The dark hours were spent doing all work required to keep their own tribe healthy, which meant that their women sewed pelts, cooked, and raised their families. The children collected and processed grains left in the fields so that bread and cereal could be eaten, and the men would hunt and fish for meat and make tools and shelter.

"The Timid Tribe's strenuous life took its toll on the people. There was not enough time to conceive and raise children, so the tribe shrunk in members. Over-work from the governing tribe meant that the Timids did not sleep enough each night. Those who did sleep enough did not work in the night, so there wasn't enough food. Many Timids dropped over dead from starvation. Timids who did not sew pelts into blankets lacked warmth. These Timids froze to death.

"The elders of the Timid Tribe were known to ask the birds for guidance twice each year. To the governing tribe, it looked like idiocy and folly.

"'Your bird friends are giving you good advice, Timid elders, so good that with this bird-brained advice, soon there will be no Timids left to work for us,' the last warring chief said mockingly.

"True to their ways, Timid elders would not defend themselves from the spoken abuse from the governing tribes. One day, the birds of the forest asked the Timid elders—both of them who were still alive—if they would like to fight back against the strong tribes. The elders replied, 'No. Never. It is not for us to do.'

"The birds tried to convince the elders that, in order to survive as a people, they would have to stand up for themselves.

"'There are only five people left of the Timid Tribe! Do you not understand that your people will be obliterated from the Earth?' the birds squawked imploringly.

"The elders sighed at the suggestion and, with long faces, the elders replied, 'It is against our nature to rebel. Our place in nature is to take care of the ignorant and foolish barbaric tribes. Can you ask a fish not to swim in the water? Can you ask a vulture to stay away from carrion, and only subsist on grass or leaves? Truly, I say to you, you will not give up flying across the heavens purely because it is requested of you. We are the keepers of wisdom—we hold all knowledge of hunting, farming, and fishing. We hold all of the skills to build villages and make needed tools.'

"The birds held a conference to discuss the fate of the Timid Tribe. They argued that the Timids might hold all knowledge of a civilized world, but they must change their ways, or they would no longer walk the Earth. They would be forgotten and all of their wisdom with them. 'We must help the Timids. We must summon the Benevolent Gwennagwir Clan. They are wise and have watched the tribes from the beginning of time.'

"The venerable Benevolent Gwennagwir Clan was consulted with the problem. They flew away to consider and formulate the solution. When they returned in the warm months, the decision was this: 'Warring Tribes have failed to learn civilized skills and how to exist in harmony. The Warring Tribes will be removed forever because they have contributed nothing but grief and destruction with their selfish ways.' At these words, all of the Gwennagwir Clan flew in a flurry, igniting a huge ball of fire. The Earth quaked and shook, swallowing every member of every Warring Tribe.

"'The Timid Tribe will be restored to rule the land,' the Gwennagwirs continued. 'Their children will be healed, and their ancestors will return. We will begin and make it so.'

"Footsteps were heard. The sound was barely audible but grew and grew, becoming thunderous. All of the woodland creatures fled from the sound, scampering every which way—up into the tallest trees, across the endless stretches of water, and burrowing into the ground to avoid being trampled. Then a magic glow appeared, and the terrifying hooves stopped.

"As the glow intensified, beautiful horses began to emerge from all corners of the forest. On their backs rode Timid ancestors, back from the Beyond and ready to use their wisdom to rebuild the Timid Tribe.

"Gwennagwir birds are no longer on the Earth but, in their place, came the horse. The moral of the story is that, from patience and wisdom, Nature provides the staunch with great resources."

Anne smiled. "And now, it is time for all LeSage tribal members to wash up and get sleep so they will be well for tomorrow's chores," she directed.

René and Pierre congratulated Georges for his performance as chairs were reluctantly pushed back, and everyone prepared for the night.

Chapter 12

Beulah's eyes were crusty and difficult to open in the first light of the morning. A gentle knock on the chamber's door assisted her in prying them open and allowed her to see the painted ceiling motif in a blurred, Impressionist watercolor way. Beulah, being more than two hundred years too early for this art, was unimpressed and was focused more on the inconsiderate intrusion on her delicate dreams and the harsh reality of the ache in her head from the previous evening.

The young girl entered, eyes cast down at the floor so as not to be more impudent than was necessary. "Begging your pardon, madam."

"What is it, Polly? What's happening? Why? Oh, what is it you want, Polly?"

"The master is ready to travel to the Ruby Oil, madam."

Beulah's head was filled with sand, and nothing was making sense. "Ruby Oil, thank you, Polly. You may go." Beulah pulled on a dressing gown and kept mulling *ruby oil* to herself as if chanting to elicit good spirits to do her bidding. "Of course! Silly nilly of a girl!" She raced down the stairs to greet her husband in the foyer of their grand estate.

"You bid me adieu, darling. How sweet of you to rise," Armand said as he pecked his wife on her flushed cheek.

"Well, if your wife had her wits at this hour, you would be leaving through a lonely and cold threshold. I declare, it has taken me the better part of my awakened day to understand that the master is underway on his journey!"

"You make less sense each day of our marriage, Beulah, and yet I love you more and more with each passing minute, dearest. You had an enjoyable time with your lady friends last night, I trust? This trek, I am afraid, to the *Rue de Royale*, could be longer this time, dear Beulah, but I will write you of every speck of minutia that one must endure with fellows of my noble profession."

"Your noble profession?" Beulah draped her arms about his neck and looked longingly into his loving, falcon-like eyes. She knew his mind was set on his meeting with the *Secrétaire d'État de la Marine* in Paris and wouldn't necessarily hear any of her contribution to the conversation. She asked imploringly, "Please, dear, if you can squeeze in a moment for your loyal wife, think of her and know that she will be pining away the days and weeks until your return."

Armand was suddenly shaken and enraptured with her words. He looked into her eyes caringly and caressed her soft, trailing hair.

"Perchance you could even remember to bring a gift," she added. "Perhaps that of the finest *ruby oil* Paris has to offer?"

"Of course, I shan't forget, *mon doux de la renoncule,* my love, but..."

"Yes, I am listening...you were saying?" Beulah impishly kissed his face. She ran her fingers through his long hair and looked as though she could be sizing him up to buy at auction.

"What, across all of earth's frothy and blue oceans, is *ruby oil*?"

Chapter 13

Goody, good, Little Johnny. You are a great smith."

John, Jr. dipped the hot metal into the bucket to cool. "Many thanks, Pierre."

He looked over his work with pride. He fabricated a small broach from scrap pieces of copper and planned to put color into it. He marked the back with a tiny stamp that imprinted his brand: a square at the center, with one of its sides extended. Opposite to that were two arcs extending the parallel side, into an S shape. His initials—reading from left to right—were L then J and the S was made through use of the J, rounding up to finish the letter. The ends of the S had points similar to the leaves of a grapnel anchor used on board a ship.

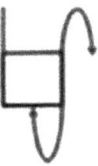

"And did you make that *pour ton amour*?" Pierre said with a chuckle.

"*Non, non*, Pierre!"

"Well, someday, little Johnny, someday a young maiden will steal your heart. You with your looks so fine and your skills, too."

Johnny turned red in the face and hoped it just looked blushed from the heat of the fire. "*Oui, Pierre, oui*. But right now I just wish I would have brought this little piece up just a bit more."

He scrutinized over his art piece with contempt as he showed it to Pierre.

"Goody, good, Johnny. Your pains will make you a rich man. Truly, we must work on this chain and have it completed by evening. No more fun and games, work, work, work. And phfft! You will be a man!"

"Okay, I was just practicing. I will get the stock iron."

Pierre was a lighthearted man that was a bit of a curio. While he explained careless mistakes and sloppy work to Johnny and his brother, the excitement in his voice, along with his thick dialect, could be construed as brash and offensive to a bystander. The two brothers took it all in stride and knew Pierre was passionate about his craft and only meant to teach through showing inadequacies. Pierre wasn't always teaching his apprentice but could sound intimidating. He would vehemently argue or discuss a topic with such passion that a listener could think the discussion would result in a vicious pummeling if Pierre's side of the story was not favored by all.

These events were daily fare at the LeSage place. Pierre would walk around the shop or yard and argue animatedly, as if trying to make his opponent see his point. He would loudly boom his position in an oration that could be heard on the far side of the Berkeley Plantation, his voice ebbing and flowing as each point in his argument was laid out clearly and assured his victory in rhetoric. Most of the time, Pierre did not have an audience for his points of view. Ranting out loud was just the way Pierre organized his thoughts.

Johnny and Joëlle had grown up listening to Pierre's soliloquies and thought nothing of the performances. It never occurred to the boys that others from the area would hear Pierre, the convictions and ravings in his tone as he screeched his opinion, but that they would never understand a word from this mad man. The barrage was hurled through the air in the French tongue. The young brothers were fluent in both languages, so what they heard amounted to a man thinking out loud to himself. They both knew that Pierre was a gifted artisan, loved his new 'family' in the Colonies, and had no desire for fisticuffs.

Pierre and Johnny labored all day into the early evening over the heat of the forge. They completed the chain, as well as an assortment of other repairs.

"Johnny, this latch is repaired for Madam Flynn. Could you take it to her estate while I clean up?"

"Indeed, Pierre. Right away." Johnny wiped his hands on his apron and started to remove it.

"Johnny, *Lavez-vous les mains...avec savon de lessive.*"

"*Oui, Monsieur,* soap."

Johnny washed and walked briskly toward the Flynn estate. It felt good to stretch his legs and breathe fresh air after working metal all day. The Flynns lived a few miles north of the center of town. Their land still had patches of dense forest in places that were eerily dark. Johnny never feared for anything and was a particularly happy boy. He was quiet most of the time and didn't say much to others, but shyness had nothing to do with it. He was genuinely entertained with his own thoughts and musings. He liked to hear what others said and let their ideas rattle around in his head for a time before concluding any opinion, for or against. He had strong opinions and convictions like anyone else, but he didn't like to force his ideals on another person.

Johnny was a sage man for his years. When he eventually sailed with John, Sr., he felt his time aboard ship with his father was the best time he had ever had. Contrary to his mother's intuitive fear for him, nothing bad happened to the crew. The short voyages were easy, and both he and his father agreed that what Anne wasn't privy to was for the best all around. Time aboard ship strengthened the father-son bond, and the experiences were enlightening. Johnny made a good sailor, but he knew the sea was not his destiny.

Johnny sailed a few more times with his dad on short jaunts to the Caribbean or up the coast to Massachusetts. Smithing was his passion, however, and his skill was evident in how quickly he could fabricate an item, and by the quality which he produced.

Johnny was greeted at the front entrance by a servant and shown into the parlor of Mrs. Kebob-Flynn. Mrs. Kebob-Flynn was working diligently on paperwork, and only stopped and looked up when the servant announced, "John, Junior, Madam."

"Ah, the young Master LeSage. Do come in and sit awhile. Clarey, bring some cool cider and biscuits for John."

The servant left the room. Johnny sat on a small chair with fabric on the seat. He smiled as he looked the room over.

Mrs. Kebob-Flynn shuffled her papers into tidiness, pushed the desk chair in, walked the floor, and sat in a matching chair with fabric next to a small table, opposite to Johnny. "Well, it is so nice to see Anne's fine son."

After an uneasy moment of silence, Johnny offered, "I needn't stay long, Mrs. Kebob-Flynn. I only came to return this." He pulled the small latch from his pocket, stood, and handed it to Beulah.

"Oh, this is fine. Did you do the work yourself?"

"No, ma'am, Pierre did the repair."

"That man is a goldmine. His talent is unparalleled here in the Colonies. I understand you have been studying with him?"

"Yes, ma'am."

Johnny liked praise, but sitting in her house was even more confining than working metal all day. He really desired to run outside like a wild animal. Just until the evening meal, anyway. Clarey brought a tray to the small table and began serving drinks and biscuits. Food had a wonderful retaining effect on a hungry lad. Wolfing three pieces down and guzzling a full glass of cider was fair payment for confinement. He realized his manners and slowly sat back in his chair, a little befuddled. Had he resembled too wild a creature in Mrs. Kebob-Flynn's parlor?

"Good for you, John. A young man needs energy, have another."

Johnny was relieved that he hadn't bungled his manners. He picked up the small latch and pointed to the repair. "This is where he replaced the spring. It's an easy repair. I could have done it myself, but I was completing a chain for my father's ship."

Mrs. Kebob-Flynn examined the work when Johnny took the broach out of his pocket.

"I did this broach this morning." He beamed. "I am just playing around with copper—just for fun. The next piece will be better."

"Master John, you and Pierre do fine work. I think smithing is your calling, son. I think you have made a good decision to stay on land. Not to mention how happy your mother is with the decision."

"Mother gets lonely when Father is at sea. I don't think she wants any of us boys to become sailors. I would be fine either way, really. Working with Father, working at home with Pierre, it doesn't matter."

"So, you don't care to explore the far regions of the Earth?" she questioned.

Johnny gnawed a biscuit and shrugged indifference. Beulah mulled this information over for a moment. John, Jr. was perhaps the most handsome boy in the area, and he hadn't an inkling of vanity. This boy could do anything in the world that he wanted to, but he just didn't seem to have the competitive edge for conquering and managing. No, a ship's captain was not a good career for John. He didn't have the wild spirit that each of his parents had for adventure. He had artistry and was compelled toward perfection.

"From what I've heard, you will be brilliant at whatever you choose. Now, take a pocketful of biscuits and scoot home before it gets dark."

Johnny stuffed his pockets and skipped and ran along the trail back to his home. His tummy was happy, his head was free and light from the strong cider Mrs. Kebob-Flynn served, and his pride sparkled. Life was as good as it got for a young boy. As the years went by and his skills as a smith developed into that of a master craftsman, life got a lot tougher for Johnny and all of Colonial New England.

Chapter 14

Boycotts. Boycotts. More boycotts," Abigail said. "Beulah, I don't know how the rest of New England is faring, given that they mustn't have a stitch more cloth or thread than we do here in Virginia. The inn is out of all of the extras we have offered our lodgers, including malt whiskey and snuff."

The year was 1781, and the people of the United States of America were tired of war and the inconveniences it created for day-to-day living. Most of the men had enlisted in the Continental Army or with the Virginia Militia.

The women contended with the usual home duties but many plantations and smaller farms had allowed their servants to enlist, putting extra work on the ones who stayed behind. It was a stressful time.

Beulah skimmed a letter that she collected on the way to see Abigail. She folded the nice parchment stationary and slipped it back into her purse. "I am sure travelers understand the situation, Abigail. Surely, comfort and information you offer, or the latest copy of the *Virginia Gazette,* is worth more to folks than a few indulgences they don't need."

"'Tis true, of course." Abigail watched Beulah

carefully fold the paper. "Is that new correspondence? How did you get that?"

"Yes, Solomon Vos had it for me. It is from Armand's sister in France."

"*Nothing* is coming into port! Why, we haven't had a shipment—" Abigail stopped mid-sentence as it dawned on her to whom she was talking. "Oh, that is special. I see. Connections."

"Yes, Abigail, some things must break through any blockade. As it turns out, my husband does receive official business correspondence more often than provisions come for regular supplies and trade. Sometimes personal items may be part of the freight, but please, keep all venom from your words. This letter is dated eight months ago, hardly an item to be referred to as 'new.'"

Abigail was ashamed of herself for thinking the Flynns were more entitled than the Trentons. The Flynns' history and fortune stretched back to the Normans. Abigail dropped her selfish thoughts as she remembered that the Flynns were titled aristocracy, but Beulah nor Armand would never allude to status. Abigail relaxed and let her face reflect her usual congeniality.

Beulah continued with germane concerns. "The attendance of guests has lessened, *n'est pas*?"

"Oh, yes, more than tenfold since last month!"

"The British are moving south. The battles are coming our way, and we will need to put all strength to the fore. Everything is in place, and we are ready!"

The whoops from the rider of a winning horse couldn't have as much enthusiasm as Beulah did that moment. She was excited that all of her rallying, encouragement, and preparations over the past years were to come to fruition.

As a strong and prosperous colonist, Abigail was worried. "Oh, this is such a strain. Do you think there will be fighting here, really?"

"Good chance. Armand said the fleet will be down and that the Spanish have joined us now. When fighting commences here, everyone knows their tasks and will be vigilant. I am going on to the LeSage place and check a few things with Georges."

"Godspeed, Beulah. We will be fine. I have courage."

"*Oui, mon petit ami, courage!*" Beulah left the inn for Anne's in her carriage.

乀ﾟ乁ﾟ

Beulah disembarked from her carriage and went straight to the root cellar to talk to Georges. Georges spent much time in the cellar. Anne had questioned his hermitage, but he averred that the temperature stayed fairly consistent throughout the highs and lows of the region. Both women knew this to be true, but they also knew of Georges's compulsion to do more work than necessary to get any job done.

He was outside and greeted Beulah genteelly. A treed animal would have had a calmer demeanor. "Madam Flynn, I have my doubts. I think I should have joined the Virginia Militia, like young John," he said as he paced quickly back and forth.

"You are needed here, Georges. Supplies must be distributed. Anne, Martha, and the younger children cannot move those barrels like you can."

"*Oh, je devrais être avec le petit* John*! Ce que s'il est tué? Anne ne pourront faire face à la mort.*"

"Nonsense, Georges! John will be fine. Pierre is with him, not that he can divert a musket ball, but they are doing what they do best—forging iron. A highly needed skill for the Continental Army."

"I am—you are right, as usual, Madam Flynn. I was just thinking of myself." Georges breathed a deep, calming breath and settled on his more peaceful demeanor. Beulah was an enchantress that could calm any savage beast. Georges's disciplined mind gripped into the task at hand. "We have moved over half of the gunpowder."

"You are a hero, Georges, and you rarely, if ever, think just of yourself. I am going into the house to see how rations are sizing up. Armand was in Richmond working with General Lafayette, but should be nearing home tonight. We are almost there, Georges. The Marquis de Lafayette is sly like a fox. I wouldn't want to be in his path as an enemy."

Beulah found all preparations in order with Anne and sat with her. The LeSage kitchen, aflutter with activity since before daybreak, was now quiet. Martha retired for rest on a soft bed as the two friends sat quietly by the hearth.

"I thought my hands were going to cramp into gnarled, unusable lumps from kneading so much dough. They look clean and fine, now, but oh, how they ache!"

"The bread will be appreciated greatly by hungry men. The aroma is heavenly!"

"I think Martha and I have done well today. I will sleep like the dead tonight." Anne closed her eyes and rocked in the chair. She was content and happy from her hard labors today.

"I have a letter from Armand's sister in France. I will read some of it to you while you rest." Beulah read parts of the letter out loud in French, first, to ensure accurate meaning and then translated the words into English. It was a long and beautiful letter, and Anne enjoyed the happy diversion.

"I don't understand, Beulah, why is Patrice sending her daughter over here?"

"The temperature of unrest is heating up. Life is becoming uncertain in their village. I am sure Patrice will sail, too." They sat in silence a few moments then Beulah laughed a little. "I do hope she has the sense not to come over until the summer months."

Anne laughed, a forced and worried sound, as she thought of current events. "The high seas are a deadly adventure with the gunned armadas trolling along the coast. Dissident French ruffians cannot be as bad."

"We, over here, seem to her to be the safest, yet betwixt and between two evils. Action, on a worried mother's part, seems to have trumped dangers that we assuredly have here in the Colonies," Beulah explained with delighted mischief in her voice. "Her daughter could be exposed to more wild and barbaric ways than could be thought possible by the bourgeoisie Continentals!"

Anne listened but didn't fully understand Beulah's insinuation.

"You know, of course, they think we run naked with savages and have other indelicate habits."

Anne laughed heartily understanding now. "When I married John, some of the thrill of crossing to the Colonies was that my family saw me as an offering to the pagan natives and prayed I would be granted a merciful death at sea! They have a better understanding now. I wrote and told them our children always wear clothing, without fail. Well, at least, always on the Sabbath!"

"You are plucky, Anne. I can't wait to introduce you to my sister-in-law and niece. We are good folks in this land, no matter what anyone else thinks. I need to return home now, but it has been such a nice visit, Anne. I am eager for Armand to be back home, so I think I will go home and clean something to pass the time. Enjoy peaceful sleep tonight."

The women rose as Beulah left the brick house and kisses her dear friend *adieu*. Beulah happily directed her carriage on the path toward home.

Chapter 15

The woods were calm like any other day. It was an unusually warm day for October. Unpredictable autumn days could see temperatures plunging sharply or rising to a balmy, southerly climate.

Nights were chilly, and folks were making the preparations for the coming winter. The thud of an axe, from someone splitting logs for the hearth or removing a stump, penetrated the air, and the smell of cook fires overwhelmed the senses. Hounds bayed and voices jaggedly ripped into the natural surroundings, aurally assaulting the landscape, only to ebb through the falling leaves, as gently as residual understanding from a fleeting thought.

The Marquis de Lafayette and his troops were in the area, readied for battle. Their subdued encroachment was eerie. All of the able men and boys of the area were sequestered with the militia. Usual daily sounds were stifled, and yet the large amount of soldiers, militia, and equipment, so near though shrouded, did not fill the silence.

Cocked tension suspended like sails in the doldrums; slight atmospheric changes sparked a reaction, reverberating through every soul; and the grit of the

Virginian people rode in the teeth of the wind.

A thunderclap *crack*! Its reverberation echoed through the brick house, jarring the nerves of the most courageous. Alerted by the sound, the two women remained motionless, resisting the impulse to flee.

"Are soldiers combating here, on this land? Where is Georges? No. I am unnerved. I am hearing ghosts from the usual sound of a hunter felling prey for winter stores." Anne's mind raced for an explanation. She rose from her rocker, a few steps her from the threshold. She was expecting a volley of shot targeting human flesh. She found stillness in the surrounding fields. No one was present. No uniforms, no commands. The blast of another musket directed Anne's attention toward the Pig Beast Inn.

Martha stood at the door. "Madam, come back inside, it isn't safe," she coaxed.

"I can't find Georges! Do you see him? I need to find Abigail." Panic sent Anne across the fields, along the path toward the Pig Beast Inn. She could not hear Martha's terror-riven pleas imploring her to return to the safety of the brick house.

The summer crops were now wilted and dying back. The shortened days and frosty early mornings sped blackened, decaying tissues of the once green and thriving flora back to the soil, feeding the microbial. Decomposing civilization required nutrients and minerals.

Anne ran toward the Pig Beast Inn, worried for her best friend. She was devoid of sense and unarmed, ironically racing to help, but lacking in the skills to mend injuries that may have been sustained. Anne's loyalty and care pushed her through the fatigue she had with immortal strength. Her trek was violently severed by tumultuous upheaval of sod and stubble.

Roiling rape of the land snared Anne in her flight, churning all matter into basic, primal ingredients. Debris was projected above the hawk's soaring arc in a cacophonous overture that hurtled Anne in its maelstrom. Soil, roots, and dried plant matter rained to the earth. Georges's beloved deer path had been erased, and the stones from the old markers had seemingly been cast back to the headwaters of the streams of their origin.

Yellow, earthy, choking air, grainy and gritty dust settled onto the now-barren landscape, and a small, broken figure lay motionless in the rubble.

Chapter 16

John, Jr. worked metal in the shop at the LeSage home. Nearly five years had elapsed since the Siege at Yorktown. Captain, John, Sr., had docked from a recent voyage from Breton and was unwell. He had not fully recovered from the loss of his wife and brother and felt guilt for running cargo during the Siege of Yorktown, instead of protecting his family at home. He sat outside and watched John work. John had recently discovered his first broach that he crafted so many years ago and was in the process of correcting mistakes he had made as an apprentice.

"Father, are your clothes readied for tomorrow night's fête?"

"They will suffice."

"It will be quite a gala, you will want to look your best." John finished the metal and dipped it into a bucket of water. He sat near his father and rubbed the metal with a soft piece of cloth, admiring it as he did so. "Armand Flynn told me that his sister is back from France. It will be nice to see her again. It seems as if she and her daughter just left to go home yesterday."

The men sit in silence, and John continues shining his metal piece.

"The Flynn family is quite a family in Paris. Patrice would be a good catch."

"Father, I don't need a wife yet."

"No, no, son, I know that. I am just pointing out a fact. A widow would probably enjoy a few dances from a handsome man such as yourself."

John kept polishing. "I will invite Patrice to the floor because it is polite, but Beulah will have Patrice's evening filled with all of the affluent men from the area, including that of a ship's captain," he added with a little salt and vinegar. "There won't be time to spend with a common smith."

"Common, you are not. *Oui, vous êtes un peu 'impertinence*," John, Sr. said with an affectionate smile. "Love is magic, son. Once you are sprinkled with its essence, all of society's rules ebb into obscurity as the spell entices you to action." The elder John thought of his beautiful wife he lost to the explosion and how he missed her. "I married beneath my class, Johnny. Your mother's charm made me lose all logic."

"Is that why you came to New England? Did the family in Breton accept Mother?"

"She was English, Johnny, but she would have learned to live in Breton and speak the language if I asked her to. My family would have 'trained' her to be one of them and would have loved her as family. But that was not Anne. She had a wild spirit much the same as *mon frère*, René. Anne desired adventure and needed her own path to blaze."

"I never knew that. Mother seemed much like other women."

"Anne was sly and savvy. Nobody in the Mishipeshu area knew her background. They knew she was a sea captain's wife and didn't question beyond that boundary. She behaved like them in a natural, convincing way. She never lied to her friends, she just didn't volunteer extra information."

"I can't imagine Mother slipped by Beulah Kebob-Flynn! She must have known."

"Aye. Beulah knew. But Beulah is too much of a lady to divulge secrets and tattle. A vital ally would have been lost in Anne, to be sure. *Elle n'est pas un traître.*"

Spending time with his father had always been a treasure for John. It saddened him to see the wizened man caught in melancholy and hoped that the sadness subsided. He pondered the possibilities that his father could pursue, hoping to stumble across a suitable suggestion to present to him and, with it, the encouragement toward healing.

It was late at night when John returned to the house. Finishing the broach was salubrious work and allowed him time to reflect on what his father told him. The captain had slumbered for several hours already. John tiredly crawled into his lonely bed. His brother, Joëlle, would share the bed when they were children. John thought of him each night and said a prayer for his soul.

Joëlle had been gone since his last valiant fight during the War for Independence. He caught a large amount of shrapnel in his legs during canon fire. The injuries became gangrenous, and he perished. The price of freedom for the United States was tragic for the LeSage family, but John, Jr. understood it. He had coped with the tragedies like most of his neighbors had and had moved ahead in his life despite it. John drifted off to sleep as the embers of the forge cooled and grew dim.

Chapter 17

The Mishipeshu community turned out for the grand fête at the Flynns' estate. Captain LeSage was announced as he entered the home. He was a bearded and distinguished man, with tricorn hat atop the compulsory white wig. He sported a blue waist coat, a double row of brass buttons shining down the front, further embellished with gold epaulets and a red baldric. White cotton breeches descended to his knee gaiters buttoned over tall black boots.

John, Jr., was handsome, in his finest linen knee breeches—buckled at the knee with his own stamped buckles—silk stockings, an extravagant silk shirt, and ascot. He had grown broad across his shoulders, making his waistcoat snug. His thick, long hair was pulled back and secured with a fine bow. Rosewater scent hung dreamily around him so that the women present needed not hear his announcement from the footman. Several quickly greeted him fondly before the cry of his name.

Father and son made their way through the festive crowd of friends and dignitaries. The room was hot and loud. Abigail Trenton was seated, sipping punch, while Mr. Trenton chatted with Daniel Plinthe and David

Ramsey. John, Jr. approached Mrs. Trenton and greeted her in a loud voice. She looked up at him, smiled, and nodded her head.

""Mr. Trenton pulled them aside. "John."

"She looks well. It is good to see her out again."

"I did not think she would survive, let alone recover from the horror."

John listened to Abel Trenton carefully. He wanted to hear each detail again so that he would not forget.

"The scars are still upon her, but her hearing has returned somewhat. I don't know if she will ever be whole again."

"She seems happy like always," John said. "Does a horn not assist her?"

"Not in such a loud gathering. It is a comfort to her when attending a lodger."

"I shouldn't have let them do it," John said. "It is my fault."

"No, John," Abel replied sternly. "The blast should never have happened. I ensured one red coat couldn't meddle, but the second one slipped by me and dove into the tunnel."

"You have told me before, and I relayed it to the captain, Abel," John, Jr. implored, "but, please, tell him again, about that day and Uncle Georges."

Armand Flynn had walked up to the group with an ambassador. The two men sensed the somber tone of the group and listen politely.

"Heaven only knows, Captain LeSage, what turn of events would have befallen us if the British secured that powder. If Abigail hadn't been injured and bleeding, she would have caught up to that soldier and met her doom from the full force of the blast."

"So, she heard Georges with the soldier down there," Armand added for clarity and motions his wife and his sister to squeeze in next to him to listen.

"Oh, yes, that's why we know what happened," Abel reported. "Once I dug Abigail out of there, and she came back to consciousness, she dictated the details to the undersecretary of Lafayette. Yes, John, Georges was heroic at the least. Georges was close to the inn and met up with the soldier."

"My word, Abel, how did he know that all the way back at the LeSage place?" David Ramsey asked.

"Mr. Ramsey, Joëlle and I used to steal pies from your wife's cooling table, do you remember?" John, Jr. interjected.

"Yes," Mr. Ramsey drawled out. "Beth always pointed her finger at you two boys, but I always assumed it was because you were two strong bucks and she was making a case against you—any excuse to keep you away from our daughters. We didn't know who the culprit was, actually." He felt awkward and off topic. "This probably isn't a good time for a confession, young man."

"Umm, no," John answered with a blushed face. "You didn't suspect us because we live on the other side of the inn from you. You probably didn't think we could get all the way home and devour a pie so quickly. But if you had been able to tail us better, you would have found that we cheated."

Armand laughed a belly laugh at Ramsey being duped by small boys. Beulah poked her husband in the ribs. "You little devils!" she added with a grin.

"Joëlle and I could hit two or three homes of fresh baked goodies before anyone caught on. It was hard to limit the easy spoils to just once a week." John reflected on the scrumptious treats and then continued. "Joëlle would have run scared at the slightest hitch, so I told him that by ingeniously spacing out the crimes it would

keep us *caché de tout,* or concealed. The last summer
we pilfered, however, we made a vital mistake and
were caught."

"Abigail! No, Sally Beth, the maid! The pies be
saved!" Beulah exclaimed with excited explanation.

"No, ma'am, neither of those fine ladies were the
wiser. Pierre got us."

The captain let out a raucous laugh, proud of his
clever sons. "It cost you boys dearly, I'm sure!" His
face lit up brighter than anyone had seen in years. *"Mon
fils avec unwhipped undivulgèd des crimes et de la justice.* Ah, Pierre, *il et taquet,* Pierre always looked out
for you boys."

The audience grew as other guests surrounded the
enraptured listeners, and the captain's face turned sober
once again as he looked at his son. "What price did you
and Joëlle pay? If I know Pierre —and I do—there was
a clever and creative price to keep his lip buttoned."

"My mentor was legendary for his mercenary ways
with us boys. The price included doing his share of
chores and some of Georges."

"Georges would never use blackmail," said the
captain of his brother.

"No, I agree. But Uncle Georges didn't know that
Pierre had us over a barrel. He just thought Pierre was
the *finest* teacher around and couldn't figure out how
Pierre tamed us. That's why we had to help Georges, or
Pierre would have sold us out."

"Tar and feathers, John. Tar and feathers. Your two
treasonous sons pulled pies right out of my mouth,"
David Ramsey said facetiously as he rubbed his large
belly.

"Those lads probably extended your life by ten
years, keeping you from overindulging," Beulah
crowed.

The guests were lighthearted and warmed by the story.

David Ramsey had an easy temperament and took Beulah's ribbing in stride. "John, how did my wife's pies lead to acts of heroism from Georges and the death of two people?"

All eyes turned to John and Abel.

"It was four people, really," Abel corrected. "If you want to count the two soldiers."

Beulah came out of a momentary reverie and explained her epiphany. "The markers. Georges used the markers," she concluded, pleased with herself at providing the answer.

"That is right, Mrs. Kebob-Flynn," John continued. "Each marker on our land was a type of blind. The builder of the inn placed glass panes at the top because each marker was hollow inside. A person could hide inside from animals or angry Indians, but still have a bird's eye on the area. When the inn was built, the region was more dangerous than today. Tunnels connected the inn to the stone markers and, at some point, connected to our root cellar."

"We don't know why Georges was watching through the glass that day, but he saw the red coats and ran through the tunnel toward the inn to warn us," Abel picked up. "After the first musket fired, he must have heard footsteps running in his direction. He yelled loudly not to come down the shaft. He didn't know if the runner was Abigail, myself, or the enemy, so he yelled the warning as he ran back toward the LeSage home."

The thrilling story had the party in complete silence now. Abigail stood and grabbed Abel's hand.

"Excuse me, everyone," Able said. "I need to take my wife outside for some air."

The crowd understood and made way for their

friends as Abel escorted his wife out of the great hall.

The group of people stood as statues. Not a whisper was uttered as they hung by tenterhooks to hear what humble Georges did that day. Beulah was delighted by the entertaining of her guests. In this short lull, she nudged her sister-in-law toward the LeSage men. John glanced her way and saw her little shrug.

"Why were there only two soldiers? Why not an entire garrison? Were they headed to Richmond to get at Lafayette?" asked Daniel Plinthe.

Servants refilled the guests' glasses as John Jr. continued.

"We don't think the Brits were deserters. Someone knew about the store of gunpowder, and they probably made a pretty penny from the information."

"We were so quiet. So careful," the captain mused. "But we had been stockpiling for years. Any of the passengers I brought over could have leaked information purely from the cargo of their passage. Some, not virtuous by nature, may have had an axe to grind, and information like that would be worth a lot to the right person. Thinking back on all those years, I can't believe the duration of our success," he said with a sad voice.

Armand patted him on his back in solidarity of the operation.

Another guest asked, "Did the soldier fire upon Georges?"

"Georges detonated the powder. He was the caretaker of the stash and knew how important it was to keep it for the Continental Army." John Jr. took a deep breath. "Georges could tell the person following him was not one of the Trentons. He had savvy, like a hunted animal. He led the intruder deeper into the tunnel. Probably, when the red coat caught up to him, he fired to ignite the powder, blowing up himself, the enemy, and the remaining store of gunpowder. Mrs. Trenton was far enough away that she didn't sustain life threatening injuries, but the blast wreaked havoc on her hearing."

The conclusion of the story left the room silent for a moment more when the ambassador raised his brandy glass and offered, "Salute, Georges LeSage!"

The people raised their glasses in Georges's honor and disbursed throughout the room to dance, as the band had begun playing a lilting gigue.

Beulah looked at John in his tight-fitting coat. He noticed her gaze and stood a little taller, pulling at the tails in his awkwardness. He put forth his arm for her, and she took it.

"Johnny, I know a young lady that could do wonders with that waistcoat of yours. Accompany me, and I will introduce you to her."

They walked toward the table that had drink and all kinds of delicious foods. "Miss Langstaff has been making alterations on Armand's clothes. She has the finest stitches, as if she was trained by Rose Bertin, herself! She has been helping with the food platters tonight."

John stopped as a simply dressed woman put a hot platter of meat onto the long table. She looked up, and her eyes met his across the room. Beulah and her escort approached the table, but before she could make a formal introduction, John released Beulah's arm and reached across the plate of steaming venison, taking the young woman's hand.

"I am John LeSage, Jr. and I shall marry you as soon as you consent."

Part 2

Chapter 18

The wedding of John LeSage, Jr., and Emma Langstaff was a small affair but a memorable event for the close-knit sailing families of Virginia. The Huguenots of the area celebrated with fervor of the coupling of the son of John LeSage Sr. and Hildegard Elizabeth Anne LeSage, neé Cassagne, and the daughter of Bernard Langstaff and Lenora Langstaff, neé Berry.

The year was 1788, and the wedding took place on the grounds at the LeSage brick house near Mishipeshu. Captain John was delighted that the young couple had wed and that John, Jr. had learned a trade that did not take him away from his family for months on end as it did for a sea captain.

The devoted couple decided to move to a town northeast of Mishipeshu to start their new life together. John, fourteen years Emma's senior, had honed his forging skills and was a master craftsman. This allowed him to put down stakes where he pleased in New England.

John and Emma relocated to the Chester area, a community south of Philadelphia. Pig iron was readily available, and a large forge in the area was in need of a smith. The captain sailed them up the coast and helped them settle in before returning to his family in Breton for good.

""John brought logs inside and placed them beside the hearth. Emma was finishing dinner preparations for the two of them.

"Emma, how are you feeling tonight?"

"I am well, dear, thank you for your concern."

"Are you certain? Let me help you with the food."

"I am very strong, John. Not yet." Emma reached up to John's cheek and kissed it as she placed a pan on the table. They ate together in silence. "After I have cleaned up, we could—"

John nearly jumped from his chair at Emma, "Yes, okay, certainly. If you think it's not too soon."

"I don't think it is possible to over strain, John, but I know some folks do. Sit tight while I finish," Emma said without emotion. She dried the cleaned dishes and glanced over at John. He had become lost in his own thoughts, a million miles away from Chester. Emma came up behind his chair and rubbed his strong shoulders. "You are too tense. You need to stop thinking about it. I don't know if I will be able to live with you when I do conceive."

"Oh, Emma."

"Honestly, you are like a big kid ready to spring on gifts. Patience, my darling, you know as well as I that all good things come to those who wait."

John reached behind him and tightly grabbed Emma by the leg. He didn't turn and face her. A moment of frozen silence passed.

"John?"

Nothing.

"Have I angered you in some way?"

John still does not move.

"What is wrong, John?"

John pushed away from the table and turned to Emma. He stood with an eerie smirk shining from his face. His bright but sinister steely, blue eyes glowed with some kind of secret—a secret Emma was now afraid would be revealed in some detrimental way. For the first time in their short marriage, she was fearful of her hulking husband.

Quick as a flash, John scooped Emma into his arms. He began walking, restraining her tightly. She began to scream and wished she could flee. John's foot kicked the door open with the force of a tempest and he took her across the yard toward the creek.

Stars shone brightly in the sky. The area John LeSage had taken his bride to live was rural, considering the proximity of the nearby industry and wharf. The onshore currents cleansed the air of stifling hearth smoke, providing clean, crisp air for the inhabitants. Intense fragrance assaulted the senses. The purified air was laden with the aroma of sweet pepperbush. John had trod over wild ginger, crushing the delicate plants, and releasing their secretive flavors.

Emma struggled from his grip and screamed with terror. John could not stifle his laughter anymore and began roaring in a jag that ended with tears streaming down his cheeks.

Emma relaxed at the closure of the dramatics and went limp in his arms. "What is in your head, John LeSage? Why have you frightened me out of my wits?"

He did not answer her but deposited her gently in the soft oak sedge near the creek that bordered their land.

This wildness accurately reflected the inner soul of the boy. Had Emma known little Johnny, she would have recognized the impish air of misdeeds that would follow such an expression as he led his younger brother on grand excursions of defiance.

As the twinkling stars shifted across the heavens, the trickster sprang into action. His moves were like a large cat stalking prey, using stealthy, calculated moves to ensure success. Emma was ravaged with silky paws as the cat's meal was devoured.

After desire was sated, the puma thoroughly licked up the residue as his prey lay motionless, transfixed by the passion of one man and the care and tenderness it revealed.

With this effort of the noblest kind, Emma conceived and, in the allotted time, a gift from God entered the earthly world as Charlotte LeSage.

Chapter 19

Frolicking and enjoying all hedonistic pleasures of the night precipitated pungent excrement from an establishment. Gluttonous patrons abandoned delicacies throughout the evening like molting fowl lose their down while escaping a persistent, hungry fox. It was, therefore, no surprise that successive nights of this inconsequential freedom for laborers and shoddy performers left behind an expected amount of "debris." There was a time when the word "reuse" was much the vogue, but the action fell short for those enjoying a miniscule amount of time off from work and, attempting to live an entire calendar page in one evening— eating, drinking, and becoming entranced by mesmerizing and accommodating Cyprians.

A small town in New England at the end of the eighteenth century, of course, had much to offer its citizens, and the seedy parts, endemic to any metropolis, were seemingly contained to a small, known area that decent folk did not stray to.

"Owie! *Maman, mon doigt!*"

Emma LeSage turned quickly, as if seen performing an unsavory or immoral task, toward the plainly dressed little girl. Now relaxed, she sighed, placing her small wooden basket on the ground and reaching for the damaged digit.

"Oh, my, *c'est une mauvaise coupe*—you have given yourself a good one today." Emma placed a neat handkerchief around her daughter's injury and engulfed the three-year-old with the warmth of an embrace, which quickly and thoroughly healed Charlotte LeSage's momentary feeling of attack and laceration. "What did you do, pet?"

"That mean piece of glass over there made my finger bleed."

"I am so sorry." Emma held her daughter close to her, the tyke swallowed by the woman's full dark brown skirt. She did not readily move, frozen in a kind of healing meditation that nourished the little girl or, perhaps, herself. Leaving her reverie, she stood, dusted off her skirt, picked up her basket, and led Charlotte by her uninjured hand out of the grimy alley.

"Let's leave this to another time and get Papa's dinner to him. *le Papa a besoin de son dîner.*"

Chapter 20

Ivory staggered slowly through the back alley of the hotel. It was mid-morning. She could be drunk, but considering the piles of dead and decaying vermin, human excrement, and ashes, even the most sober person would sway to and fro while traversing this small urban capillary.

Ivory was dressed in a jaundiced cotton night gown with cardinals embroidered on the yoke. The garment was intended for a shorter figure as Ivory's knees were available to tell of an abusive lifestyle. Her makeup was in need of great repair or removal, and she had boots on with no stockings. Her henna hair was long and untamed, and her eyes, an unhealthy crimson color, moved lithely over the rubbish as she looked for something. She shifted some debris while mumbling to herself. Then, snapping her fingers, she began moving toward one end of the alley. Spying a few cider bottles, she pushed them around with her foot.

Finally, her hand shot forward into what looked like "fresher" trash—more bottles, nut shells mixed with goo extracted from a spittoon, and a small metal box. Looking carefully while opening the trinket, she saw a highly polished, mirror-like surface, and powder within. Ivory was elated and schlepped up the back stairs, evaporating into the building.

Chapter 21

John LeSage was overheated and drenched with sweat as he waited for his irons to come to just the right glowing temperature in the furnace. He had become an imposing figure of a man, with strong shoulders and hands. He took a determined breath, and reached for his hammer with a heavily insulated hand—the girth of his forearms showing the powerful strength he had. Selecting the proper iron from the intense heat, he quickly pummeled it into shape. Plunging the horseshoe into a bucket of water cooled the newly shaped iron.

John wiped the sweat from his brow and removed his gloves. "Henry, Joe! Can one of you bring that nag back in?"

"Here she is, John. She is a little spooky today, so watch her."

"These plow animals are always spooky when they come into town and leave their fields."

The other worker, Joe, stepped over to help Henry with the horse. The three men represented average American blacksmiths. Henry was a taller individual with a goliath-sized frame who outweighed the other men by at least forty pounds of staunch muscle. Joe, on the other hand, was about the same height as John but was several years older. He was quite proud of his well-fed stature.

As they steadied the horse, John checked the fit of the shoe and then hammered the nails for a proper fit. Once done, Joe led the horse out of the smith area and secured her to a post.

The morning was nearly over. The men enjoyed a cool drink of water from the barrel outside and mingled a moment together, shielded from the hot fire within. A fourth smith, Danny, relaxed with them.

"So I thought if we had a couple of cows and goats the wife could sell the extra milk. The extra green-backs could ease—"

Danny shook his head. "No, Joe. It won't work that way. Firstly, it will only amount to a few halfpennies—and that's only if you can find a buyer."

Henry couldn't resist butting in. "Aye. And the coins will probably have King George's face on them, at that!"

"Thank you, Henry." Danny rolled his eyes. "Most folks have their own animals that provide for them. And just where do you think you're going to keep them? In your pocket?"

Henry always tried to keep the peace and was *pro bono publico* on a daily basis when Danny needled Joe. But sometimes it was more relaxing to get a minor dig in to keep the conversation light. "Joe ain't goin' to keep 'em in his pocket, Danny. No, he's goin' to keep 'em in that big corral on that fancy homestead of his!"

"Leave him be, Henry. You can't spite a man for trying to get ahead in this life." John had a good sense of humor but couldn't help but think that, perhaps, he too, should have plans in the works for extra income. A blacksmith's wage was hearty, but not so generous as to joke about. Still, Joe had enough ideas each week for earning his fortune that it did become laughable. "As for me, I think a little extra to spend each week could really put us in clover!"

"Whoa, yeah! I could do with a little extra and buy me some of the finest leather gloves ever seen by a middling man."

"Danny, you could get some of them gloves that smell nice, too. You know, the kind you slip into and it's all soft, warm, and broken in..." Henry's face glazed over in thought, and his voice dropped to a low whisper. The images Henry brought to mind were honest at the outset, but as he spoke, the arousal of a more tender application drew him in.

"Henry, that's enough of *that*. Will you guys never change?"

"You just miss it, John, that's all, admit it. Danny and I ain't got no women in our lives—"

Danny nodded, "That's right, Henry, not the marrying kind. You don't know how lucky you are to have Emma. You and Joe don't need to...well, dream."

"Oh, oh, oooh! Joe, did you hear these two? Did he just insinuate that we are old? I think he just put you and me out to pasture!"

"I think you are right, John. These fellas must think your life is over when you hit old age—"

"Yes. I had no idea I was creeping up and about to hear the ominous knell of Death when I turned twenty-eight last October."

Chapter 22

Emma was a wonderful wife and mother. She was driven by a Puritanical force to complete her responsibilities. Her parents were older and had immigrated to America to improve the quality of life for their family. The move was successful. Their children assimilated easily into the new culture. Daily chores of procedure and cleanliness that had been ingrained by the ancestors followed this new generation. Imprinting of this kind was difficult to lose and, therefore, Emma's tenacity for cleanliness and order was unlike her peers of multiple generations.

Women of her age in their early twenties had increasingly lost this trait as energy was redirected to other tasks. Not that they were slovenly, no, just not as obsessive as their grandmothers. This younger generation focused their time on pursuing more handicrafts, which allowed women to spend more time together at sewing bees or putting up preserves and the like. This, of course, resulted in stellar amounts of gossip being broadcast, the breadth of which no Chinese aerial firework could compare.

Charlotte's three-year-old legs were aching as she attempted to keep up with her mother's clip. She was fixated on her wrapped finger as she flew down the dusty town lane, so the usual whining at this mode of travel was subdued. As Charlotte and Emma approached the blacksmith's, Charlotte pulled free of her mother's hand and ran full force to the barn door. She peeked into the building but pulled right back.

"What's the matter, Charlotte? Are you afraid of the men?"

Charlotte looked at the ground, seemingly immobilized from the scene she had spied, as Emma approached.

"That Devil—the hot one," Charlotte managed to convey in a laudable display of theatrical whispers.

"Oh, of course. You are right to be afraid of the fire and its bellows. What if we stay on this side, away from Papa's work area, by the door, and wave to Papa?"

Charlotte decided that would work well, so she stepped inside, making sure to keep one hand touching the frame of the barn door, and waved wildly.

John saw the tiny speck, took his gloves off, and started toward her. Joe, Henry, and Danny begin to remove their work gloves and heavy leather aprons as they followed John's lead toward Little Charlotte and Emma. John's family was always a good reason to take a break from work.

"Well, if it isn't Mrs. LeSage and Miss LeSage, out about town."

Charlotte thrust her wrapped finger up as high as she could so that John could examine it carefully. "Papa, kiss my finger."

John took her tiny hand and squatted down to Charlotte's level. Her father looked all over the finger wrapped with the large handkerchief.

"Why, this finger is bundled up and ready for a snow storm!"

"No, Papa, it is not bundled up. It is owie and it hurt!"

"Oh, I see. And Mama brought it here so I could heal it?" He looked up at Emma and smiled. "Let me try." A series of magical waves with his hands made Charlotte and Emma laugh.

"Papa is funny!"

Chapter 23

John and Emma sat on a couple of hay bales as John began devouring dinner.

The crowd of three other men inspired Charlotte almost immediately to request sanctuary in her mother's arms, and, at the approach of the other men, she burrowed her face deeper into Emma's blouse for added safety.

"Why, Mrs. LeSage and the beautiful Charlotte." A seasoned blacksmith with a jovial and sprite-like sense of humor, Joe was welcomed into any conversation. "It is so good to see you today. I missed church on Sunday, but you probably know all about it." This comment from Joe elicited a bright glare from Emma. He laughed. "Oh, has there been a lapse of communication of the women's prayer meeting? I cannot believe Melody hasn't passed this tidbit on."

Emma's eyes sparkled brightly. "Are you relying on a story to cover up guilt? Honestly, Joe, the devil has his claws on you."

"John, I don't think any event or occurrence is lost to dust in this community with the steadfast dedication of our wives. The good women treat this holy vow of information as if the honor had been ordained upon them from a priest. Why, I bet the efficiency of their grapevine has the ability to make any disciple—yes, any—blush in comparison to their own works, the way every little speck of information, for miles and miles, is distributed to each awaiting pair of ears."

As John tried to stop Joe, Emma beamed a many-dimensional stare at Joe. Charlotte pushed her finger out for all to see, successfully diverting attention to her woes.

"As I live and breathe! What is this small tentacle that protrudes from your bosom, Mrs. LeSage?" Joe took the hand and began walking his fingers to the elbow. Charlotte's face was still nested. "Why, this looks just like—" Joe tickled Charlotte. "—yes, yes, I believe it is. Oh, my. It is a beaut!"

As Joe tickled Charlotte, she turned toward him, giggling. Then she stoically held her injury up for serious inspection. Joe gently petted it. "…and they are so tasty!" He proceeded to "gobble" Charlotte, which made them all laugh.

"Joe, you certainly have a way with Charlotte. She is so shy."

"Don't worry, John, she'll grow out of it. Just as soon as that second baby arrives."

John looked at Emma at this remark. Emma sighed to let her husband know that she did not take any offense to the older man's traditional "small talk."

"Danny, Joe, we should leave these folks alone and tuck into our own dinner. I—I could use a little help with the harness I'm mending, too."

"Certainly, Henry, but it's me. Come on, I need help with my work."

"Oh, right. I forgot about that…um…that little piece of…" Henry said.

"All right, Henry, you don't have to go and make

something up. There's no bruising from Emma's flirting with Joe."

Realizing how obtuse they have been made Henry and Danny blush. A little chuckling was heard from the duped men as they stepped away from the LeSage family. Joe laughed a belly laugh and slapped them on the back as they left John to his dinner.

"*A ma Poupée été en soignant sa Maman ce matin?*" John asked as he pried Charlotte from her mother. "Has my doll been looking after her mama this morning?"

"Yes, Papa. *Oui*. Bad, bad bottle!"

John's big brown eyes locked onto Emma's. "I just thought I could make a little extra vinegar, she said. "It might be worth a few coppers."

Leaning over to kiss his wife, John whispers commandingly, "You are very thoughtful, but I'd rather not have my wife and child lurking through alleys behind the taverns seeking the odd bottle. I make quite enough for our needs."

"Well, if it's all the same, I'd like our daughter to have warm clothes and shoes this winter," she said, her gentle, blue eyes more akin to molten steel.

John reached for Emma's hand. He held it softly in his strong hands, his thoughts cloistered deeply. He brought her fingers to his lips and kissed them, smelling Emma's essence. Taking her into his arms, he would make love to her and show her what he could not articulate. He would caress every corner of her beautiful shape, melting the previous, careless, personal comment—dissolved and forgotten. Any worry Emma possessed of their future was disarmed as she surrendered everything to him.

As the adrenalin subsided, he spoke gently, nearly inaudibly into Emma's ear, "You are a hard worker,

Emma. Always thinking of others. Now, you and this precious princess need to skedaddle on to our castle so your prince can earn a full day's wage. When I am home tonight, you will push aside fears that any mother would hold for her family as I confirm to you again that you make me the wealthiest man alive, and that we want for nothing. *Je vais vous remplir de la force que Dieu m'a donné; forces opposées qui me permet de forger le fer et la force qui me permet de te caresse tendrement. Seul Dieu, dans Sa sagesse, saura comment fusionner les cadeaux ensemble de sorte que je suis l'homme tout entier qui a la capacité de vous fondre dans l'acquiescement et jamais besoin de remettre en question ma masculinité.* I want to make love to you right here, my dearest, and kiss every part of you. I will fill you with my firm strength until you melt and never question my masculinity." He stepped back from Emma: she did not move. He looked at her admiringly. "I've the Griffin's draft horse awaitin' to be shod, and a couple of yokes to mend."

Emma took Charlotte's hand and turned to leave. She stopped and turned to face her husband. "I love you, John."

His nod and smile communicated his desires as husband to wife. The intimate connection was an ablated and unequaled force of love.

"I will not tarry: expect me as soon as we close the smith's tonight."

Emma smiled, nodded, and left with Charlotte in her arms.

Chapter 24

The afternoon wore away gently, as a cool breeze gently blew through the cobbled streets, urging the first casualties of the stolid woods down the lanes, reminding townspeople that seasons, like life, were ever changing.

At the blacksmith's, John was nearing the end of a hot, but accomplished, day. He was pounding red hot iron into the first bend of a horseshoe. John was a valuable employee to the owner, Mr. Waling. He was a skilled blacksmith and a farrier. John had knowledge in both trades. He could build anything from iron and trim and shoe any horse.

He hammered nail holes into the rough iron and placed it back into the fire. It was hard work, besides being hot. John removed it again and completed the bend over the large anvil. He filed it so there were no rough edges. The shoe must fit the animal's foot exactly. The beast pulled a wagon. In itself, it was a heavy load, but weighed with cargo put a lot of stress on the team's feet and legs. The horse's owner put much trust into John's ability—an error could mean crippling the horse and the owner's livelihood. John had completed the shoe and cooled it in a bucket of water. He wiped his brow with a cloth, took out his pocket watch, and looked at the time.

Good. I should be at home on time. Fitting this last shoe will only take a couple of minutes," he mused. He walked over to the horse and patted its strong flank. He puts several nails in his mouth, picked up a hammer, and the shoe. A loud banging noise was heard outside, and the horse jumped and whinnied.

"That's okay, girl, you're fine. Don't let city life bother you." John had taken her lead and was petting her and talking to her until her ears settled to a normal position and her feet stayed still.

Now John took her rear hoof, checked one last time to make sure it was filed the way he liked. The shoe fit just fine, so he began nailing it in place. Another loud bang was heard, and it spooked the horse again. She jumped and kicked with her back feet.

John fell backward and lay motionless. Blood trickled down his face, and a black bruise began almost immediately.

Nearly ten minutes elapsed before Joe found John.

"Henry, Danny! Come help me. John's down."

"What is it, Joe? Holy Mother of—what do you want me to do?"

"Henry, John is dead. The horse must have kicked, and it knocked him back. He hit his head on this."

A large anvil on the floor was near John's head. Picking up his head revealed a large pool of blood from the impact. The men stood over John in disbelief. Danny stepped closer to the body and nearly heaved when he realized how much blood had oozed from John's bashed skull.

"I'll—I'll go tell Mr. Waling, Joe."

"Good, Danny. Henry, could you—I don't know, Henry, we have to get the word out. Me and the missus will go to Emma. Can you tell the townsfolk?"

"Sure, Joe." Henry wiped a tear from his soft but dirty cheek and left.

Chapter 25

Death truly was a way of life, but the human spirit shrouded any thought of it which, perhaps, made death more traumatic. Nearly a week had passed since Emma buried her husband, John, and it still left her in a dream-like state. She carried on dutifully each day for Charlotte, but the intense pain seared within her. Friends came to visit each day to check on the two and bring food.

> *O death, where is thy sting?*
> *O grave, where is thy victory?*
> *The sting of death is sin;*
> *and the strength of sin is the law.*
> *But thanks be to God, which give thus*
> *the victory through our Lord*
> *Jesus Christ. Amen.*

The women sat, holding hands. "Emma, I am so sorry for what has happened. The Good Lord does His work in strange ways. What plans have you made now that—now that you are on your own?"

Emma looked over at Charlotte as she played with her doll near the hearth. She had thought about the answer to her fate and Charlotte's. "I don't think I can get enough for passage back home by selling off our goods. We don't have much to offer. But if I can get back to Europe, John's family would be able to offer a sturdy roof over our heads—"

"*Oo, Papa? Grand-père et grand chien, Maman?*"

"*Oui, mon fille.* Grandfather with the large dog."

The other woman disregarded the little girl's statement and stared at Emma in disbelief of her naivety.

"—and food on the table. I can take in mending and get a job. Hopefully in a year or two—"

"In a year or two? Land sakes, child, you two could starve to death in that time! Where are you going to get a job?"

At that moment, Emma was shaken back to the real world. She had pushed aside the fact that there was no job for her. Sewing and laundering were trifles to the amount of living costs for her and her daughter. Emma sat across from the woman with a new type of emotion—one mixed with depression, despair, and fear. She now looked at the woman with intense hatred, as if it were she who took her loving John away. She stood quickly. "I thank you for checking on us and spending time with me, but I think you should be on your way. I have to prepare a meal for Charlotte and get her ready for bed."

Emma gently pushed the woman out of the door and shut it firmly, just missing the woman's skirts. Emma turned and faced into her small abode, tears streaming from her eyes. She ran to her cold, empty bed and sobbed.

The weeks went ploddingly along as the autumn colors deepened, the shrinking amount of daylight pinched the soul, and the equinox cold took hold and squeezed a body's essence. It was an unusually cold November, which always brought questions to mind as to the extent of brutality of the coming winter. The sage, with her crystal ball and tarot cards, could only verify for the attentive listener that it would surely be a cold winter. Useless information given for a small sum of pennies, but the costliest price was that of wasting one's time.

Emma did not waste time, but she seemed to have a surplus of it in these weeks since her husband's death. Her home and Charlotte were immaculately cleaned, the affairs were in order, and she had a steady influx of mending jobs to do for neighbors. The stream of jobs was more like a trickle, each request was quick and did not amount to much money. Throughout her day, Emma had too much time to worry about Charlotte and finances. She could hardly sock away anything each week after she paid for their needs.

One evening, after putting little Charlotte to bed, a knock on the door pushed Emma from her comfy chair by the hearth. She had completed the day's chores and was snuggled under a blanket about to read from the *Book of Esther*.

"Good evening, Widow LeSage."

"Hello, Henry, come in quickly. I didn't expect you tonight. It's so late, and the icy wind howls. I did finish your mending, though."

"Thank you, Mrs. LeSage."

"I will get your shirt. Please, warm yourself by the fire." Emma grabbed a man's shirt from her sewing pile and stepped over by Henry and the warm fire.

Henry handed Emma a few bills "It was awful nice of you to take care of that for me. I never was too handy with a needle."

"Oh, Henry, that's far too much. This is a small

fortune, and it was only a little tear."

Henry stepped closer to Emma. "You know, you always have looked out for all us at the smith's. Taken care of us if we ail, bringing us sweets during the season…"

"Henry, what are you getting at?"

"It's just that poor little girl of yours and John's— brought up fatherless, hungry, and all. I can't help bring him back, Emma, but I can help make sure she don't starve."

"We aren't starving, Henry."

He put his strong hand on her shoulder and caressed her petite arm. Emma saw the truth in what Henry said. She put the money on the table and led him to her bedroom.

Chapter 26

Nearing the end of the second year after John's death, Emma had proven that making money was a simple matter. She was an experienced and prosperous prostitute. Since being forced from her home, she and Charlotte now roomed with two other whores, above the tavern that offered much to its patrons.

A man left Emma's bedroom, tucking in his shirt and putting on his wide brimmed hat. Charlotte was busying herself with a toy on the floor. The man passed the little girl but took no notice of her.

"Mama, when are we—"

"Get what you need, we're going down to the saloon for the evening."

"Yes, Mama."

Her mother's curtness showed the decay of Emma's moral fiber. She was barely aware of Charlotte herself and could not nurture her child. Charlotte knew Emma loved her, but she could not remember the kindness and affection she was bathed in in her first three years of life.

What was obscured from both of them was the anger Emma had for herself, for how she had been swayed into an addictive habit, and how she seemed to lack the discipline to save her money. Every time she looked at Charlotte she saw John. It was this daily dose of pain that Emma believed serves as a reminder of her evil ways. Emma did love Charlotte, but when she came out of an opium high, she saw the child as a burden, barring her way from incessant ecstasy.

⸲ᘓ⸱

It was after midnight on a successful evening. Emma sat in the parlor of her flat with Ivory, one of her roommates. Both women wore brightly colored, exquisite robes and lounged on the sofa. Ivory was smoking opium, and Emma was nibbling on a crust of bread. Both women looked much older than their years. With their jaundiced pallor, they resembled fresh cadavers. Both had reed-like figures and wore heavy, bright makeup.

Ivory took a long drag on the pipe. Her head leaned back, and her eyes rolled into the back of her head. Silent and relaxing, neither spoke for a number of minutes.

"Emma, you gotta get rid of the kid."

"What? My Charlotte?"

"Yeh, who else in our line of work has a little brat?"

Emma thought it over. Ivory handed her the pipe. After a long drag, Emma was visibly more relaxed.

"They got them zoos for children up north. You could just leave her with them God-loving women."

"Nuns?"

"Yeah, that's them. They'll bring her up real proper—you know, like a little princess, or a holy woman that does good deeds for mankind." Ivory began giggling and rolling around on the sofa. "Oh, that's us. Emma, we are holy women doing good deeds for mankind!" Having extensive learning in the Bible, Emma looked horrified at the blasphemy. Ivory shrugged. "Meanwhile, you can do something good for the good of mankind, with no interruptions and no snotty noses rubbing on your silks and none of that shit." Emma sat in silence. "Oh, Emma, I don't mean Charlotte will grow up like us, in our trade. I was just having a laugh. But since she watches us every day, she probably won't be marryin' a prince or even a farmer's hand. Her future don't look to be all that rosy, the way I sees it."

"I don't know, Ivory. My baby girl—"

"Look, kid, she don't bring in no money, and dibblers don't like ta fuck when little eyes are lookin' on. She's going to get hurt one of these times, anyway."

Chapter 26

Emma took several days in considering Ivory's advice. Charlotte was her child that she loved more than anything. She would do, and had done, everything to protect and provide for her. Ivory was right, however, in that raising her daughter in an opium den and red-light flat would surely lead Charlotte down a dismal path, with no hope for a life with a loving husband and children like Emma had had.

"Oh, dear Lord, what have I done in the name of raising Charlotte? I have failed her, and I have failed You, Lord."

Emma's prayer was heard by Charlotte. She did not understand who her mother was yelling at, so she wrapped her tiny hands and arms around her mama's waist and cried with her in sympathy.

Within the next few months, Emma had located a place to leave Charlotte forever. She was forced to save some of her money to provide herself food, lodging, and drugs while she took Charlotte away and was unable to work.

Emma packed Charlotte's things into a small carpet bag. She added a few things of her own, from when her papa was with them. Emma hoped Charlotte wouldn't forget her mother and father. Her hands shook as she tried to write in her Bible. Frustrated and strung out, she tossed it in the bag and began sobbing and sniffling.

Her roommate, Belle, came into the room. "Goddamn! What is happening in here? What kind of shit are you up to, Em?"

"Sorry if I woke you, Belle."

Belle spotted Emma's tears. "Hey, it's okay. Here, let me dry your face." She took a rag and wiped Emma's tear-stained face. "Okay, let me get you some—"

"No, no, Belle, I have to leave with Charlotte."

"Oh, is that today? Well, you can't have a send-off all shaky and shit. Here, just a little bit of this laudanum."

Emma took a little swig and calmed down. "Okay, that's enough. I can't go out messed up." She grabbed the bag and Charlotte and headed out the door.

The stagecoach ride was bumpy, dirty, and noisy. It was unbearably long for Emma, but Charlotte was fascinated by the trip.

Emma questioned why her life was as it was. *This long journey is excruciating,* she thought. *I want to think of Charlotte in these last few hours, but all I can think of is that damned elixir.* She then removed a small, blue bottle from her skirt pocket. She studied it a little then looked over at the tiny bundle, curled up asleep on the opposite bench.

Passenger after passenger had crammed into the coach and crowded the LeSage girls. It was agony— driving for hours with a fidgety, hot body on her lap and enduring the overwhelming stench of unwashed, corpulent travelers.

"We are finally travelling alone," she mused. "What a sinful wretch I am! But, oh, I need this medicine!" Uncorking the blue bottle, she put it to her lips and drank a strong draught of laudanum. It was a common enough prescription for a plethora of what ailed a woman, but she was uncomfortable taking it in front of strangers. Perhaps they could read her mind? A horrible thought! Through strange powers, might they somehow see through the façade of the devoted mother?

The opiate settled her and her delusional thoughts. She felt this a great success, because now Emma could focus on Charlotte. Her child was the prettiest girl she had ever seen and growing like a weed. Emma was pleased with herself and the accomplishment of such a wonderful baby. She treated herself with half of the contents of the nearly full bottle.

The concentrated elixir she ingested was enough to drop a buffalo. Emma slept. She dreamed that she ran through an open field in the sunshine—the fragrant flowers ubiquitous, the breeze refreshing, uplifting. The sky was a beautiful indigo, and the sun, beginning its descent, was easy on the senses.

Emma was happy and carefree, leaping and running in the meadow. John came toward her and took her in his arms. He held her, his strong arms sliding across her every curve. She was happy, drunk with love. John pulled away, and fear struck her. Looking across the field, every tree was ablaze, glowing like an iron. She looked at John, but it was not John. It was someone else, but she could not tell who it was. He was not to be trusted. He was dangerous. He was not pleasant to look at: The experience was terrifying. The man wielded a heavy hammer, went to the glowing-hot beech trees, and pounded his hammer on them.

Now Emma's attention caught on the many figures approaching her. Horrified, she tried to run but couldn't leave the spot. She worked harder and harder. The figures neared. They wore dark robes and hoods. The woods still glowed with fire.

As she attempted to get away from the onslaught of strangers, their robes turned from a dark color to a darker, more ominous shade as black as midnight tar. She feared them less, and her breathing slowed. A feeling of euphoria took her, leaving her with an apathy toward the cloaked crowd.

These figures—Emma felt there were maybe ten to fifteen of them—approached her and began disrobing her. She stood stark naked before them. Her apathy held her steady as she watched them. Then uneasiness captured her as she witnessed the robes changing to a deep, sticky, scarlet hue. The figures were laughing, drooling, and carrying on like a crazed mob. They did not seem human. The robes appeared to liquefy but not erode. The macabre spectors neared her and, as though by magic, the viscous and sanguine fabric defiled her flesh and colored her in their likeness.

Emma's horror and fear escalated. It was blood. Her death was eminent. She could not withstand these ghouls and the terror she could not control within her mind. Then she fell. She fell down into an abyss, accelerating to speeds beyond comprehension. Emma was tired and accepted her fate. She did not fight. She let it carry her away into the Unknown. Anything was better than being with the cloaked, bloody figures.

The stagecoach gave a lurch and groaned enough to awaken Emma. She gripped the wooden seat of the coach and steadied her mind. She looked at her sleeping beauty and wondered when this ride through Hell would end.

Tall, dark shadows fell from the narrow slit of moonlight when they arrived at the Good Samaritan Orphanage for Waifs in New Hampshire. Charlotte slept like a wee babe as her mother carried her through the stagnant darkness. It was well beyond the Witching Hour. A darkly clad figure opened the door and took the child and her belongings. Not a word was uttered. Emma had corresponded with the orphanage—her story laid out, along with her needs. The nun disappeared behind the heavy door with Emma's child.

Part 3

Chapter 28

Eleven-year-old Charlotte finished cleaning up a large amount of dishes. She had grown to a good height for her age and was an obedient ward. She had a sturdy, but lean, build and had dark hair and eyes. The assortment of dishes had chips and scratches and were generally plain, institutional kitchenware. They had served the convent school well and would for many years to come. Completing her task, she removed her white apron and hung it on a peg to dry then ran outside to meet with her best friend, Elizabeth.

"Charlotte, I'm so glad you are here. I thought you would never finish those dishes after that slimy meal!"

"Sister Mary Ruth helped me. She said it was unfair that my dish night 'included pasty and oily food that wouldn't even be found in trials of the Old Testament'!"

Both girls held on to each other and giggled as they walked together. It was a beautiful June evening.

Elizabeth was the same age as Charlotte but much more at ease with people, therefore, more outgoing. Her perky disposition was partnered well with the shining red-blonde hair upon her head and her crystalline blue eyes.

Charlotte fell into character immediately. "I want to be queen and have a royal court when I grow up!"

"Yes, but what about all of our own dishes? Who is to clean them when you are queen, Elizabeth?

"I will have my servants do them, of course, or better yet, we'll just throw them away when they are dirty and command a new set to be made."

"Oh, your majesty, I never dreamed of such riches."

Charlotte stopped walking and performed an honorable curtsy. "Silly of me to even suggest such chores. Hey, Elizabeth, let's see what Bartholomew is up to!"

The girls laughed as they raced to a stable.

Four strong horses were munching their evening meal within a corral. A young man of seventeen tended the animals. He wore brown trousers with dark brown, leather suspenders and dirty boots. His long-sleeved, heavy cotton shirt was well worn. The multitude of washings it had been subjected to had faded it to a faint buckskin hue. The sleeves were rolled up as far as possible to keep him cool, but his arms had a large girth, making it only possible to clear above the elbow. Mousy brown hair covered his ears, and his head was topped with a tired bicorn hat. He carried a large bucket and waved to the girls as they approached. He was a plain-looking youth, neither handsome nor ugly, but in the evening dusk his features were illuminated and showed the potential in the powerful facial features to be a stunningly handsome man.

""Bartholomew set the bucket down, pushed his hat up off of his forehead, and leaned against the rail. "Girls! How now, Miss Charlotte?"

"Well, thank you, Bartholomew," Charlotte said quietly as she looked carefully at her hands to avoid eye contact.

"Don't you two have lessons to tend to?"

"We just finished dinner, but we do have an evening lesson," Elizabeth offered eagerly. "Sister Mary Ruth is taking us out today to study nature. I just love being outside in nature. All the wonderful smells—the flowers and grass—even the air is better!"

"Well, that sounds like a good time. What about you, Charlotte, do you like to study outside?"

"Yes, I like it very much," she said, attempting a quick look at his face as she answered.

The two girls followed Bartholomew to the barn. He put the bucket away and began raking some of the straw back into a stall.

"Oh, Charlotte," Elizabeth gushed. "Summer is so wonderful with quacking flocks of birds back for feeding and fattening, the warm breezes and the—"

"Mosquitos," Charlotte said in deadpan.

All three of them laughed heartily at such a true observation.

Charlotte was emboldened to urge her friend, "Liza, we should probably get back over to the pergola. Sister Mary Ruth is going to think we forgot."

Bartholomew nodded. "Well, Miss Charlotte has a good point. If you two don't trot off to the evening lesson, Sister Mary Ruth might have you praying penitence for a month of Sundays. But promise me you'll come back tomorrow and see me again?"

"May we brush the horses for you?" Charlotte managed to look at Bartholomew's face to convey her hopes.

He looked at her and scratched his stubbly chin. "How old are the two of you now?"

"Eleven," both answered together.

He grinned "I think eleven is just the age for young girls to learn about horses. 'Sides, these horses

wouldn't hear of anyone else doin' it but yourselves.
Now, git on afore your backsides get tanned."

The girls squealed delightedly and ran over to the
field where classes met for nature lessons.

Chapter 29

All of the girls were waiting at the pergola when Mary Ruth started her lesson. The lesson drew attention to all of God's creatures of the insect world. As Mary Ruth led them toward the beaver pond, the tiniest little girls were dragged along by two of the bossier ten-year-old girls. The three-year-olds generally delighted in studying bugs, but they could only wonder why prayers and bedtime seemed so difficult to achieve during this warm season.

Charlotte and Elizabeth listened carefully to the sister describe the active insects at dusk. Fish in the pond jumped for their meal while industrious animals worked along the banks in search of theirs. A raccoon rinsed berries in the water and ate them while the last glimmer of the day's light reflected off of its small, black eyes.

As the sun set, the class sat quietly, observing the activity of the pond. Sister Ruth began walking back to the main building, which was a sign that the girls should follow. Charlotte and Elizabeth walked arm in arm, whispering.

"Don't you just think he's handsome?"

"Yes. But how many footmen and servants does he have, Queen Elizabeth?"

Both laughed enough to make the girls at the front of the migration turn around and stare. The two friends ignored them and continued laughing, enjoying the magical summer evening.

The dormitory was quiet and still now that the last resident returned from the outhouse and settled into her soft bedding. Moonlight shone from high in the heavens through a paned window as a nightgown-clad figure stole across the hard maple floor and slipped under the quilt next to Charlotte.

"Charlotte, are you asleep?"

"Naturally, I am asleep. I cannot awake to know that my best friend is out of her bed and is going to get us in trouble."

Elizabeth laid still. Their faces were four inches apart. Elizabeth's breathing was loud and excited. She tried to quiet herself, and her pounding heart slowed its tempo at Charlotte's tone.

"An evil witch has put me under a spell and I cannot move," Charlotte said with a soft giggle.

Tension melted away.

Elizabeth chuckled. "Oh, you poor princess. Will a handsome young prince rescue you?"

Charlotte attempted to reply, but both girls began to giggle and retreated under the covers.

"Sshh!" was heard across the room and made the two freeze.

"You better go back to your bed before we get penance," whispered Charlotte.

"Okay, Charlotte. I love you."

"I love you, too, now go on!"

Chapter 30

The sun rose early and began warming the air. It was nice to tread on ground that was neither frozen nor muddy. Charlotte stroked the broad nose of Sammy, a large and gentle draft horse, while Bartholomew finished his work in the corral and moved into the stable. Charlotte picked up a brush in one hand and petted the ears of the horse in the opposite stall.

"They take a lot of brushing, especially after being rigged up to a wagon. They like it, though," Bartholomew opined. Charlotte was silent. "You also have to take pains with their feet."

"Their feet?" Charlotte asked quietly.

"The hooves get rubbish and gravel pressed into them. It's a lot worse than when you have a stone in your shoe."

Charlotte absorbed every word of horse care from Bartholomew.

"Here, let me show you how to brush her."

"Is this Appleshell?" she asked.

He nodded. "Yes. She is a hard working horse."

Charlotte watched as Bartholomew brushed her dark coat.

"She is one of our biggest animals, but she is probably the most gentle of the lot."

She considered the large creature. As he continued to brush, the animal's back rippled, and she threw her head up and down. "Why does she do that, Bartholomew? Is she angry?"

"No, she ain't angry—she likes being brushed and talked to. When you see her back do that little dance and she moves her head like you just saw, why, she's telling you that she is happy and excited. There's nothing to fear when a horse does that."

"Should you fear a horse, Bartholomew?"

"Oh, they let you know when they ain't happy. The trick is to know it ahead of time, so all this muscle don't pound into you." He gave Appleshell a good pat on her back and stroked her. "Mighty strong creatures, these horses. They can trample you and kick you and snap your body like a twig."

Charlotte took a step backward.

He chuckled. "She ain't going to hurt us right now, Charlotte. Come on now, take the brush and do the legs. Just keep talking to her, and pat her with your other hand so she knows what you're doing."

Charlotte visited the horses every chance she got. Bartholomew showed her how to comb out the long hair on Appleshell's feet, mane and tail. She learned how to feed the horses and fit them with bridals, harnesses, and saddles. She talked to the horses as much as she did her best friend, Elizabeth.

Chapter 31

A year of learning and growing had elapsed at the Good Samaritan Orphanage. It was a particularly fine August morning, and the two friends lay on their backs in the tall grasses and watched puffy, white clouds move silently across the deep blue sky. The sounds of summer hummed through the air. The tones were complimentary and caressed the girls with warmth and well-being.

Butterflies flitted from flower to flower as they attempted to alight on every bloom of meadowsweet, fragrant goldenrod, and Joe Pye weed. Bees and ladybugs worked diligently at their tasks, so as not to waste any summer flower.

"What are you going to do when you grow up, Elizabeth?"

Elizabeth lazily rotated her hand and fingers as she watched a ladybug making its way to no avail. "Ahh, eee, oowoowoo…"

"Is it funny? Are you going to be a clown? Have you decided to be the court jester instead of the queen?"

"Oh, you are so funny, Charlotte! Okay, fly away home, ladybug!" The beetle escaped to a nearby flower and resumed its tasks. Elizabeth took in a deep breath and let it out.

"Do you ever hear anything I say to you?"

"What? Of course! I heard you, Charlotte. Let me see…well, I won't be queen, so I guess I will get married and have children. My house will be beautiful and clean, too. I can't live in a dirty house. And I will make luscious pies and sweets. The best in the area. Of course, that's why I will probably marry the most handsome man in the county. He probably won't be the wealthiest, but he will think I am the prettiest, and he will work hard so that he can earn my pastries. Why?"

"Would that man be *Bartholomew*?"

"No, no, no. He is very handsome, it's true, but he has too much wealth."

"Too much wealth? He's a stable hand!"

"I know, but I think his uncle owns the stable."

"How do you know that? You *are* sweet on him, aren't you?"

"Charlotte LeSage, you take that back! I have just listened to the adults when they talk. It's not my fault I'm smart."

"Eavesdropping is a sin. You *like* him, *don't you*?" Charlotte noticed the blush extending up Elizabeth's face. After a moment of silence, Charlotte pleaded, "I'm sorry I said those hurtful things. Will you forgive me?"

"Well, uh, what are you going to do, Charlotte?"

"Oh. I don't know. The sisters trained Matilda Loy, and now she is a teacher down in Louden. Maybe they will train us, too. I don't think I could do it, though."

"Why on earth not? You won't be so shy forever. You rally around when you need to, Charlotte—like the other day when you licked Sally Jo."

Charlotte had a big grin on her face from the

memory. "She had it coming," she said with a subdued voice. "Picking on little Amy like that, and making her cry."

"I think that was the bravest act any of us have seen in a long time. I think you would do fine as a teacher but—and I won't say this to anyone else, I promise—I don't think you should take vows to join the Church. I think you may be quick to take up the rod so the children will be safe from being spoiled."

At this statement, Elizabeth got up and ran as hard as she could toward the orphanage. Charlotte arose, brushed off her petticoat, and trotted in the same direction, laughing.

Chapter 32

Being twelve years old made some things easier for the girls. Chores were reassigned each autumn. As the girls graduated toward adulthood, they received more dignified chores. This helped the sisters manage the brood, and allowed girls to feel more mature by having more responsibilities.

Some things remained difficult at any age. Winter hit hard and fast that year. Ice seemed to creep into the river forests weeks before the maples and heath shrubs changed to their final, deep colors. Snow flurries stung uncovered cheeks and fingers. The older girls quickly learned that graduating to things like bringing in wood for the fire and filling buckets with water were more akin to torture.

"Goodwife Esther Agnes, it is too cold for us to go outside."

"Elizabeth, if you do not fetch more wood, you will be much colder than you are when the fire burns out."

"I suppose you are right. Once I get my coat on I will go." Elizabeth donned another layer before braving the out of doors. "When you find my body in the courtyard as stiff as a bronze statue, will you lament my demise?"

"Of course not, Elizabeth. We will pray your soul crosses over to be with our Heavenly Father."

"Naturally," Elizabeth mumbled to herself, still unhappy about going out in the unseasonable cold.

"Let me get my cloak, Elizabeth, and I will help you." Charlotte jumped up to get her coat.

"See, Elizabeth, the Lord will provide. Remember: Content makes poor men rich, and discontent makes rich men poor."

"What book is that from, Goodwife Esther Agnes?"

"It's not exactly from the Bible. Benjamin Franklin penned it. But it is good advice."

"Okay, Elizabeth, I'm ready."

"Good, Charlotte, prepare to be extremely rich from being discontented in the cold."

The girls braved the cold and retrieved several logs each to resupply the hearth. Elizabeth removed her warm layers. "Oh. I don't think even January is this cold!"

"January is worse. I am going out to check on the horses. The barn isn't very warm. I can add another blanket to Appleshell."

"Bartholomew will have the horses blanketed just fine, Charlotte. Stay inside."

"It won't take long. I can talk to them, too."

"They don't care what you say. It's cold for them, too."

"I'll be back in a jiff." Charlotte slipped out the door and ran to the stables. When she arrived, she found the barn much warmer than outside, and the animals were fine. She checked on Appleshell and spoke quietly to her.

The barn door opened and brought a chill in before it slammed closed. The light from a candle lantern alerted Charlotte that the person was not Elizabeth.

"Hey, now! What brings you out in this weather?" Bartholomew hailed the girl as he entered the barn. "Is Appleshell warm enough?"

"Yes, I believe so. I just thought I'd talk with her before I turn in."

"Do the sisters know where you are? It's a little late for orphans to be wandering about."

"I'm big enough to go about. I'm one of the oldest girls now. Elizabeth even has kitchen duties with Sarah and Rachael."

"Ahh, yes. You are really growing up. You will be a woman soon."

Charlotte continued to pet Appleshell, and watched her dark eyes as the lantern light flickered off of them. Bartholomew gave one of the younger steeds a few oats and came to stand by Charlotte.

"Is that your desire? To cook in the kitchen?"

"I like it outside. The kitchen is too hot and crowded."

"The barn is full of flies and vermin. And the livestock smell."

"I don't mind the smell at all, and I think the mice are cute and soft. One day Rachael screamed when she opened the flour barrel. Sarah quickly grabbed the mouse with her hand and threw it to the mouser! It was so mean and heartless."

"Well, Miss Charlotte, they may be soft and furry, but they're nothing but a nuisance in the granary. You sure have a soft side to you." Charlotte blushed at his praise. Bartholomew stepped closer to her. "I wouldn't'a thought it, the way I seen you lick that Sally Jo."

Charlotte was a bit embarrassed that he witnessed the fight but proud of her victory. "Well, I'm just glad you are on my side."

Bartholomew took Charlotte by the hand and led her to a stall filled with straw. She was confused. "Miss Charlotte," he said. "I sure appreciate the attention you give to these animals."

"I love animals, especially horses. They are so strong and beautiful. What are you doing?"

"They sure are." He pulled Charlotte closer. He felt her cheek and then cupped his large hands around her face. "You know, there are other things more important than horses."

Bartholomew was one of the few people Charlotte was comfortable with. His behavior was odd, but she found the attention exhilarating. "Yes, silly," she said. "Like warm, summer weather, apple pies and sumacade!"

"I can keep myself warm in the cold season. But a man's got to have his appetite taken care of—and apple pie's a good way to fill it." He pulled her head forward, ran his hands down her shoulders, and pulled her waist against his. He nuzzled her neck and whispered, "But sometimes a man don't get his fill at the table and needs a little dessert."

Charlotte relaxed enough to be unconcerned with his forwardness. "Apple pie *is* dessert, you!" She didn't understand his game and pushed him away playfully.

"Sometimes a pretty girl is the only way to satisfy his sweet tooth." He tugged his suspenders off of his shoulders and pulled her back to him. Bartholomew placed her hips against his.

She felt his crotch grow and harden as he rubbed it against her. Charlotte was scared and did not understand what he was doing. She tried in vain to continue the conversation. "Goody Esther Agnes says we should be grateful for even the smallest amount of luxury. Bartholomew, I need to get back. Please let me go."

"Goody Esther Agnes don't know what a man needs."

Bartholomew pushed her down and continued his assault on the girl. As he forced himself onto her, tears trickled from the corners of her eyes. She began to struggle and wished to get away, but it only made him hold her tighter. She never considered just how strong he was and how roughly he could treat her. Charlotte laid in the scratchy straw and knew she was at his mercy.

His pungent odor seemed to intensify with every movement. It was wild and unbroken. She tried to distract her mind from the immolation—rape was unlike anything she could imagine. She focused on the flame in the candle lantern that was on a post above them. She fixed her thoughts on the bail wire with black smoke easing above it from the vent holes. She noted the graded black soot on the glass panes and how the soot thinned nearer the flame as each candle melted down.

As he forced into her, she let go a little whimper from the pain and quickly refocused her mind on the sturdy wood frame of the lantern. Pegs had been fitted and hammered into each panel to hold its shape. It was a valuable item. At the orphanage, they did not have anything so grand. They had many candle holders and a few iron betty lamps that burned fat.

Focusing her mind did not take away the vile act or memory of it. Once the ordeal was over, Charlotte lay still like an injured and frightened animal.

"I am grateful, Miss Charlotte. And I'll be even more grateful if we just keep this to ourselves." He wiped his hands on his shirt tails as he tucked them into his trousers. He pulled up the leather suspenders, put his hat on his head, and put his cloak on. As he left the barn, he turned to Charlotte and reiterated, "Our secret, right?"

She nodded as if nothing out of the ordinary had happened, and he left into the night.

Chapter 33

Charlotte crept inside as quietly as possible and shut the door carefully behind her. She removed her shoes and headed to the stairs to retreat to the dormitory.

"Put your shoes by the hearth, child, so they are warmed for you in the morning."

Charlotte froze on the stairs at Sister Esther Agnes's comment. The two tired women sat by the fire with some mending before retiring to bed. Charlotte turned, picked up her shoes, and placed them with all of the different sizes of shoes, scuffed and ratty though they were, that sat dutifully for their young owners when they arose. She stared at the women and could hardly move. A pale look of horror reflected from Charlotte's face. She could not speak.

"We thought you returned with Elizabeth when the wood was brought in. You haven't been ailing, out at the outhouse this whole time, have you?"

"No, Goody Esther Agnes. I didn't think it would take so much time...I...I was just going to check the horses and run right back, Sister Esther Agnes. Please forgive me?"

"Charlotte, you haven't done anything wrong,

dear," Good Mary Ruth said, "but I must insist that when it is so dark and cold, please put chores and tasks *before* supper."

Sister Esther Agnes nodded. "You are going to catch the grippe going out in this cold, dear child. Heed Goody Mary Ruth's warning." Returning her attention to her colleague, she noted, "Oh, Sister, we could have a rough go at it this winter, to be sure. Bitingly cold even before Advent and three little ones with fever. Our dear Father presents us with such trials!"

With the sisters safely back in their evening routine, Charlotte skulked up the stairs to the dormitory. All of the girls slept securely in their beds. She poured a bit of water into the basin on the stand near her bed. She didn't notice how cold the water was on her hands when she dipped the rag into it. It offered gentle relief to her face as she cleaned the tear stains and grime off. Quietly, she rinsed and wiped her skin. Moonlight revealed her legs and crotch were a horror—blood and semen, mixed with bits of straw. The irritants came off readily—the pain was still numbed from the trauma of being raped.

Chapter 34

The early autumn did not properly announce the winter's cold. Snow fell in its usual way in New Hampshire, but it wasn't a particularly harsh winter. The orphanage continued on the day to day routine, with only one death that season. One of the newer toddlers, Amias Aaron, became ill with croup. Several different women from surrounding communities came to help nurse him, but he succumbed after a short week.

Charlotte did not feel well that winter. Sister Mary Ruth had her drink hot, herbal tea several times each day and made her pray extra each evening. She was put with several other children that had come down with a variety of complaints. Charlotte thought the tea helped with nausea, so she followed the sister's remedy. Charlotte prayed in earnest, too—she felt her sins substantial and required divine forgiveness. By the end of February, she felt much better and was happy to return to her own bunk. Storms still came down from the northeast and were cold, but the earth began to show signs of rebirth.

Elizabeth knew that with the coming of spring her friend would be fine. There was so much to look forward to now that they were thirteen, and nearly courting age. Elizabeth was excited to have fresh new culinary ingredients as the earth revived, and she nagged the sisters, Sarah and Rachael, daily about what could be made with the fresh ingredients from the woods. The outdoor opportunities were gaining in progression: cold would settle into sugaring temperatures, and the Lenten season would emerge to see hopniss and checkerberry vines awaken. Fox grape vines on the pergola will soon begin to sprout leaves, and the warm breezes and smells of summer would envelope them all.

Warmer weather did improve Charlotte's mood. She felt newly awakened and had energy to race through her chores and lessons so that she could spend more time with the horses. She seemed to be lighter of heart and laughed more with Elizabeth.

A day late in March saw Charlotte happily walking the quarter mile to the stables. It was early morning, and she enjoyed the symphony performed by songbirds, toads and crickets. Solitude offered time to think. She watched Cole as he trotted in the corral. Some said he was a Narragansett Pacer. Bartholomew disagreed with what others said and stood firmly with him being a thoroughbred.

The animal was completely black and handsome. Bartholomew said he would reach at least fifteen hands, and a pacer would be lucky to reach fourteen, if you could even find one these days. Charlotte considered what he said about them being long gone and not as good riding anyway.

Cole jumped and played without care, the warm air of his nose emerged as steam as it burst into the chilly air. She wondered what went through the mind of a young horse. *Does he dream about grand things like she and Elizabeth did? Do the horses chat and tell se-*

crets to each other? Does he pretend he is a dragon as he plays in the cool air?

Charlotte continued on to the barn to see her favorite horse, Appleshell. She petted the animal and talked to her. Bartholomew entered and did his work at the other end of the barn, but he did not say anything. This was surprising since she had spent so little time with the horses over the winter. She thought a more heartfelt greeting would have been offered. The two of them had a bond—Charlotte knew it wasn't a virtuous union, but he had selected her to spend time with that evening so many weeks ago. There were older, prettier girls he could have chosen.

As his work neared Appleshell's stall, Bartholomew said good morning. He never mentioned the evening that he raped her. He didn't seem to treat her any differently, either. He tended to his duties and made small talk as in the past.

"Where is your sidekick Elizabeth, Charlotte?"

"She is with the others at Chicktoah Ranch. They are helping Mr. Apgar collect sugar." She turned to him and studied his face. It was hard for her to talk to him now, and wasn't sure how to start. "Bartholomew, do you like me?"

"Sure, I like you fine."

Charlotte went back to brushing Appleshell. She nodded her head as she thought to herself. It was a feeble attempt, but she needed him to talk to her. After a few minutes of silence, she ventured, "I didn't feel well this winter. That's why I didn't come to see the horses as much. I heard that you danced every dance with Rachael at the Hopsing's wedding in January. Elizabeth and I get to go to weddings and dances, now that we are thirteen."

Bartholomew repaired a rail that had loosened. He

did not comment, he continued his work as if she wasn't there.

"Have I made you angry, Bartholomew? I'm sorry if I have. Why do you ignore me?"

Bartholomew put his tools down and stepped toward Charlotte. The rancorous, sinister odor loomed in the air where he stood. Her heart began to race. He took her hand as gently as he would a halter from a horse's head, but she drew it back quickly anyway. She started to back away from him and said quietly, "Don't, Bartholomew. Please don't touch me."

"But, Charlotte, remember? I got needs and you are here to take care of me. Now, be a good girl, go into the stall, and pull aside your pantaloons."

"No, no, let me leave. Please don't. You hurt me so much last time."

"I promise I won't hurt you. Now, do as I say."

It was inconceivable to Charlotte that Bartholomew would violate her again. Loyal to his friendship and grateful for all that he had taught her about horses, she pushed aside the known treachery that lurked within him and mentally tried to continue on as before the assault. She offered forgiveness and continued amnesty to this man she revered for the equine savvy he shared with her. In spite of her amicable resolve, her heart plummeted at this second attack. It did not give the same feeling of besiegement. The previous experience had tempered her spirit, so she acquiesced. She watched him with more disgust than fear as he removed his garments. She knew not to struggle or he would thrust against her small body with painful malice.

Her cooperation made no impact on the severity of the torture. Bartholomew wielded his strong lance and rubbed it on her. It was red and pulsing: the warmth of him touching her vagina left a strange chill through her body. It seemed endless as he rocked her back and forth and pushed into her. It was painful. With a few final jerks, he withdrew the sabre, red with blood. Glistening semen dripped from the tip.

He stood, dressed, and left the barn without a word. Charlotte vomited, composed herself, and went back to talk to Appleshell. She did not cry this time. As she stroked the horse's nose, she wondered why Bartholomew did this to her. She knew she could never tell anyone, not even Elizabeth. She felt the sin was her own and did not want to complicate it by complaint nor lay blame to another person. Anger mixed with sadness swelled in her. She felt keeping the secret from Elizabeth was the worst sin of all, and she wished that she had more courage.

Chapter 35

The Lupine Dance was anticipated by all in the Merrimack area. The wildflowers were everywhere across the region, and in some open places, the blooms seemed to create a lush blue carpet. The oldest girls at the orphanage primped and talked about nothing else for several weeks before the event in early June.

Cooking chores were extended to younger girls and boys during this time, in order to prepare extra pies and cakes required for the celebration. The priest from Concord would attend and auction live fowl, as well as preserves, maple syrups, and several jugs of brandy Sister Esther Agnes and Sister Mary Ruth were famous for. It was a splendid time for all, and the best chance the orphanage had in raising money for needed supplies.

"Charlotte, when we finish cleaning the baking dishes, let's go down to the creek and collect berries."

"Okay, Elizabeth."

"You aren't going to drag me over to the horses?"

"No, I talked to Appleshell earlier today."

Charlotte sat in a chair while Elizabeth dried the last of the pans. She hung her towel neatly by the hearth so as to dry in time for the dinner dishes, and she took the apron off and returned it to its hook.

"Charlotte, wake up. I'm ready now."

Charlotte was groggy. She had slipped deep into sleep in the few minutes waiting for Elizabeth.

"Are you okay?"

"Yes, Elizabeth, I'm fine. I haven't been sleeping well the past few nights. Did you get baskets?"

"Right here. Let's go!"

As soon as they left the kitchen, Elizabeth started running toward the creek. She stopped, turned around, and found her best friend far behind her. She ran back to Charlotte.

"You are *not* okay, are you? Do you want to go back?"

Charlotte grabbed her middle with one hand and reached out to Elizabeth with the other. "*Oh, la douleur. Il fait mal tellement*!" she cried feebly. She seemed better in a few moments and could talk again. Elizabeth was terrified but walked with Charlotte slowly and took her up to bed.

"I'm sorry, Elizabeth. I know you wanted to collect those berries for something special. If I lay here awhile, I will be as good as new. We can go back to the creek tomorrow morning. I'm just tired. Will you fetch me a scrap of bread and some water?"

"Sure. Do you want me to get Goody Esther Agnes?"

"I'm just not strong, yet. I'm sure it is the same thing that ailed me over the winter. It will pass. Please don't bother the sisters. They have enough to do with the unexpected cases of pox that have crept up."

Elizabeth sat with Charlotte while she nibbled on bread. She looked Charlotte over while they sat together. She did not look well.

That night, Charlotte stayed in bed and missed supper. When all of the girls crawled into their beds, Elizabeth crawled in with Charlotte.

"Do you want me to bring you something from the kitchen?"

"Goody Mary Ruth brought up some broth and tea earlier. I'm fine."

"Everyone missed you at Vespers. Do you think you will be able to go to the dance next week? You still don't have any spots. It will be our first, real dance."

"I'm sure I will go."

Elizabeth put her arms around Charlotte's neck and held her. "You are telling me everything, aren't you? You're still my best friend, right?

"Yes, Elizabeth, you are my best friend. I'm just tired, that's all. I need to go to sleep now."

"Are you sure nothing is bothering you?"

"No. Nothing."

"I love you, Charlotte. Promise me that we can stay together, always."

"I promise."

Elizabeth got into her bed and thought about Charlotte. Her behavior of late confused her. Her passion for life had faded. She didn't even seem as interested in the horses. Worry was overtaking Elizabeth's thoughts and resulted in many nights plagued with nightmares.

Another week went by, and Charlotte did not improve. She slept most of the day and only left the dormitory to relieve herself outside in the privy sparingly—it was exceedingly draining on her energy to walk down the stairs and out back to it.

She craved fresh air, and she found using the chamber pot unsavory.

Elizabeth was exhausted from worry. She tried to focus her energy on her own tasks and Charlotte's chores, too, but nothing seemed to pry the state of her friend from her thoughts.

One morning Elizabeth woke, and Charlotte was not in her bed. Elizabeth quickly dressed, combed her hair, and washed her face. Running down the stairs, she hoped to find Charlotte healed and ready for the day. Sister Mary Ruth was sitting by the hearth with one hand gently caressing the cross that hung from her neck. The other hand was tracking text quickly as she read from the Bible. Elizabeth stopped cold and felt the blood drain from her face.

"Good morning, Elizabeth. Shall we start on breakfast?" Elizabeth could not move or speak. "Charlotte is fine, Elizabeth. She has been moved to the hospital room. Goody Esther Agnes will care for her. We have the best midwife in the area. She arrived early this morning, full of energy and enthusiasm. She began dictating orders to us as soon as she stepped through the door." Mary Ruth reflected on her experience with this dynamic personality and grinned a wide grin. She looked up from her studies and beamed at Elizabeth. "The Lord is with her; He will guide her skills!"

Elizabeth could not believe how stupid she had been. Everything made sense. Four days passed before she was allowed to see her friend. Worry had subsided, but anger soon filled the void. "She couldn't confide in me? Haven't I been with her through everything? How many secrets can she keep from me?" Her thoughts formed a thick canker of anger within her soul. When the sisters said she could see Charlotte, she would not go. She decided that Charlotte was not a true friend, and she might as well get closer to some of the other girls.

Three weeks elapsed before Charlotte returned to be with the other girls. The Lupine Dance had been a great success as anticipated, and life settled back to its usual hum. Charlotte knew Elizabeth was avoiding her, so after dinner one day, she went into the kitchen. Elizabeth was busy preparing a crust as a couple of the younger girls finished drying dishes.

"Hello, Elizabeth. I'm much better, now."

"That's good. Abbey, I need that dish. Put it on the table when it's dry." Elizabeth's anger still simmered.

She was cold and curt with the younger girl and took little notice of Charlotte. After sitting silently and listening patiently to the clatter of dishes being replaced on shelves for a few minutes, Charlotte rose from her seat.

"I will let you get your work done, Elizabeth, see you later this evening." Downcast from Elizabeth's unspoken discontent, Charlotte left the kitchen.

Chapter 36

Charlotte walked slowly toward the stable. Her mind was preoccupied with what she had been through. She was saddened by Elizabeth's behavior, but she wasn't thinking about that. Monumental problems overshadowed friendship spats. Once she sorted out the bigger problems, she would mend the chasm-like rift that had opened between the two best friends. She needed desperately to talk to Bartholomew. Bartholomew would make everything right. She knew he would help her.

She saw the horses in the adjacent pasture, so she diverted her path toward the field fence. She sat down on a rail and watched the horses graze peacefully on the dark green clover. The clover had many bright, pink flowers, abuzz with bees. It was so good to be back outside again. She watched blue damselflies flit by in their quick, unpredictable way.

"Appleshell! Come over here, Appleshell!" The horses looked up in the direction of the voice. Most lowered their heads and resumed their meals. A strong buckskin with blonde mane and tail continued to look in Charlotte's direction, with her ears pricked and facing forward.

The equine took a few tentative steps in her direction.

"Appleshell, come to me!"

Appleshell rippled her back and flanks, made a leap, and trotted to Charlotte. Charlotte stood and hugged the massive head, trying to keep her balance as Appleshell returned the greeting.

"I've missed you so much, Appleshell! Oh, such a good girl. I have so much to tell you." The reunion lasted for nearly half of an hour with both girls happy and satisfied. Charlotte felt she could not drink in enough of her friend and lost track of time.

Bartholomew approached with his lasso. "Evening, Miss Charlotte. It's time I brought the herd in."

Charlotte jumped a little when he spoke. He had approached the pasture in his typical silent manner, but she was so preoccupied adoring Appleshell that she hadn't noticed him. "Bartholomew! I was hoping to see you. Is it really that late that the horses have to go back in, now?"

"Yes, and you missed supper." He could see her anxiety and calmed her. "It's all right, I said I'd bring you in, too."

"Oh, thank you, Bartholomew."

"Appleshell missed you, too. I think they all did, but she missed you the most."

"Bartholomew, I had a baby. She was beautiful. They took her away from me, and said I couldn't keep her."

Bartholomew looked out at the horses and whistled to them.

"Did you understand me? Don't you care, Bartholomew?" The horses started walking toward them. "She was so tiny, but the midwife said I did fine and didn't crush her or nothing. Bartholomew!" She reached up and grabbed his shirt. "What are we going to do? They took her away!"

"Why, Miss Charlotte, it sounds like you got yourself in a heap of trouble. You should have been paying closer attention to Mary Ruth's scripture lessons. Sinful girls like yourself don't have any business being around upstanding citizens. There's only one thing left to do with wayward girls like you—" He grabbed Charlotte roughly and threw her to the ground. Ripping her clothes, he forced himself painfully through her tender, healing perineum, leaving her bleeding and in agony.

He left her in the grass and led the horses to the corral. She cried from this betrayal. She could not avert weeping. When her crying ebbed, even though her body was taxed and exhausted, another jag would involuntarily spill forth again without respite. Her eyes were swollen and her vision blurred, which made walking difficult. She tripped on the uneven ground, staggering this way and that to keep from falling. It was difficult to navigate, but she made it to the creek and sat down on the bank by the gently moving stream. The rippling water soothed her, and soon she managed to compose herself enough to apply the cool water on her renewed wounds.

Solitude revived her. She reclined against a maple tree and tried to clear her mind. The constant chanting of a whip-poor-will comforted her. She thought of her life, and the abuse she has had to endure. A few tears fell from her eyes, but she had renewed strength and pushed them back, maintaining her composure. She was optimistic that the violence she knew did not need to be an option for her future. Charlotte's mood improved with these thoughts that empowered her. She mentally sketched out a plan that would get her away from harm.

When it was very late and the moon had moved far across the leonine sky, Charlotte returned to the dormitory. Leaving her shoes on, she crept up the stairs silently, having the skill to avoid boards known to squeak.

Stealing across the room, she squatted next to Elizabeth's bed. Elizabeth was sound asleep. Charlotte watched her as she lay, breathing sweetly, with a cherubic smile on her face. "Elizabeth, wake up, I have to tell you something." She gently wiggled Elizabeth's shoulder as she spoke, hoping not to startle her. Elizabeth's eyes opened and stared at Charlotte. "I see your eyes, but are you truly awake? It's important."

Elizabeth nodded, her face dropping into a serious frown.

"I have to leave," Charlotte continued.

"What are you talking about?"

A moment of pause revealed tears forming in Charlotte's eyes. The delicate moisture ran down her soft cheek. She was strong and wiped them away, but hoped that Elizabeth couldn't see them in the dim lighting of this witching time of night. "Just know that I will always love you. I will never forget you." Elizabeth's eyes told Charlotte that she heard and understood. "I'm going tonight. Just cover for me in the morning, so I get a good head start."

Within a few minutes, Charlotte was out of the house and across the field. She stopped in the barn to see Appleshell one last time. It was a brief visit so that she could flee all the sooner. She grabbed some of Bartholomew's work clothes as she left, because her own garments were uncomfortably snug. Absentmindedly, she grabbed work gloves and Appleshell's harness, then she set out walking on her own.

She followed the river and walked with vigor, as if

in a hurry to arrive somewhere. Had another traveler been encountered on the path, that person would interpret the fervent pace of the young girl prudent for one on her way to help with altruistic works or for delivering important information to an intended destination. Oddly, her mind seemed focused on one thought as she moved.

It hadn't settled on abuse, or on the fear of what unknown things she would meet along the road. These pertinent themes would be natural, but didn't surface nor distract Charlotte. Her thoughts were bathed with two words rattling and chanting in her mind: benevolence and Gwennagwir.

The words seemed familiar, but she couldn't recollect any reason for them. Her mind occupied with foolery, she pushed forward optimistically. If the strength of her armored façade was dissolved, exposure would divulge that she had no idea where she was headed nor what was to become of her.

Part 4

Chapter 37

Charlotte walked all night along the river. She stayed back from the bridal path because she was afraid of meeting anyone. As the sun came up, she found a renewed strength to push forward on her journey. She was tired, sore, and hungry.

"Honestly, if Elizabeth was with me, she would never let us starve. She would say, 'Just look around in nature's pantry, so much good food all around!' Well, I better get started looking for my breakfast." Charlotte sat down on a rock to rest and survey the bounty of food that should be here, according to her make-believe traveling companion.

"I think I saw checkerberry bushes back somewhere." She thought she must be going mad. She had imbibed so much checkerberry in the teas steeped for her when she was ill that it might be better to be hungry. She spied some elderberries and got up to pick some. She tasted a berry. "Yes, elderberry. Not my favorite, but I won't starve."

Sallying slowly and steadily, and feeling as though she had command of her direction, she reached the outskirts of a town. She quickly dropped the remaining tart berries, inspired by the prospects of proper food. It was an imposing city to Charlotte, who had spent most of her childhood at the rural orphanage.

Charlotte wasn't sure what she needed to do, so she leaned up against a storefront, out of the chaos of people going every direction on foot, on horseback, and on carts. Food was not going to be handed to her. She needed to earn money to buy food and pay for a place to live.

The first place she tried was a mercantile. She went in confidently to the register. A skinny, unattractive young man was busy doing something below the large brass machine.

"Excuse me, sir?" she inquired.

The man mumbled something to himself before he surfaced. "Yes. May I be of assistance?"

"My name is Charlotte LeSage. I have never been in your town, and I would be beholding if you could give work."

He looked at her for a moment, shook his head, and replied rudely. "I am sorry, but Master O'Malley does not need your assistance. Kindly leave if you do not wish to purchase any of our fine products."

"I beg your pardon, sir. I shall not take up any more of your time." Charlotte dipped a short, heartless curtsey, and was happy to exit the mercantile. She continued down the boardwalk into town. She thought the man was odd. The energy of the city lured her on. The next storefront was a mortuary. She peeked inside and decided that the Lord must have something else in mind.

After being turned away from eight different establishments, she was disappointed and had only a fragment of hope remaining. Most places did not regard her with much credibility. Indeed, most of the people working were men. Women did not contribute much to the workings of this city. This was a harsh reality she had not considered.

She had been raised and schooled by women. The midwife who took charge of her delivery was a woman, and the main adult male she had contact with did unspeakable things to her. As she walked, she considered herself for the first time as a suspicious character. She thought herself a perfectly normal thirteen-year-old girl. She was not dangerous, and quite able in many tasks. She did not quite know what it was that she could offer, but every person, surely, needed socks darned, water and wood brought to the hearth, and food prepared.

A loud roar of running feet neared her on the boardwalk. As she turned to see what was happening, one of the men pushed her aside. "Get out of the way, boy! Can't you see?"

Charlotte had no idea that she was an imposition on the walkway and stared as the men distanced themselves from pursuit.

She moved along the boardwalk, deeper into the heart of the village. A group of boys loitered at the end of the walk. She was afraid of them and wished to cross the street. She hesitated, but decided it would be better to pass them and to get as far away as possible. Charlotte's tummy was making noises, and she felt weak. She gathered her courage and walked past the group, trying not to look at their faces. Success had been achieved without incident.

She was safely on her way when she heard comments thrown in her direction.

"Hey, kid, Arthur could use you on his team. Come back, new boy. Sammy needs you to buckle his shoes, the 'ittle bittle mama's boy!"

Their laughter made her feel bad, but she decided

the comments were idle nonsense, and that boys were mad. Charlotte hurried along.

She turned down a pleasant-looking side street, hoping her luck would change by going a different direction. After walking nearly to the end of the street, she looked into the shop window of another mercantile. This shop was more interesting because it had fewer fancy items, and more goods like hammers, canvas, and barrels stacked upon each other with blankets laying across them—saddle blankets.

A sign in the window advertised the need of a hand. She immediately thought of Bartholomew and sighed. He was a hand and a good one with great skill. She was the only one that she knew of who had a complaint against him. Still, it seemed that she had put in a hard day's work and shouldn't spoil it by thinking of him. She stood looking in through the glass, somewhat mesmerized in thought.

"Young man, I just asked you if you needed anything."

Charlotte looked up quickly and saw a man in his late thirties with red hair quickly turning white and a matching mustache. He was looking at her. She nodded her head slowly.

"Are you here to apply for the job?" Again, she nodded. "Well, come inside, and let's find out what you are about."

He led her through the store and into a kitchen that had a small round table with a blue tablecloth. There was a bowl with sugar and a salt cellar in the middle. The man sat down and motioned for her to sit, too, and so she did.

"Well, do you have any experience? Are you from Concord? I don't recognize your face. Maybe we should start with your name."

It was well after dinner time. Charlotte hadn't had a decent meal since dinner the previous day. She felt faint, and it was difficult to stay in the conversation. She couldn't help staring at the table. Sugar and salt were not unusual, but to have a cloth on the table was reserved for special times and those times did not usually include the young girls at the orphanage.

"Son? Son, what do I call you?"

Charlotte looked into his face blankly. Growls emanated from her belly and seemingly echoed like a canon.

"Have you eaten? Would you like a bite to eat?"

Charlotte nodded, her spirits perking up at the prospects of nourishment. The man excused himself and stepped into the next room. When he came back, a woman followed him and began preparing food.

"My wife, Emmaline, will get you fixed up. It's probably hard to answer a lot of pesky questions when you are hungry."

Charlotte jumped on the plate of food like a lynx on a brook trout.

"Whoa, slow down there, boy. Don't you want to take your gloves off and wash up?"

Curbing her hunger was the only thing in her mind, and she didn't realize that she was sporting Bartholomew's leather gloves. Considering her dainty hands, she shook her head to removing the gloves. After Charlotte ate her fill, the room stopped spinning, and she was able to think better.

"You should tell me your name. It will be a lot friendlier than calling you 'boy.'"

To this, she slowed her chewing and swallowed. A cool sip of water rinsed her mouth before she said, "Livery. Charles John Livery is my name, sir."

The interview revealed that Goodman Ezequiel

Hutchins owned this dry goods store. Sales had been increasing of late, so he was looking for a second driver to help with deliveries.

"I ship goods to all parts of the county, and I expect all deliveries on time and delivered with courtesy. Can you read and write, Charles?"

"Charles" nodded yes.

"I'd like to see you handle a horse and hook up a team before we make an accord. Do you have a place to stay?"

"Charles" shook her head no.

"Well, assuming you can handle the job, you are welcome to live in the stable. There's a little nook that has been used as sort of a bedroom before. Nothing much, but I won't charge you for it. I like having someone with the horses, anyway."

"Charles" smiled at Goodman Hutchins.

"You seem pretty young to handle a team, but Jack can watch you with the horses. That will tell us if you can do the job. I reckon you haven't a bunk, so you are welcome to spend tonight in the tack room. Jack will be back first thing come morning."

Chapter 38

Charles awoke after a long and needed sleep. She slept like a corpse the moment she cozied into the pallet of hay the evening before. She lay studying the beams above her and watched as a few nesting swallows flew this way and that, as they kept their loft home built to perfection.

The town was already alive. She heard the clop-clop of hooves on cobblestone, which she thought was a beautiful sound: It had a rich tenor that was amplified compared to the same action on dry dirt roads. She heard the sounds of a young, vibrant horse, and low voices. Pulling herself up, she went to the door and peeked out to find a man working with a horse in the corral while Mr. Hutchins watched from the fence.

"Top o' the morning to you, Charles! The privy is just behind me, next to the house, and Goody Emmaline has a plate waiting for you. Come straight out when sated, and we'll get you started. This here's Master Jack. He's the one you will be working with."

Jack's hands were busy with the spirited horse, but he managed to nod and presented a friendly smile.

Charles gave an uncertain wave and scurried into the familiar kitchen as the men talked.

"Well, Jack, how is young Squamsauke doing with the lead?"

"Just fine, Mr. Hutchins. Still a little skittish, but she's coming around fine."

"Good. Jack, I know how you feel about help, and I know you are able to do it all, but I'm going to hire another driver."

"Yes, sir. I'm sorry to put you to that expense."

"You are not the cause for need, Jack. Please don't take it that way. Think of it from my point of view. If you're on a delivery and something goes wrong, I have to handle it, which takes me out of the store. Emmaline can't be expected to cover for me all the time. No, another hand will be good all around."

"Whatever you say, Mr. Hutchins." Squamsauke was slowing down and, as Jack moved up the rope toward her head, she reared up and stomped. "I won't mind the extra help. And when you put it that way, well, I don't want to add duties to Goody Hutchins. She's got her hands full with those boys of yours."

"Boy, you're not kidding." Mr. Hutchins chuckled, thinking about his sons as he watched the strong horse. "I've got quite a few regulars around the county, plus quite a bit from the state from their projects. Yep, we're doing all right. A new hand will be a good investment and will give us more flexibility in the business."

Jack worked steadily with Squamsauke. It was frustrating because she was so spirited. Two men a few years Jack's senior approached the fence.

"Good marrow, boys. Fresh coffee in the kitchen if you'd like some."

"Thank you, kindly, Mr. Hutchins," James replied. He surveyed the energetic horse as he continued, "I had my fill at breakfast."

"Thank you, sir," the second accepted but held his

ground. "I just wanted to witness Jack, witness Jack earning some blisters."

"Dusty, when are you going to admit that I work harder, faster, and with more skill than you ever will?"

"I don't know, Jack. When I see your hands blistered a bit and a little dirt, a little dirt on your nose." Dusty kept a straight face.

"I've got tough hands, Dusty, and the only men that have dirt on their noses are usually the ones poking their noses into places they don't belong." Jack slackened the rope and squinted at Dusty. "Dusty, on your way in for coffee, you should use the towel on the pump over there to clean your face. You don't want to give Goody Hutchins a fright."

Mr. Hutchins grinned. "Oh, oh, Dusty, he's hot today. I wouldn't tangle with him. This wild horse seems to be transferring his energy into old Jack."

"Plain skill," Jack added. "Plain skill."

Chapter 39

Charles stood in the corral and spoke to the horse that was there. When she came out from breakfast, the yard was empty, with the exception of the buckskin mare she was getting to know. She was gentle and friendly like the other Haflinger horses she had been around.

Mr. Hutchins walked over from the kitchen. "Charles, you can start harnessing Sophie right now. Jack will be back shortly. Her tack is on the fifth peg."

Charles retrieved what was needed from the tack room and stepped back over to the horse, Sophie. Charles continued talking with Sophie before she started with the bridal.

Jack brought the wagon and team into the yard and walked over by Mr. Hutchins. "Now, who's the kid again?"

"That is my new hand, Charles."

"Kind of small. How old is he?"

"He's old enough, I expect. Watch him with Sophie."

The men watched Charles with the horse for a few minutes.

"You convinced?"

"He seems to have a way with horses. Can he lift a load?"

"I expect he will. No family here—either orphaned or a run away. You'll look after him?"

"Surely, Mr. Hutchins. I'll take care of him." Jack turned to Mr. Hutchins, displaying a contented grin. "I'm looking forward to a little extra fishing time this spring."

"Atta boy. You're a good man, Jack."

Chapter 40

Concord was a large city that offered many diversions to its inhabitants. Jack Harrison enjoyed his hometown. The city was large compared to most of rural America, but the people were friendly and worked together as if it were a small community. It was urban enough to provide locals with a mélange of artistic entertainment.

This evening, Jack escorted a young woman as they strolled along the boardwalk. The storefronts were dark, and the town lamplighter had nearly completed his task. Many people were about, enjoying the dusky, candle-lit and balmy romantic evening.

"It has been a lovely evening, Jack. I'm so glad you asked me to accompany you."

Jack was silent for several minutes before he answered his date, Rachael Rutledge. "I just wanted to see you again. I'm sorry we couldn't go to the theatre."

"Yes, that would have been nice, but the drinks were lovely, and we had such a good chat. Are you planning on anything special this Sunday, Jack?"

Before Jack had a quick second to formulate an answer, Pearl Ann Marchand and Mrs. Wanda Spruce approached the couple as they navigated the boardwalk.

"Well, I—Evening Pearl Ann, Mrs. Spruce."

"Good evening to you, Jack, Rachael," Mrs. Spruce said.

"It is such a lovely and romantic evening for a stroll, isn't it, Wanda?" Jack thought he had an opportunity to avoid Rachael's Sunday question, but Pearl Ann's comment struck him like an omen.

"Indeed. Oh, Rachael, please tell your mother to come over soon. I need her to help me with the cause."

"Yes, Mrs. Spruce. I'll mention it as soon as I'm home tonight."

"Good girl. Jack, don't keep Rachael out too late."

"Oh, no, ma'am. Just heading home right now."

"Jack, since you're retiring so early, could you stop by on your way home and help me for a bit?"

"Certainly, Pearl Ann. I will come straight over after I walk Rachael home. Good night, ladies."

The quartet bade each a good night, and as Jack and Rachael continued leisurely on to Rachael's home, she beamed a glassy stare into Jack. "Jack, you didn't answer me."

"Huh? Gosh, that Pearl Ann never quits, does she?"

"Jack. You are free this Sunday, aren't you? Mother said it would be all right if I asked you to supper. You *would* like to come and have supper with us, wouldn't you?"

"I—I think that would be awful nice, Rachael but—"

Sensing Jack's reluctance, she knew his reticence was due to her sister, Prudence, who was a meddling nuisance. "Yes, Jack, my sister will be there. It will be all right, she won't fuss."

"Rachael, it's just that—well, I've been...ah, Mr. Hutchins has a lot of work, and I don't think he should

do the hard stuff. You understand, the stuff a hand
should—"

Rachael was put off by Jack's less than gallant behavior. "Well, you don't have to go to all that trouble
just to say, 'no.'"

"Now, wait, Rachael, I didn't exactly say no—"

"Good! Mother will expect you at three Sunday afternoon. I think if you play your cards right, there might
even be some special, tasty treat made just for you,
Jack."

Jack escorted Rachael up steps to the door of the
Rutledge family home. The federal style structure was a
grand home, apropos for an affluent family. The servants kept an excellent shine on the hardwood floors that
are renown in the community. The Rutledge family often offered their conservatory for teas and dramatic
readings, as well as for political events.

Jack took Rachael into the large entryway. A servant appeared to greet and assist Rachael. Jack was uncomfortable and wished to end the evening with
Rachael. "Oh, okay, Rachael," he finally consented.
"But I feel so uncomfortable around Prudence."

"You don't have anything to worry about, Jack. I
will take care of you."

Chapter 41

Jack stood in the hallway, looking into a bedroom. Hearty grunts and groans rolled forth as Jack's expression remained unchanged.

"I know it's here somewhere. My Justice *never* threw anything out if it could be used again. Aha!" Pearl Ann's resonant voice echoed off of the birch floors and plastered walls of the building.

Jack's evening was not ending soon enough, but he wondered, *What the devil is she doing?* This was the second of two of the most prominent houses in Concord he had visited tonight. This home, when he visited, offered the most unusual experiences, and tonight proved to be typical. Pearl Ann's home was several years older than the Rutledge home and had an aristocratic air. It was built in 1760 by the owner, Giles Marchand.

Marchand immigrated to the Colonies from France. He built an empire with his skills in business and trade. The mansion originally was built Georgian, with a five-bay façade. For the most part that was how it remained, but after enumerable fires, wars and other economic burdens, the interior wasn't quite the boxy shape known to Georgians—it had taken on its own personality through necessitated reconstruction.

A few more moments listening to strange emanations, and Jack offered, "You know, Dusty is the man you need to help you with this."

"Oh, posh. You are big and strong and quite handsome, I must say."

Brushing aside the compliment, Jack said knowledgeably, "That doesn't ensure know-how."

Pearl Ann emerged from her hunt. "Now, this is what he used." She held two metal taps up for Jack to see. "But I don't remember what he did with them, exactly."

Jack took a resolved breath and lowered the eyebrow that had raised at the sight of the old hardware being stored inside Pearl Ann's boudoir closet. "Well, it's pretty easy. You just drill a hole, insert this, and hang a bucket on the hook." He took one from her and mimed the procedure. "But I still think you want Dusty to do the surgery this spring—he has the knack to insert it just so."

"All righty, then. Dusty will just have to come over and help. Now, Jack, you toodle on home so I can get my beauty sleep. Thank you for stopping by." Pearl Ann ushered Jack to the massive front door. "Sometimes I'm just so lost without my Justice."

Jack stood patiently and respectfully.

"Two years now," she continued. "But, like all pain, it heals with time. Our stolid maple trees wouldn't serve year after year if the scars didn't heal."

"We all miss Justice. You are a strong woman—"

Pearl Ann swept away Jack's humble courtesy. "Head on home now, Jack. And a word of advice: you date a heap of girls, but you need to know, there is the right person for everyone out there. Make sure you find *her*."

"Yes, ma'am. Good night, Pearl Ann."

Chapter 42

Charles obtained several sheets of paper, a quill, and a small bottle of ink from Mrs. Hutchins. She considered her first day of work and was pleased. She missed Elizabeth and Appleshell terribly. She was not sure of the magnitude of her crime. She remembered other children who were discontent with the sisters and ran away. At the memories of their capture and return, she shuddered. Others who fled—they went missing, at any rate—were never heard from again.

"Maybe I am hiding like a villain or highway man. I love being responsible for Mr. Hutchins's horses, and he is such a nice man." She weighed each point in her head. "No," she avowed out loud. "I must not be taken back to the orphanage. It is strange being thought of as a boy, but if it keeps me safe, then it is prudent. It should not be too much of a crime. Sister Mary Ruth would have me do penance. I will do that and keep the horses for Mr. Hutchins until I devise another plan. Caring for horses is honorable work. Horses mean safety."

Charles wrote a few lines to Elizabeth to tell her everything was okay. She made sure not to include where she was, or what she was doing. No names were mentioned. She did tell Elizabeth that she worked with horses and that she was well. She concluded, "Love, Charlotte."

Chapter 43

A cool morning enveloped two men talking in front of the dry goods store. Each nursed a strong cup of coffee while they witnessed the manifesting spectacle. The town was waking slowly. Dogs barked and roosters crowed. A drift of swine were encouraged down the road by two brothers wielding canes. A surly man from a tallow shop pressured the boys to keep their animals out of his shop and as far away as possible.

It was a sylvan late summer morning that the men drinking coffee enjoyed. Josiah Spruce, however, was troubled. "I don't know, Ezequiel, it just doesn't seem to be."

"You've given your matrimonial best, I'm sure."

"Oh, yes! Of course. Maybe I'm too old."

"I doubt it. Have you considered taking a child in somehow? There are needy families where urchins prove more of a burden than a gift."

"I think I've convinced her that adopting a bairn is the way we have to go. We can get a young boy for our own, train him. He'll be good help for me. And if we get him soon, we won't be so old the kid will have to care for us in his teens."

"I think it a wise plan, Josiah." A team trundled by. The men waved to the driver and the faithful shepherd dog by his side. "Hey, the missus has been agog planning this dance coming up."

"That fever is burning at our place, too. Not too long now and the womenfolk can settle back into the usual routine. We hardly get supper before bedtime with Wanda and Alma Mae planning the attack."

"Yes, they do get excited about these things. Still, it has been a nice excuse to get out of their way in the evenings."

"Indeed, Ezequiel! I am going to miss meeting at Simon's for cards."

The coffee cups were empty, and the sun was now peeking above the granite outcrops. The men began stretching to inspire their bodies to get to work.

"Josiah, we men should start formulating how to sow the seeds for the next social event," Ezekiel said and winked in syndication.

Chapter 44

Mrs. Spruce sat in the family parlor, reinforcing buttons on one of her husband's linen under shirts. Modern wallpaper of a light cream color kept the room bright. Maroon and gold ribbon sprig pattern decorated it, trailing from the ceiling to the mop board of the maple floor. An elegant rug covered the center of the hardwood floor. Staunch geometric shapes of gold and maroon formed an epaulette with rosettes, framing the border. Over the soft beige palate, limber olive green acanthus and laurel leaves secured within more geometric frames waved the eye across a regiment of quatrefoils. The visual crescendo brought the beholder to the center medallion whose repose was as proud as a cocked hat.

Final instructions for the day have been given by Mrs. Spruce. Alma Mae, the head domestic, was a lean woman in her early fifties. She was loyal to the Spruce family and was a valuable servant. "Mrs. Spruce, it's probably time we start to put up some of the season's vegetables. If you don't mind helping me?"

"Of course, I'll help, silly, don't I help every season? Unless I'm more of a burden in the kitchen to you than moisture in the sugar bowl."

"Heavens no, Mrs. Spruce. I'll check the pantry to make sure we have enough sealing wax. Oh, the Good Lord save us! We have a lot of work ahead of us."

"Oh! That reminds me. I have to go next door and talk to Pearl Ann this morning, before she goes into town. I need to check on a few plans for the Auxiliary's Cause."

A black head of hair with distinguished accents of gray entered the room. His age was a bit older than Al-ma Mae, but she and Zackary Joseph had been together with the Spruce family since their arrival to the Colonies as indentured servants. "Ma'am, just wanted to let you know the order is in. Mr. Jack and a new hand are at the kitchen door."

"Good. I've been waiting for that order, and I need to talk with Jack, too." Mrs. Spruce set the sewing aside and exited to greet Jack.

Chapter 45

The ending to a fine day of work was one spent with friends and drinking a pint or two together. Jack tossed his hand of cards down on the table while James collected the deck.

James began shuffling. "Ante up. Let's make this the last pot."

"That's fine," Dusty said. "I don't have much more, more to lose."

Jack gave Dusty a frustrated look. "You're losing *my* money, now, remember?"

"Ah, ya know, ya know, we just play for fun anyway, Jack."

"Enough talk. You open, Dusty?"

Dusty shook his head no.

"Jack?"

Jack tossed chips into the pot to open the bet. "All right, I can. Pathetic."

While the men continued the game, a strong man with a side arm and badge approached the table. "Simon, how's the evening going?"

Jack's eyes never lifted from his cards as he acknowledged the sheriff.

"Evening, boys. Peaceful as usual. For such a big town, it's usually quiet."

James nodded in greeting to the sheriff as he passed out the draw cards. "Is that a problem?"

"Oh, no, not for me. I don't need any excitement. I do need to head for home. Susan is expecting me for dinner. Lamb stew!"

Dusty could hardly contain himself hearing the menu at Simon's.

"Simon, you may kill Dusty with talk like that."

"Jack, what are, what are you—"

"Dusty, I think we would all agree, right, Jack?" James interrupted. "Susan is the best cook in town, and always brings the most scrumptious dishes at any pot luck." He tossed his hand of cards face down atop the pot and sat back in his chair with a disgusted look on his face.

All the players faced Jack to see his reaction to this turn in the game.

"Couldn't agree more. And I win. Flush. Beat that."

Simon laughed as the other two men groaned at the outcome. "Well, if pistols are staying in the holsters, I'm going home. My stomach is growling."

Dusty threw his cards down in defeat. Jack signaled the barkeeper to refill their ales.

"You men want to get a little hunting in?" James asked.

"Sure. Umm…roasted duck, tender and dripping, dripping with grease. Hot baked bread to mop it up with. If we go before daybreak, Julia will never notice, never notice I went."

James grinned. "Good. Sounds like Dusty is in."

Dusty was still contemplating a feast.

"Dusty, what does it matter to her if you go hunting?" Jack asked. "I don't see a collar around your neck."

Dusty's smile broadened into something more mischievous.

"Hey! You *don't* have a collar, do you?" Jack said as if he had been betrayed.

Dusty's face turned serious. "Not yet, not yet."

"Uh, oh, James, we may be losing one pretty soon," Jack observed.

"Then we better all go hunting before Dusty makes any regrettable commitments."

Jack nodded. "You know, I think I will. Mr. Hutchins has a new hand, so I think I can relax a little more. Mrs. Hutchins would probably appreciate fresh meat to feed her boys, too."

"Good, just afore daybreak, men," James said. "I just hope we aren't bagging Dusty's final meal."

Chapter 46

Flocks of geese flapped, their honking and cackling shrieking through crisp morning air as if alerting the river valley of danger. Their flurry did not hide the presence of the countless other species, like the yellow-headed blackbirds that added their music from the wetlands, opposing symphonic strains of the *pit-ti-tuck* song of content summer tanagers above in the canopy. Foliage was tinged with yellow as night temperatures had begun to drop, the first bars of an overture that would crescendo into deep yellows, oranges, reds, and purples before the final strains resonate, leaving the woodlands defoliated, quietly sleeping safely through the cold, wintery season.

Mr. and Mrs. Spruce were dressed in fine togs, as if going to a special ceremony. They each had on an extra layer this morning to shield them from the cold. It was well above freezing, but the breeze was strong. Zackary Joseph had detailed each chore completed for the Spruce's journey and wished them well.

"Oh, one more thing, Zackary," Mr. Spruce said. "Remind Alma Mae to have the nursery ready. This is the day!"

"Indeed, sir. Everything will be as you wish. Have a delightful trip, sir."

The couple drove down the cobblestones and out of town. Each was silent, either soaking in the beautiful day or, more likely, anticipating life with a child of their own.

"I have waited for this day—how old is he?"

"I think she said about four to five weeks, but it's not a boy, darling."

"Oh, Josiah, a baby girl? But our plan was—and you need—"

"I know, we wanted a son to do work for us. But you've waited so long. I have not been truthful, I'm sorry. I didn't commit to the baby being boy or girl and allowed you to think…well, whatever made you happy. I hope you are not sore with me."

"A baby girl. I love you more than anything, Josiah!"

Chapter 47

The exhaustive journey, taken along ruts etched into the hardwood forest, took exceedingly long, and the couple was relieved at their arrival. Mr. Spruce brought the buggy to a halt in front of a sizable building. The structure was two stories with clapboard siding and wooden shingles on top. A single chimney rose from mid-center and emitted a lazy whirl of smoke. The second story overhung the first and had four small casement windows. Mr. Spruce assisted Mrs. Spruce from the buggy, and they walked to the door. Two wooden steps led just above the stone foundation.

A woman let them in and seated them. "You are Mr. Spruce, of course. Your correspondence stated that you wanted a baby girl?"

Mrs. Spruce's eyes glared at her husband. He had known all along what the institution had available.

"My wife and I have wanted a family, but the Lord has had other plans."

"Sister Esther Agnes will bring the little girl down in a moment. We thought we had another home to receive her in Boston, but in the end, the family was unable to take her. Can I offer you some tea while you wait?"

The Spruces agreed that hot tea would warm them and would be appreciated. The woman left the room. Mrs. Spruce had tears of joy in her eyes, and Mr. Spruce was pleased that his surprise had gone as he had planned.

"Oh, Josiah, a baby girl!"

"If we had our own child, be it boy or girl, we would still be unknowing until the moment of birth. We would have loved it without reservation. I thought you would agree." He took Mrs. Spruce's hands in his and caressed them lovingly while he enjoyed her untethered delight.

A different woman entered the large room and had a working apron on with a familiar and stunning broach against her neck. "Why, Pearl Ann! What on earth?"

"Why, Wanda and Josiah! So good to see you here. Oh, it's just my day here to help. You know it does a body good to help and minister with these children."

"Well, Pearl Ann, if you don't beat all. Have you been helping here for long?

"Land's sake, no, I've been helping out the sisters for the past three years or so." The woman returned and offered cups of tea. "Thank you, love, I could use a boost from freshly brewed tea. Well, I don't do much, just a little here, a little there. Whatever they need the most. Tell you the truth, I think I get more from them than I give."

Sister Mary Ruth beamed at her. "Pearl Ann is a true blessing. She comes in anytime there is need, midwifing and nursing at all hours of the day and night."

Pearl Ann cast away the praise. "Well, a person has to have duties to keep going strong."

"I don't know a stronger woman than Pearl Ann."

"Indeed, and she is one of our best neighbors."

"Oh, are you taking our littlest babe home to stay?" Pearl Ann asked. "Oh, she's a dream! What a lucky little baby to go home with the Spruces. The Lord works in wonderful ways!"

Chapter 48

Just take it easy on them horses."

"Yes, sir."

"Stick to the schedule. When you get there, find Old Hannigan, the shop keep. He'll tell you where to unload."

"I will, sir. Won't take too long, sir."

"Cut it out with the 'sir.' My name's Jack. Just be careful. I want those animals back and rested for tomorrow's loads, understand, Charles?"

"Will do—*Jack*."

"One last thing. I know you probably don't shave yet, but have you thought of getting your hair cut? People are going to start calling you 'miss' in the coming weeks."

Charles nodded in agreement. She was eager to take the team by herself all the way to Penacook Brook. It wasn't a long or difficult drive, but it was the first time that Jack had not gone along. Charles was excited to go but anxious that she might do something wrong. She climbed into the wagon as Jack snugged the lines one last time. The wagon pulled out.

Charles's nerves settled down within a few hundred yards out of town. Driving the beautiful team of

Sophie and Mi'kmaq was the best. She thought nothing was quite as pretty as Mi'kmaq's dapple gray coat and dark mane and tail. The two Haflinger mares eased her mind as she enjoyed the ride. She considered horses to be the most divine animals on the planet.

"They are true to you, and they never pretend to be something that they aren't," she muttered aloud. "It's strange that, even though they led me straight into—" Charles stopped talking when she rummaged over the bad memories. The pain seared through her soul.

She realized her fear to speak out loud, as if there was someone near that could hear her deepest secrets. This was silly, and she proved it to herself by shouting, "Ha, ha! Sophie and Mi'kmaq, you are the best friends ever!"

As they continued down the road, she wondered why her past *hadn't* poisoned her against the large animals. "They are just good," she shouted out loud as she sorted through her mind. "There is something magical about them. I don't know…but I sure feel good when I'm with them." She shrugged and was truly happy and proud of herself.

The air smelled fresh as she and the horses moved toward Penacook Brook when a thought hit her. "Get my hair cut? What?"

Then she realized one reason why everyone thought she was a boy: short hair. Many boys and men had long hair that they pulled back, but the fashion was old and moving toward a cleaner cut. The girls at the orphanage usually had their hair cut short for ease of handling and to limit head lice. It was easier to keep clean in general, too. She had been wearing Bartholomew's things, but had noticed that they were much too big, now. Charles had lost a considerable amount of weight since arriving in Concord.

Chapter 49

Nothing could turn an otherwise neat and organized home upside down quite as fast as a new baby. The servants cleaned and prepared the nursery and the house. Then they returned and did it all again. Alma Mae was a general, leading an army into the biggest battle in history. The rest of the servants were ready to be done a half an hour after the Spruce's left town, but they knew Alma Mae was excited about the new arrival and understood her fervor.

Finally, the horse and buggy drove up the drive, and Alma Mae and Zackary Joseph were there to welcome them home. "This is Miss Charlotte Spruce!" Mrs. Spruce said as she beamed as she leaned over to show the two.

Alma Mae took the bundle so Mrs. Spruce could dismount from her seat. "Oh, if she ain't beautiful! I have her nursery all ready. Zackary Joseph, come and see this miracle of the Almighty. Help bring her things in. Let's get her inside, Mrs. Spruce, we don't want her to catch a chill."

"I think she will be fine, Alma Mae. She just spent nearly two hours in a buggy. All right, let me have her back."

"Here, gentle with her, do you have her okay? Zackary Joseph, get all of Mrs. Spruce's things. Hurry up, now!"

"I'm getting all of it. Lord, woman, you're gonna put Gabriel outta a job someday with that voice of yourn. Oh, Sweet Mother Mary, if that isn't the tiniest thing I ever seen. What's her name again?"

"This is little Charlotte, just three months old tomorrow. Alma Mae, we need a toasty bath in the kitchen and all the fixin's for a little princess."

"Yes, ma'am." Alma Mae scurried inside the building, her excitement couldn't be contained. Orders to the staff echoed from the kitchen, the clarion-cries probably reaching the people of Canada.

"Come along, Zachary Joseph, and help me unload the packages. Never knew such a tiny thing could require so much."

"Yes, sir, Mr. Spruce. Yes, sir."

Chapter 50

New Hampshire was known as the granite state. A wagon path was never straight, from one town to another, because of the sheer outcrops of hard granite. Besides New Hampshire's hardwood forests, the supply of granite was surely a reason the British did not wish to lose the American Colonies in the War for Independence. Many stonemasons would have obligingly loaded British vessels to the masthead with their product, ending the Revolution sooner. The British navy wouldn't do many battles from the bottom of the ocean. The stone was a valuable resource, but it took muscle to form it.

Dusty and James were skilled stone masons and were working together on an order. Simon Bernard approached and gave the men a reason to rest from the laborious work of chiseling.

"Right there, Dusty," James said, "one hit should do it. Hi, Simon."

"James, Dusty. Hope the day is treating you boys' right. I have an official question that I have to ask you. Do you know anything about some cobbler that went missing?"

Dusty grinned. "If he works on shoes, shoes, no. If

the cobbler is something to eat, I wish, I wish I did."

The sheriff smiled. "Just have to follow up."

"What happened?"

"Well, James, Mrs. Mueller had a couple of cobblers cooling out of doors. They just 'walked away.'"

"Who would steal cobbler?" James thought it odd, Dusty thought it reprehensible.

"Well, maybe you boys would. No wife, no family. You work hard all day, with no time to make something like that."

"I can assure you that we did not take a woman's cobbler," James declared. "What about her sons?"

"No, they are out trapping. Been gone a couple, three days now. She made four cobblers for her boys' return."

"Like James said, we would never, would never do such a low down thing. But cobbler does sound tasty, sounds tasty."

The other men watched as Dusty thought. They never knew what he might say. "I wonder if Julia and, Julia and her mom could use a bushel of fresh peaches, peaches."

Sheriff Bernard shook his head. "Thanks, men, sorry to trouble you. Carry on with your work." He left to continue with his investigation.

"Maybe your girl could use *two* bushels, Dusty!"

"James, I think that's a great, a great idea."

Chapter 51

Pennicook Brook was not a formal town. There was a small community of people, mostly men, who logged the area and floated the timber down the Pennicook River to a mill below. Maple, birch, and hemlock were milled in the Brook area. Charles, with the help of Mr. Hannigan, had unloaded the wagon at the small building used as a storehouse and mercantile. Since it was one of the only buildings at the site, it served as the area's tavern and meeting place. Mr. Hannigan suggested Charles get a bite before his return.

Charles entered the bar area and sat down on a stool. An older man entered and got his culinary items ready to fix a meal.

"What'll ya have, stranger? Mr. Hannigan says you've come up from Concord with supplies."

"Yes, sir. Name's Charles. Brought the load up for Ezekiel Hutchins. Sarsaparilla, meat, and crackers, please."

"Ahh…good man, good business sense. Here's the drink. I'll cut you some dried fish and cured pork, if you give me a minute. Pump's out back if you want to wash up."

Charles ate her meal silently. She felt success from

doing the journey and that she earned the special beverage. The older man cleaned his counter and didn't mind the silence. He was content to get his work finished. In a few minutes he offered, "Can I get you anything else? You didn't eat enough to keep up your size. Pie? It's left over from last night, but it should be good."

Scars that were still tender began to itch and throb in Charles's mind. She pushed their echoes out of her mind and smiled at the old man. "Pie would be nice."

"Here you go. Enjoy. How come you eat with your gloves on?"

"I don't know. Is there anyone around this area who can give me a haircut?"

Chapter 52

Jack was confident in Charles's ability but felt relief when his wagon rolled back into the yard. He helped Charles with unhooking the horses and brushing them down. The two went to Jack's favorite meeting place to celebrate this first solo delivery.

The tavern was the bulk of the basement of a large building. Lighting was provided by casement windows along the tops of the walls that contained diamond-shaped panes with thick leading. There was a hearth and iron betty lamps on the structure's supports, as well as a few candles on tables in darker corners. Mostly men were dining, but there were a few women partaking of an evening meal, too.

The tavern was known for excellent food. The chef filled the room with delectable odors, but unfortunately, as with most establishments, the unwashed bodies of patrons emitted a noisome contribution that eked through the strongest aroma of kitchen fare.

Dusty was at a table, savagely dining on a partridge or ruffed grouse stuffed with Johnny cake, hazelnuts, and chestnuts while washing it down with a tankard of rum. He had a fair complexion, with rosy cheeks, and his blond hair became lighter in the summer sun.

His large, hulking frame was made more immense from chiseling and lifting stone every day. Incongruous was the clean, bright red shirt he wore.

James sat next to him. His working clothes were dirty from chiseling stone all day. James's dark head and light skin tone complimented his Irish ancestors. He was a large man if not compared to Dusty, and, like his mate, was a stonemason that carried broad, strong shoulders. Charles observed him rise to fetch more Madeira for himself at the bar. The barkeeper refilled his tankard from a large hogshead that had many kegs piled around it, before returning to his fish, crusts of bread, and root vegetables. Jack carried two drinks as he and Charles joined Dusty and James. "Hey, Jack, how's business, business?"

"More than you can imagine." Jack handed Charles the drink and noticed Dusty's dandy attire. "Hey, are you sporting a new work shirt?"

"Yeah, ripped the old one clean off today, clean off. See?" Dusty held up an identical shirt to the one he was wearing, rather a shredded rag that used to be a shirt.

"Business is really picking up with all of the timber orders coming in. Good thing we hired Charles, here."

Dusty wiped his greasy hands on his trousers and reached out to shake hands. "Dusty Johansson, good to meet ya."

Charles offered his gloved hand.

"Jack's a good man, Charles, good man," Dusty said. "Good level head on him—even if he can't spit, can't spit a lick."

"Oh, now! Dusty's just jealous 'cause I spent my time learnin' more important skills, Charles."

James had returned to the table and heard the introduction and the derogatory comment about Jack. He held out his hand. "James Wheeler. Glad to know you, Charles. Yeah, Jack's a bleeding heart, right, Dusty? He'll do anything to save even the smallest of pups from a grim demise. Yowl!" he howled freely, which made Charles look at Jack with concern.

"All right, boys, how about buying my new driver a drink? And knock it off. Charles don't wanna hear no dumb stuff like that."

"I'm sorry, Jack—even if you can't spit a lick! But here's a glass for you and Charlie."

Charles took the glass and looked at Jack.

Jack raised his to toast. "Well, here's to a fine day, Charles."

Charles lifted his glass to his lips. The strong drink made his eyes burn.

"Go on, drink up, kid!"

Charles recognized it was rum. She had only previously had very small medicinal amounts and thought it awful. She did not wish to be rude, and she did not want to call attention to "himself," so she wetted her lips with the liquid throughout the evening to appear like the men.

"So are you gonna tell him the story, or are we?" James asked.

"Now, now, there ain't no story, James." After a little more nagging, Jack relented. "All right, but nobody butts in, hear? I will relay the experience so that Charles hears it the right way." He began his story, and the other three sat silently.

Dusty and James had their mouths full finishing their meal, but Jack's version was embellished with details that they had never heard, so they kept quiet and enjoyed the show.

"...so I hear this sound, sort of whining and scratching, down around the base of the water barrel and the stable. I heard it for at least three days."

"And the cur—tell him about the yellow cur."

"*Shh*, James, I'll get there. Okay, we had this big yellow dog hanging around. She was okay—didn't really pester anyone and 'she didn't have hydrophobia—she came around looking—"

"Yeah, and she waddled and moved funny, moved funny." Dusty was excited and couldn't resist adding to the story.

"And James here, he kept saying she was a pregnant bitch, and we were going to be flooded with a bunch of pups, yapping and carrying on."

"No, I just said she was big enough to have a litter of twenty-five, and with Dusty's Dukie she didn't have no chance but to be in…in a family way."

"You leave Dukie outta this. He's a gentleman, he is, a gentleman. 'Sides, that yellow bitch wasn't his style."

"Quiet, you two. So, look, Charles, with all this evidence—"

"And the fact that the yellow dog disappeared—"

"James, let me tell it! And the yellow dog disappeared—that sound could have been pups hungry for their mama."

"Yeah, so Jack, worrying about pups like a beefhead, stuck his hand back behind the barrel and pulled out a—"

"It *was* a pup!"

"But it wasn't quite the soft and cute little doggie, cute little doggie he had expected."

"No. It wasn't that, was it?" Jack was a little embarrassed but enjoyed the drama and suspense the men brought to the event.

Charles was swept away by the story and had sipped more of the rum than she had planned on. She jumped into the conversation a little louder than she would normally have offered. "So, Jack, what was it?" She realized her outburst, sat back nonchalantly, ruing her lack of control, and sipped more rum.

"Charles, you should be proud to be working alongside a real hero. Yes, sir, the most gallant of King Arthur's Court."

"A man who would give his right arm to help you."

All three men felt the spirits loosen their tongues and enjoyed the performance for Charles.

"Or at least a finger. A finger *nail*, that is."

"Well, boys, that's it for me tonight: I have to get up with the cocks." Jack stood and pushed his stool under the table. "You coming, Charles?"

Pushing a nearly half-full glass toward James, Charles stood to a stagger, steadied herself, and hoped it wasn't noticeable.

"Ah, come on, come on, Jack, sit down and tell him, tell him!"

"It was an opossum's nest. When I reached in, I grabbed one of the pups. It scared her so bad that she bit my finger. It turned blue, and the nail fell off. That's it. Nothing more."

"But we had to hear Jack whining: 'What if they are pups, are pups, and the yellow dog died, died? They'll starve.' And, 'They'll be cold with no mother, no mother, lookin' after 'um.'"

"And the next time you're hurt or scared, I'll tell you I can't help because I don't want to be laughed out of town. You might just be an opossum exercising in the rafters. Come on, Charles."

Jack and Charles left the tavern and walked down the boardwalk. Charles felt a little light-headed, but it was clearing. "Did they make you mad, Jack?"

"Nah, not really. It's a funny story."

Two young ladies approached from the opposite direction, arm in arm. Jack and the girls greeted each other as the groups passed. Light giggling was heard from the girls before Charles asked, "Just not a story you want your new hand to hear? I would have done the same—I mean, if I'd a thought, thought an animal was in danger."

"Little too much rum? You're starting to sound like Dusty." Jack smiled. "I guess I just think it would be nice to have your pals tell a new kid how great you are, sort of build him up."

"Not tear him down?"

"Yeah."

"They didn't tear you down. I can tell those guys think you're the greatest. If they had done otherwise, it would be like they felt they had to make you more than you are."

"I suppose so. I guess it's okay as long as you don't mind working with a 'hero.'"

"Don't matter. I like the *horses* just fine."

Chapter 53

Charles was in the corral talking to Sophie. She put her gear away and was brushing her coat. Jack approached and leaned against the fence, watching him. He yelled across to the boy, "Charles, when you're through, do you want to grab a bite?"

Charles rubbed Sophie's nose and walked over to Jack. "Sure. What?"

"Well, the Women's Auxiliary has a spread out. Usually some good vittles."

Charles nodded and put the brush away. The two walked to the commons area and were greeted by several women.

"Why, hello, Jack, who's your friend? Did you come to support our Cause? Here, come and get yourselves some dinner and punch, oh, and don't forget some of Adele's rolls—softest you'll find anywhere in New Hampshire. Come on over here—scoot over, Mr. O'Leary, make some room for these hungry boys." The woman put two plates on the table heaped with stew, sweetmeats, and fritters.

Charles was less impressed with the food than the perpetual flurry of the woman who greeted them. Charles's discomfort with being in the company of so many strangers prevented her from most of the details of the experience, but she would never forget the woman's energy and the most beautiful broach around her neck. The piece of jewelry upstaged nearly everything at the picnic that day, with the exception of the woman, herself. The broach had tiny swirls of gold swimming in a sea made of the most beautiful blue stone Charles had ever seen.

"Much obliged, Pearl Ann. Well, Charles, if you weren't hungry before, you are stuck in tar now. Can't let all this good hospitality go to waste. You don't want to hurt these ladies' feelings. Tuck in!"

The food was good. Charles was introduced to Seamus O'Leary and learned that he owned the lumber mill. Not much else was said before the energetic woman flapped back to the table and squeezed in to sit next to Charles.

"Now, Charles…it was Charles, wasn't it? Or do you prefer Charlie or Chuck? My great-great uncle Charlie went by Zeb. Really! We don't know where he came up with that—not even in his Christian name at all—Jack, will you and Charlie be coming to the dance tonight? We'll have an auction, and, of course, Shilling-a-Dance is always a favorite. Proceeds to help our Cause. Charlie, of course, you'll be there? There are so many sweet young ladies that will be fighting over each other to get your dance, I just know it. And just think of all the people you will meet. Charlie's new to town, isn't he, Jack? Where do you hail from, Charlie?"

"Now, Pearl Ann, that's awful nice of you, but Charles is pretty quiet. The evening you have planned for him might be a bit much for a shy gent."

"Oh, now, Charlie, there is nothing to be afraid of. No wild ones, I promise, only good and decent, Christian manners from our local townsfolk. Jack, look how pale he is. Doesn't he get out much?"

Jack's eyes said it before he could whisper, "Golly, Pearl Ann, give the kid a break. He's new to town, and don't know nobody. You'll scare him to death, talking about buying dances and all."

"Well, maybe he will come for a little while. Meeting a few folk is all Charlie needs. Charlie, don't let me push you into anything you don't want to do. I understand completely. I used to be quiet and shy myself, once."

Chapter 54

Molly Boulanger, with her ten-month-old baby Jane, followed by Jane Tisdale, entered Hughlett's Mercantile to shop. They greeted Mr. Hughlett, who was busy counting his supplies and making marks on a sheet of paper with a pencil. Jack and Charles entered behind the girls. The women stop and chat with Mr. Hughlett, so Jack leads Charles around the group to start looking for what they need.

"Hello, Molly. And how is our little lady, Janie, today?" The baby giggled and wiggled. Her smile showed her excitement before she dropped her face into her mother's arm.

"Janie is growing like a weed, of course. Just the sweetest thing a mother could hope for."

"Well, Miss Jane, maybe there will be the patter of feet in your house soon."

"Oh, Mr. Hughlett! Please, you are putting the cart before the horse."

"Really, you silly man, her wedding is not for three months, yet."

"Mr. Hughlett loves babies, girls." Mrs. Hughlett entered and couldn't resist the youngling, either. "Little Jane has him wrapped around his finger already. Our grandchildren are all in Boston and practically grown. They just don't stay little for long, do they?"

Molly nodded. "I see what you mean. I could swear Little Jane grew two inches just over night. She will be running in the school yard with the other children before long."

Mr. Hughlett stepped over to assist Jack. "Hello, Jack, going to the dance this evening?"

"Yes, I thought I might stop by. This is Charles, a new hand that is working with me." Jack requested to have his horn filled with gun powder and to have a good deal of fishing line.

"Planning a vacation, Jack? Going hunting? You are going to have to hurry to get the last few fish before the heavy frosts."

"Well, I always try to make time for fishing. Charles and I thought we might try my favorite hole in Parson's Creek on Saturday, right, Charles?"

Charles was distracted and stared in the direction of the baby. She nodded at Jack absentmindedly then walked to the other part of the room.

"Not a very talkative chap."

"Quiet, soft spoken. Real good with the horses."

Chapter 55

The dance was lively and had decorations and a fiddle and bass player. Jack was having a good time dancing with nearly every girl in attendance, but Charles had stayed off in the shadows, drinking punch. She saw Pearl Ann moving toward her, and she turned away from her direction. Charles knew she was trapped.

"Why, Charles! It's so good to see you tonight. Have you danced yet?"

Charles shook her head that she hadn't, knowing it would not suffice to deflect the attention.

"Well, I'd be delighted to dance with you, if you want to put your work gloves down, and you don't mind dancing with an old widow."

"An old widow? You are not old."

Pearl Ann grabbed "his" hand to dance. "Well, come on, then."

Charles knew she had to, so she put her hands up to get it over with.

"No, you lead, Charles. You've only danced with your father, I guess. There you go—you are a fine dancer, Charlie. So graceful. Where do you hail from? We are all dying to know."

"Virginia."

"What part? I have cousins in that area, I think. Have you been in Concord long? Whew! It's hot tonight, let's go get some punch."

The sheriff stood at the refreshment table as Pearl Ann dragged Charles over. "Simon, you better keep an eye on Susan. Charlie is liable to sweep her off her feet if he gets a chance to dance with her." Charles turned beet red. Pearl Ann sighed. "I'm sorry, Charlie, sometimes I speak before I think. That was very rude of me. Simon, have you met Charles?"

"Nice to meet you, Charles. In town long?"

"No. Few weeks."

"Hope you like it here in Concord. This town has the most friendly, most brave, and most hardworking families in all of New England. Aye. We are a proud lot. Let me know if you need anything while you settle in."

The sheriff tipped his hat and walked back in to the dance as Jack and Rachael walked out.

"Pearl Ann, that new dress you gave me is stunning," Rachel said. "It's too much, I really can't accept such a gift."

"Stuff and nonsense, I insist. It's just going to hang in my closet and feed the moths—Lord knows it won't ever fit me again."

"Well, it's awful nice and I—"

"And you will wear it to perfection."

Jack filled two cups with punch and handed one to Rachel. "Charles, you know which punch to drink, right? That bucket is rum punch. I don't think you want any."

"Yes, I have been drinking from the other. Jack, it's getting late. I think I'm going to turn in."

"It's not that late, Charles. Besides, I need to dance

with Rachael, and you need to meet a few more people. I'm sure Pearl Ann will take care of you." Jack took Rachael back inside, and Charles attempted an escape.

Pearl Ann took his arm. "Okay, Charles, let's take our punch over to that log and get some cool air." They walked away from the barn and sat apart—Pearl Ann on the log, and Charles on a bale of straw. "I don't mean to be too nosy, Charlie, but you seem familiar. Virginia?"

"Yes, I was born and lived there as a small child—then I came to New Hampshire."

"With your folks?"

Charles looks off into the starry night. "No."

"You don't have any family?"

"No, Goodwi— er, *ma'am*."

"Well, you do now. I can tell Jack has taken a shine to you. He is a very caring man, stick with him. He is loyal as the day is long, just like my Justice. Justice is my—was my husband. He died of a fever."

Charles breathed a sigh of relief at the jibing of Pearl Ann's interrogation.

"I loved my Justice more than anything." She continued. "He was a gift, and I am so fortunate to have had ten years with him." She looked at Charles and noticed his mind seemed far away. "What's your age, son?"

"Nearly fourteen."

Pearl Ann sipped punch and looked Charles over. Charles stared off into the night sky, wishing to be elsewhere. She noticed his clothes were too large, and he had the trousers belted to keep them up.

"Your clothes look like they were meant for a larger man, Charles, but that is a fine silver buckle on your belt. It is so delicate."

"I don't have anything nice to wear to a party. Jack

loaned me his old things." Charles looked down, grabbed the buckle, and ran his gloved fingers along the leather. "I had to make a belt from an old harness. The buckle is mine. I think it belonged to my mother."

"Well, shall we go back in? I've cooled off, and I'm ready for more dancing."

"I—I think I'm going to turn in. Thank you for the dance."

Pearl Ann bid him adieu and watched him walk away. Simon and his wife Susan emerged from the hot barn as Pearl Ann stood by the entrance.

"Hello, Pearl Ann. You look like you are this close to solving the secrets that the moon keeps."

"Oh! No, just thinking quietly."

Susan inquired if Charles was well since he left so early. Pearl Ann, still mulling over a mystery in her mind, replied, "He just…well, I'm sure it's nothing. Nice boy."

"Jack seems just fine with such a sprig of a sapling. You know, having to break him in and all at the dry goods store."

A large, compulsive grin drenched Pearl Ann's countenance. "In truth, Susan. It's not *'Don Juan's* cup of tea, is it?"

"Oh, stop that, Simon! Jack's a good man. Mr. Hutchins is lucky to have him in his employ."

"I think my husband thinks, well…" Susan tried to be delicate. "Jack doesn't have a lot of experience with younglings. Now, if he had a good wife—"

"Okay, who is ready for some more dancing?" Pearl Ann was too busy thinking about important puzzles and, rather than have hints of matchmaking thrown in her direction, she abandoned the couple, and re-entered the barn.

Chapter 56

Charles walked alone through the dark town. She 'didn't notice the chilly air as it was such a great relief from being in the hot, crowded barn. It was late, and the lamplighter had extinguished the lamps. There wasn't any activity in the streets, but she heard loud voices. She turned down an avenue and spied a group of young boys loitering on the boardwalk. They were bored with the evening and were smoking and drinking.

"I tell ya, I'm headed for great things in this life. My uncle says—"

"Put a stopper in it, Ren."

"Hey! What's eating you? All's I was sayin'—"

"Jesse, knock it off, let Ren say his piece. Hey, who's that?"

Charles approached the group, and one boy acknowledged her. "Howdy, stranger."

Charles nodded and continued walking.

"I said, 'good evening, sir.'"

Charles stopped and turned to face the boys.

"Hey, who are you? I've never seen you before."

"I work for Mr. Hutchins. I'm Charles," she replied. Her reply was soft spoken, but she impressed herself that she did not cower and stood her ground with the strangers.

"Hey, he must work with Jack. You're not from around here. Where'd you come from?"

"Men, stand down. We don't want any trouble, kid—Charlie."

"I'm Martin, this is Ren and Jesse. What are you doing on this fine evening?"

"I'm headed home, I was at the dance."

"Early for leaving the dance. It was a good dance, wasn't it?"

☙

"Jack, why are you walking so fast?"

"Am I, Rachael?

"Yes."

"I just want to get you home safe and sound."

"And? Do you have something else planned?"

"No! No, not a thing. I do want to check in on Charles at the livery. You know, make sure he made it home, and see if he had a good time."

"I'm sure he made it home fine. He's a big boy, Jack. My, my, how you coddle that boy!"

"Coddle? Rachael, he's barely thirteen. Ah, you know what I mean. He's just a pup and new in town, don't know hardly no one. I think he has had a rough go of it so far."

"I am sorry, Jack. You are kind to keep track of him."

Jack and Rachael came upon a crowd in the shadows of the dimly lit night.

"Jesse, *you* need to put a stopper in it." The boys' voices were edgy.

"Charles, is everything okay?"

Charles was visually relieved to see the other couple. Jack was some kind of hero to the riff-raff boys, so he made small talk and diffused any differences of opinion that might have arisen between them and Charles. They parted ways, and Jack and Charles walked Rachael home.

"Making some great friends, there, Charles. You planning on spending a lot of time with them?"

"Hopefully, not."

"Good. Not some of the most virtuous kids around. Not bad, just not entirely sober most of the time."

"They smelled less than virtuous—not that I'd judge anyone," Rachael said. Her mien softened when she realized her tone sounded haughty.

"Rachael, I think your opinion is widely shared."

Chapter 57

Charles sat on the edge of a small creek. She had fishing tackle but was carefully surveying the surrounding forest rather than preparing her line. She spied a snake-like animal sticking out of the water downstream. She eyed the spot and watched the reeds move quickly and unnaturally. Charles smiled because she knew the mystery was just the slim tail of a muskrat that waved like a flag out of the water as the small mammal chewed on cattails under water.

The displaying colors of the tall wooded canvas was stunning—yellow and orange with hardly any of the summer green left on the leaves. White oak, river birch, and silver ash dominated the view. The thick, fern-covered floor of the forest was nearly all dark with a few spots of yellow foliage peaking from more protected locations.

Leaf litter was beginning to settle like drifts of snow, and sedges poked up along the stream banks, seemingly naked without the ferns about them. The water was low in the creek, which should offer success in catching fish at Jack's favorite hole.

Jack noticed Charles hadn't placed his line in the water. He yelled to him from several yards upstream.

"What are you waiting for? You act like you've never
fished before!" Understanding the truth in his comment,
Jack walked back to Charles, helped untangle his line,
and set the tackle. He decided that Charles would never
be successful with his protective, leather gloves on and
knew that Charles would not remove them, even for
fishing. "You're going to have the fish laughing at us
before long." The line was readied, and Jack tossed it
into the water. He sat down next to Charles. "Did you
have a good time last night?" Charles nodded that he
did. "Did you dance with anyone? Besides Pearl Ann, I
mean."

"No. She's nice."

"She's a piece of work. A pillar of the community." Charles's head again cued understanding, and Jack
continued. "She and her husband, Justice, were the life
of the town. They hosted all kinds of parties and activities, never a dull moment. And I've never saw two people more in love than Pearl Ann and Justice. Didn't
have any kids, and they loved to be with people. Having the kind of money Justice had didn't hurt, neither."

"What did he do?"

"I don't rightly know. I guess he was just a 'gentleman.' I've heard that Pearl Ann came from a titled
family from France, so the money could have come to
her that way, but that's just hearsay." Jack and Charles
enjoyed the peaceful, susurrous water as they each reflected on their experiences with Pearl Ann. "In love.
No better words to describe the two. You just don't see
that every day."

Both Pearl Ann and Jack were gentle and amazing
people. "Does she have a beau now?"

"Nah, it's too soon anyway. No telling Pearl Ann's
path right now. You don't have to know her to know
how much his death hurt."

"She likes you."

"Yeah, but she's older than me by a few years. I...you know, I never thought about Pearl Ann that way." Jack considered the relationship. "No, she's too much like a sister to me. Anyway, I can't take Justice's place, that's for sure." He stood and stretched. "I'm going to check my line and then walk up the crick a bit to catch more fish than a marten could digest in a fortnight."

Charles was pretty sure the fish would take care of themselves, swimming around her hook. She leaned back, comfortable and contented, and remarked, "Suit yourself. I can't get up."

"Sweet dreams, don't let the fish bite."

Chapter 58

Charles's sleep was restless and plagued with nightmares. She bolted upright from her bunk and realized the fear and terror she had been experiencing were just illusions her mind had been churning through. Rising from her bed, she lighted a small candle.

Normally, a dark room had not scared her since she was small. Tonight, she was grateful for the luxury of the miniscule amount of light offered from a lump of wax. It comforted and reassured her. She poured water into the basin and washed her face. She peered at her image in the small shard of looking-glass on the wall.

Soft, normal sounds come from the horses bedded down in their stalls.

She was safe. It took some moments still, to quiet her heart. She paced in the small room and, when convinced everything was in order, she climbed back into bed and warmed her chilled limbs under the covers and finally drifted back into a peaceful slumber.

Chapter 59

For eight years the seasons had cycled, and the town of Concord had strengthened in population and industry. Amoskeag Falls plunged eighty-five feet and provided the power to run a mill, which, in these first decades of the Industrial Revolution, began changing the economic landscape to industry from an otherwise agrarian country. New Hampshire embraced opportunities such as mills for textiles because farming, such as that done in Virginia, could not be done with the intrusion of granite within the landscape of this northern state.

Mr. Hutchins's business continued its success. Local requirements were met, and he had the opportunity to contract with out of area deliveries as well. Jack and Charles made a reliable team for him with nary a bad word from customers. Hutchins resisted some of the easy success because he was content. He made plenty of money, paid his hands handsomely, and life seemed to tick along with balance. It was nice that he could grant time off to his employees in addition to the Sabbath.

On a lovely day outside of work, Dusty helped Charles set up a beehive. Charles read from a small pamphlet. "'Bees will pollinate the local flora. This will determine the flavor of your honey.'"

"Yah, the bees will collect from all the flowers around here."

"Even the maple trees?"

"Yah, but you won't get maple-flavored, flavored honey." This comment made Dusty stop to think. "Maple-flavored honey. That sounds kind of, kind of good!"

"Yuck. I don't think anyone around here would buy maple-flavored honey. Clover is fine with me, or whatever these flowers around here will make."

"Now, these little guys are gonna hibernate in the winter, the winter, Charles, so you gotta get 'em started, started before the first snow."

Charles and Dusty finished the set up. Dusty stepped back and admired the project.

Sheriff Bernard walked up and watched them.

Charles studied the bee hive. "Okay, Dusty, what do I do now? Afternoon, Sheriff."

"Sheriff, Sheriff, how-de-do. Well, the bees will do what they have to do. You have this hive set up nice, Charles, the way they, way they like it. They'll settle in and then hibernate. Production will really get going, going in the spring."

"Boys, we've had an incident. Seems Mrs. Sprague has lost some of her husband's under garments and a shirt."

Charles and Dusty found the information humorous, but they silently waited for the sheriff to continue.

"Off the drying line, is my first explanation. I reckon the wind picked up or she dropped them." The sheriff's thoughts became more creative as he explored the mystery. "Then again, squirrels have been known to scavenge civilized bits and pieces to cozy their nest for the coming winter—"

Dusty comically cut the sheriff's wandering thoughts short. "Sheriff, we are your men. We will keep an eye out for said undergarments and report back to you, back to you directly." His call to action was finished off by saluting the sheriff.

"Good. The town needs upstanding citizens like yourselves to keep everything safe and in order. Carry on, men." Sheriff Bernard walked away, happily chuckling to himself.

"Thanks for helping me, Dusty," Charles said.

"No problem. My family has had bees for ages. Nothing to it. Nothing to it."

Chapter 60

Charles slept soundly in the tack room. She had not found it necessary to move to a home of her own. She liked to be with "his" horses and knew that Mr. Hutchins felt more secure, knowing Charles was so close to them all night. Most nights were as quiet as if she lived in the outskirts of town. The location of the dry goods store and stable was down a side street away from the center of town, so it was always quiet after the shops closed and the inhabitants returned to their residences.

Her sleep was still, as if she were hibernating. If she had been dreaming, it would have been about squirrels stealing honey. They reached into the honeycomb and scratched out handfuls of honey, laden with squirming bees. The sound got louder and louder until a resounding crash pulled Charles's consciousness into the tangible smells of the corrals and tack room.

Charles was immediately frightened by the unfamiliar sound. She got out of bed and slid into the shadows. There was an intruder attempting to come through the door. The unwanted guest managed to slip the hasp open and enter. The invader's movements were familiar, but clumsy. Charles quickly identified the suspect as Jack, staggering into the room, moving toward the bed.

"Charles—Charles, you sleeping?" Jack whispered loudly. "It's just me."

Charles moved toward Jack and put her bare hand on his shoulder. Jack was not expecting this and it made him jump. He tripped and fell onto Charles's bed. "Oh! What are you doing over there?"

Charles grimaced at her ungloved hands and knew exactly where she was and why she was there. *Jack cannot see well in the dark room and won't notice anyway*, she thought.

"Hey, I was wondering if you'd ever skinned a pelt off of a beaver?"

"No, Jack. What do you really want?"

Finding himself supine, he decided it was comfortable and did not try to rise. His situation had appeal for one who had earlier, attempted to drink an entire cask of rum. "Oh, Charles, Charles, Charles…What am I going to do? I have women dripping—yes, dripping—off of me. And you know what? I don't want 'em." His arrogant tone quickly changed to a sarcastic tenor. 'Come to dinner, Jack, meet the folks, Jack, do what I say, Jack…' Why, just answer me this—why do we need women?"

"Can't answer," Charles answered curtly. Jack was making her nervous.

"That's okay, I can." Jack began to opine like a young disciple. The spirit influenced brogue of the sermon, however, would have deceived the humbugger to any astute harkeners. "Listen. Charles, we need women to realize just how happy life is when we go off and spend time with other men."

"Jack, I think you need to go home to your own bed. Now."

Jack laughed a belly laugh at the irony, "There you go—'Jack, go to bed now.'"

"That's not what I mean. I'm not telling you what to do. Come on, get up. You don't want to tell me any of this stuff." *Please, don't tell me this stuff.*

"Boy, oh boy, oh boy. Now even you sound like a woman. You can't do that to me, Charles. We men gotta stick together. I know, I know, you're still pretty young, but take it from me. Men…men…men, sheesh. Charles, I don't feel too good."

Jack leaned over the side of the bunk and began heaving. Disgusted but wide awake now, Charles wet a cloth and wiped his friend's face. Jack's eyes were closed as he muttered, "Ah, Rachael, you are so kind to me, but, sshh, what if Prudence sees us? What about all of the others? You don't *know* about them? But you love me *anyway*? Kiss me, Rachael."

Jack tried to kiss Charles, who was repulsed by the smell of Jack's breath and the stench of vomit. Jack quietly fell asleep.

Chapter 61

Mr. Hutchins valued input from his oldest employee. As he figured on paper, he showed it to Jack for his opinion. "So, by my calculations, we can do this if we focus here rather than there. What do you think?"

"Well, it looks good on paper."

"Oh, Jack, I almost forgot. Pearl Ann needs some help—Oh, this memory of mine. I can't remember what she said, but she should be home later this afternoon."

"Ahh, I had a feeling this was coming up. That woman," Jack said with a sound of finality.

"What do you mean, '*That woman?*' I thought you two hit it off really well?"

"No, no, Mr. Hutchins, Pearl Ann has been getting a bit spooked by all of the missing preserves and such, that's all. She probably needs a small task taken care of at home and wants me to do it."

Mr. Hutchins stared at Jack blankly. Jack stared back motionless with an equally vague look.

"Oh. That's all." Mr. Hutchins raised an eyebrow, insinuating that there is more to the story.

"No! Nothing but a little handyman work for an old friend's widow. Nothing else."

While Mr. Hutchins summed up Jack's story, Sheriff Bernard entered the store and waved to the two men. "Pearl Ann is an eligible catch, Jack. She has more than enough to offer a man. Howdy, Simon."

"I'm fine. She's fine." Jack was flustered. "Don't tell me you've joined the old hens and their gossip sessions?"

The sheriff felt he had walked into a hubbub. "Uh, oh, what's got his feathers all ruffled, Ezekiel?"

"Nothing. It was my fault. I overstepped my bounds. I'm sorry, Jack. I won't say another word about it. It's none of my business."

"I just wanted to let you know the good news, men." Sheriff Bernard stayed true to his task and was eager to fill the men in on his progress. "I think I know who the perpetrator is that is swiping small articles around town. I think it's that buddy of yours, Jack, but I can't figure a motive."

Chapter 62

Jack and Charles worked together for Pearl Ann, repairing her front entry. Leaning against the house, supervising the men, she held a small piece of jewelry in her palm and studied it before she replaced it on the ribbon around her neck. She was silent as she watched them work and noticed a hulking figure happily loping toward her home. Dusty walked up to the crew with an apple danish in each of his hands. With his mouth stuffed full, he managed greetings and inquired what they are working on.

"Just securing the latch on the door. There. It's easier to move, but it won't undo itself. It aligns better so I don't think there are any open spaces, now, so the mosquitos can't make an interior assault, either. Let's look at that kitchen window."

"Bravo! Right this way. Simon, how do you fare?"

The sheriff had just walked up to the work party and followed them around the house. "Pearl Ann, I need a word with this lot."

"Okay, mind if I get a swallow, a swallow of water to wash these down?"

"Go on, Dusty."

"What's wrong, Sheriff? What do you need us for?"

"I told you the other day, Jack, we think Dusty may be taking things around this area."

Charles looked at Jack for an explanation, but Jack only shrugged back and offered his own puzzlement.

Dusty returned from the water well.

The sheriff pointed. "Dusty, I notice that you are wearing a brand new shirt."

Dusty smiled proudly about his new garment. "Yes, sir, I had to buy one, buy one to replace the old one. Luckily, Mrs. Hughlett just got these in, got these in. I bought two—both red."

"Uh, huh. What were you just eating when I walked up?"

"Apple danish! Julia Tisdale baked them just for me! Delicious."

"That was nice. What can you tell me about the preserves, underwear, shirt, and cobbler that went missing in the past few weeks?"

"I told you we'd keep a weather eye out for you, but nothing has come up to report on," Dusty explained in earnest.

"I think you've been taking things from people, Dusty."

"I haven't!" he shouted. "That's slander, slander."

"Dusty, tell us the truth." Jack could not believe the accusation but pushed Dusty to clear his name. "Have you been needing things? Wanting things?"

"No, Jack! I—I wouldn't take anything that didn't belong to me."

"Sheriff," Jack pleaded, "why would Dusty take food and clothes? He makes good money as a stone mason."

"Like I mentioned the other day, I don't know. Things just point to Dusty."

"Because he eats sweets?" Pearl Ann thought Simon had lost his marbles. "He buys new shirts every month. He can't help ripping out of them. You know how big he is and the hard work he does. That's absurd, Simon." She threw her hands up in frustration and walked into the house.

The sheriff called after her. "I know, I know, Pearl Ann. I guess I just—dog gone it, men. This is so trivial, but *someone* is breaking the law, and I have to find the answer."

"Sheriff?" Charles asked quietly.

"Yes, Charles, what is it?"

"Dusty didn't steal those things."

Pearl Ann returned to the group and was excited to hear Charles speaking up. "Oh? What do you know, son?"

"Dusty always does things in twos. He bought two red shirts, not just one, or even a red one and a blue one. Miss Julia gave him two danish because of it."

"Charles is right, Simon, *il est brillant*!" Pearl Ann interjected.

"In fact," Charles continued. "Dusty always repeats something twice when he's speaking."

Pearl Ann was proud of Charles with his deduction skills and happy that the sheriff was wrong about Dusty. "That was very clever of you, Charles."

"In two's? What do you mean, two's? Pearl Ann?"

"If Dusty had taken those things, Sheriff, he would have naturally taken two of everything," Jack stated with judicial defense.

"You have a point there, boys, and I'm glad Dusty has a jury of friends. But whoever is taking things is driving me batty!"

"There you go, Simon. Dusty's a good man. Go follow your trail a little farther and let Jack get my repairs done. Oh! I almost forgot. Post this letter for me, won't you, love?"

Simon took the letter from Pearl Ann and nodded.

She headed off of the porch and shouted, "Come around the other side of the house, boys. Good bye, Simon."

Sheriff Bernard was left standing by himself and sighed, thinking, *Dead end. Again.*

Chapter 63

How on earth do I balance this silly cup and saucer on my lap, Mother?"

"You won't have to most of the time, Charlotte, but practice will prepare you if you have to."

"Must I really attend teas and such?"

"Yes, dear. A lady must be educated in the finer things in life."

"Then I don't wish to be a lady! I wish to climb trees and play with bugs!"

"That's enough, Charlotte. Pass me a cookie, and wipe your chin."

The education of Charlotte Spruce had been thorough during her first eight years, but her mother often encountered snags. Life as a Spruce meant living with luxury, but also having manners and poise. Charlotte was more active than her mother thought a young girl should be, but Mr. Spruce was delighted nonetheless, that Charlotte was well-liked by other children and was healthy and robust.

Mrs. Spruce employed the best tutors for her daughter. Most wealthy families prepared their sons with early education in the hopes that they might go on to study at the Deerfield Academy. All of the New England colonies insisted that education be offered to the residents' sons. Concord complied, of course. The schoolmaster was almost always a man, and girls did not share in public education.

Mrs. Spruce saw this standard as less than ideal for her daughter. She knew Charlotte would thrive in the company of her peers and possibly whither from being isolated at home. If she did not, she would drive her mother mad from her excess energy. The first opportunity to hire a new teacher put Mr. Spruce on the selection committee. The mind of Wanda Spruce was lithe and sprang into action. Mr. Spruce's presence insured that her choice of teacher was placed in the community, and a female teacher for her daughter was her choice.

The opportunity to have a small amount of teaching time devoted to girls would be easy to enact. Time was devoted each teaching day, as deemed by Mrs. Spruce—and an army of strong mothers and wives—for very young boys and girls who could afford the tuition. The boys were taught basic skills like colors, numbers, the alphabet, and playing games. The girls were taught etiquette, dance, and sewing. It was progressive for a town north of Boston, but Mr. Spruce's wife was a happy woman because of it.

Chapter 64

Another day was coming to a close, and Mr. Hutchins's loyal employees were nearly done cleaning up and putting away everything from a busy day of making deliveries in the area. Both Jack and Charles had served the dry goods shop well, and they worked together with ease. Jack suggested the two of them visit the tavern for a cool drink and supper.

Jack ordered food for both of them and grog for himself. He asked Charles what his choice of drink was.

"Water's fine. Pretty dry."

"And a water for Charles, Artie."

The tavern keeper started on their order as the men met up with friends.

"Heya, Jack! Jack!"

"Dusty! How now?"

"All righty. All righty. Cutting some troughs, but next week we are going to start on some curbs."

"Yeah? For who?"

"Town of Boston. They want to line, to line their streets."

"How do you get the granite down to Boston, Dusty?" Charles had seen the size of some of the cut rock and never considered that the commodity would have to be loaded and hauled to some destination.

"Team. A *big* team. Much of it floats down the river, but it's not a, not a straight shot down. Stuff ain't light. Ain't light. Costs almost as much to ship as to cut."

Artie brought their food and drink. Charles began to eat when Dusty noticed a problem. "Hey, hey, ain't you going to wash?"

Charles's head did not turn from his plate. "Nope."

"In the eight years I've known him, he never takes them gloves off, Dusty. Leave him be."

"Yes, I guess that is, that is the way you do eat, Charles. A man's gotta do what a man's gotta do. Gotta do."

"Best hand I've ever had. Got a real way with horses. I like the way he works with them, and I think I may have even learned from him. Why, he even tamed old Meditation." Jack's praise of Charles was solid.

"Hey, Artie! Let's have a couple more of what Jack has to eat."

The tavern keeper was ready for Dusty's appetite and brought another tray of food for him. "No! Isn't that the horse that couldn't, that couldn't be harnessed?"

"Same one."

"Well, we must have a real prodigy with us. 'Charlie, the tamer, tamer of lions and beasts.'" Dusty devoured the tray of food and emptied his tankard. He sat back and emitted a rumbling belch and sigh of relief. "Well, I have to move on now, gents. Julia will be expecting me for supper."

Jack and Charles stayed behind and finished their meals. "My, oh my! That Dusty has a hollow leg."

Charles nodded in accord with Jack's observation.

"It is amazing how much food Dusty can eat and still feel good. And that was to tie him over until supper."

The two ate silently and, when Jack finished a particularly satisfying mouthful, he asked, "Well, what activities will entertain you , come the evening, Charles?"

"I don't have anything in mind. I will probably read some and then go to bed. Why, do you have a scheme? Will you be meeting Rachael?"

Jack drank his grog and went to the bar to refill his glass. Charles noticed how Jack was evading him and asked plainly, as his friend sat back down, "You've been seeing Rachael since I came to Concord. Are you going to marry her?"

"I don't want to get married." Jack's voice was low and irritated.

"Oh. Why not? I mean, to Rachael? Or not to anyone?"

"Like you said, Charles, I have been seeing her for over eight years."

Chapter 65

Jack and Charles left the tavern and walked along the boardwalk. It was a cool spring evening filled by the aroma of newly born flowers that recently burst through their bulb lair and pushed through the warming, dense soil, silently waving their colors in truce to the winter's cold. The community's activity buzzed steadily alongside the awakening foliage. Sugaring weather in March stirred a town's activity— lambing season brings new creatures into the fold, sheering begins, and in the blink of an eye, life has segued into the balmy summer.

Charles enjoyed walking with Jack. She enjoyed doing *everything* with Jack. Jack was more than a best friend. When they reached the street that the dry goods store was on, they said goodnight to each other, and Charles walked to the end of her street while Jack continued on to his home.

She tried to read from the Bible. Concentration fled as soon as she had the text in the candle light. Charles decided that perhaps her addled thoughts needed the poetry book that was nestled safely in a hidey hole. She retrieved the well-worn book and said aloud, "'Lady Mary Wortley Montague, I hope you can help me settle my thoughts." The poetry was beautiful. It put into words feelings that were difficult for Charles to arrange in her head.

> *For constancy is Nature too.*
> *Can all the doctrine of the schools,*
> *Our maxims, our religious rules,*
> *Can learning to our lives ensure,*
> *Virtue so bright, or bliss so pure?*

The beautiful words that described billing doves could not anchor Charles's restless thoughts. She set the book down and blew out the candle, and then she crawled into bed. She thought of Jack and wondered what exactly he meant by his comment about not wanting to get married. Jack hadn't been on many dates in the past several months, with Rachael, or any other girl. Charles couldn't get her mind off of Jack.

The more she thought of Jack, the more miserable she became. Her life was secure and comfortable, yet it was putting a strain on her after eight years of deceit. If she could have admitted to herself that she loved Jack—nay, *was in love* with Jack—it would surely have propelled her into a dismal hell that would silence her breath for eternity.

"If I'm discovered," she pondered, "the likelihood that the misery I experienced before I came to Concord will accost me again, without mercy."

After much of the dark night eroded, Charles's mind ceased enough to allow her tired body to sleep.

Chapter 66

The power of the hind legs of a grasshopper, their trigger-quick unfolding that blasted them aloft to another leaf of another shrub, could describe the gray matter in her head. The controlling of every thought, every emotion, and every sensation seemed to be destined to always, without fail, land on Jack at any resolve.

As Charles worked the following day, she was as able as any other day, but her mind worked tediously as a machine whose end goal was meant to effectively and efficiently return to the same mark and repeat the task over and over again. By the late afternoon, Charles felt that her mind was a loom in one of the new textile factories, with the agile way that it hopped between thoughts of anything, yet landed every time magnetically on Jack. She understood that she needed to snap out of it. Jack didn't cross Charles's path much during that particular work day, but he drifted across Charles's thoughts until she knew her mental health was at stake.

"Hey, it's late, Charles. You're done for the day."

"I just want everything neat when I'm back in the morning."

"You're a good worker, maybe even too dedicated.

But you know you never leave, so 'coming back in the morning' isn't really the way it is."

"I know. But you know what they say—a stitch in time saves nine. And dedication to your job is...well..."

Jack came very near Charles while she was hanging up the tack. Charles could not speak. She could feel the warmth of Jack's body, but she was not afraid. This was a surprise to her. She was nervous, however, and dropped a harness.

Jack leaned over to pick it up for Charles, just as Charles squatted down to retrieve it. Their eyes locked and they gazed deeply into one another. For Charles, time stopped. *If you could see into my soul, you would see my all-consuming love that runs deeper and wider in breadth than any human heart can contain under their breast.* Within this caesura, Jack could have touched her, held her, and in Charles's hypnotic tranquility, taken her anywhere. *C'est lui pour moi, moi pour lui dans la vie.*

"Yeah, well, I never was too good with women's work. Here, I have it." Jack stood up and hung the harness on the peg. "You want to come with me tonight to the Opry House? They got a new show. I hear they got some buxom women with a lot of curves," Jack's description was unanimated.

"Thank you, but I'd rather stay here with old Thunder."

"Suit yourself, but I hear it's a really good show."

Another pause between the two made Charles uncomfortable, so she fidgeted with her gloves. Jack started for the door to leave but stopped. He turned back to look at Charles. "Charles?" he stalled. "Sure you don't want to come with me?"

She *did* want to go. "Well...maybe I should get out

more. See new things." It seemed feeble when she uttered it.

"Great! Be ready to go at seven. I'll come by. You
know, we can walk there together."

Chapter 67

Dirty, dirty, Dicky.
He's stinky and's all icky.
Wash your face, comb your hair,
Or for our team we won't pick ye!"

The school yard, filled with little boys and a variety of girls, displayed the less than ideal setting for the fledgling attempt at coeducational learning. The older girls, with an air of supremacy, saw the obvious opportunity to thwart the male species while given this new setting of unity. One little boy, in bedraggled attire, was surrounded by taunting. He was only four or five years of age, but was learning the callous lessons of the sin of being less affluent than others.

A painful jab was ironically delivered by descendants of the women who sent their husbands and sons to 'die for the Constitution' in seeming retribution of the unheeded words of Abigail Adams, "Remember the Ladies," from which she pointed out that women were blatantly left out of its protection.

Fortunately for the lad, some of the bystanding lassies saw his treatment as a crime. "What are Betsy, Matilda, and Fanny doing to that little boy?"

"Dicky stinks and didn't wash before school. He's like that every day."

"So they push him down into the dirt? He's just a little guy." This plucky lass ran to Dicky's rescue. She freed him from the badgering older girls, helped him up, brushed him off, and walked him to the school's water trough.

The young girl tried to console him. "Here, Dicky, just a little on your face and you'll be okay. Don't you have a comb or brush? Well, let's just use a little water—there! It's taming your mop pretty good. Now you are respectable. You shouldn't let them tease you like that. You can stand up for yourself! There—Brave Dickey!"

The incident was quickly relayed to the school marm Miss Pomery who, knowing how she earned her bread and butter, was quick to make sure the report was taken to the intervening girl's mother before the town's tongues convulsed a rendition such that it would be detrimental to Miss Pomery's livelihood.

Miss Pomery left immediately after this auxiliary class was dismissed and went straight to the home of the interloping girl. "It is so nice to visit, and the tea is delicious." She was well trained and appeared professional in every way but was uncomfortable with the chore of informing parents.

"Miss Pomery, you should stop by more often. We would love to have you stay for the next month."

Many teachers of this time floated between the homes of his or her pupils for room and board and usually stayed for approximately a month's duration before moving to the next family.

"That is so kind of you. I have made arrangements to stay with the John Goddard family until next Tuesday, but I would be grateful to return to your lovely home and hospitality at that time. I do want to tell you of an incident at school today. Some of the children were picking on a small boy," Miss Pomery squeezed the information in like taking a swig of stiff medicine.

Mrs. Spruce betrayed her status with friendly rapport. "Oh, I bet it was little Richard Gibbs. I keep telling his mother that he needs a little more attention from her. He's just not as quick as his brothers."

"The very same, the poor dear. Anyway, your daughter, Charlotte, put a stop to it."

"My little Charlotte! Such high morals, such an obedient Christian regarding her peers!"

"Yes. Unfortunately, she shoved three girls of our finest families."

"*Shoved?*"

"Yes, Mrs. Spruce. Well, you could call it that— Okay, she really walloped them."

"Oh."

"I'm sure you can appreciate my position. She was helping a little boy, but I can't condone fighting for any reason."

"Of course not, darling. I will have a chat with her right away. Josiah and I try to encourage her toward a more refined and lady-like disposition."

"Naturally. Of course, you do."

Deep relief was felt by both women after all was said regarding this delicate task. Their brains proceeded logically on the topic presented, but the essence of the event revolving around the precocious and dynamic personality of Charlotte Spruce could not be viewed as anything but the typical breach of etiquette often displayed by the lass in the most public of times. Sniggering by the two women turned into full roars of healthy laughter in the brief silence.

"That girl is something else! Just the other day, I

found an entire city of snails she was keeping in her doll house! Come with me to the kitchen so I can tell Alma Mae to set an extra plate for supper— you really must stay and sup with us."

Mrs. Spruce led Miss Pomery into the kitchen and informed Alma Mae of the plans. The sound of a wagon approaching the compound piqued the women's interest. The servant peeked out the kitchen window. "It looks like supplies are here from Hutchins's. Excuse me, ma'am, so I can let Mr. Jack in."

"Certainly, Alma Mae. Please have Jack bring the dry goods in and put them in the pantry."

Jack entered the house with an armload of goods. "Afternoon, Mrs. Spruce!"

"Afternoon, Jack. Jack, have you met Miss Pomery, our school marm?"

"Glad to make your acquaintance, Miss Pomery." A gentle but electric feeling was felt as the two met for the first time.

"*Elizabeth* Pomery. It is so good to meet you," she said informally to this handsome man.

"Jack, you should take Miss Pomery to the auction. Had you planned on going, Miss Pomery?"

Miss Pomery was clearly abashed at such boldness.

"Well, I'd be obliged to take Miss Pomery anywhere she wants, but I'll be tending shop that day while Mr. Hutchins is away."

"Well, you two would have a fine time together, at any rate. Perhaps something else will come up," Mrs. Spruce concluded with a meddlesome air.

Chapter 68

M r. Hutchins had the day off to spend time with his boys, so Jack was tending the counter. He was comfortable indoors working with stock and figures. His family devoutly supported education, ensuring that Jack and his brothers could all read, write, and figure. His sisters did not go to school, but were taught the basics by their mother.

Miss Pomery entered the dry goods shop.

Jack straightened. "Why, Miss. Pomery! What can I do for you?"

"Hello, Jack. I just need a few items." She handed him the list, and he began collecting the products. They chatted and filled in the answers to the usual light topics. Miss Pomery's marketing time was not proportional to the small number of items on her list, but the two could not pull themselves away from each other.

"I would love to treat you to dinner tonight, Miss Pomery, if you do not have other plans."

"I am being boarded with the Spruce family."

"I don't wish to upset your routine. I, ah, just thought—"

"It would not upset anything, Jack, I would love to! I will let Alma Mae know not to set a plate for me."

Charles walked into the store and saw the two at the counter. She did not wish to have communication with anyone new, so she stayed in the far corner and hoped they wouldn't notice her.

It was nearly time for a break and a meal, so Jack wrapped Miss Pomery's items and carried them as the two left the building. Charles was concerned, but she hoped the woman was in Jack's family or, at least, in the Hutchins family. Jack was polite and was expected to be cordial to a guest. *He is very polite.*

Chapter 69

Charles was in the corral with two horses as Jack escorted Miss Pomery into the yard.

"How do you fare, Charles? Have you met Miss Pomery?"

Charles recognized the woman. She dropped her head and hoped that enough time had elapsed and her costume would protect her. "Nice to meet you, ma'am." She moved to the other side of the horse.

"Have we met?" Elizabeth only got a whisper of a feeling of the young man.

Charles shook her head and continued with her work. Jack and Elizabeth left the area, and Charles prepared Sophie and Mi'kmaq as they stood together. They were harnessed and ready to take the wagon out for the last delivery of the day. Mr. Hutchins came out to the corral and patted Sophie along her broad shoulder and back to her hip. Charles stepped around the wagon and greeted him.

"Charles, I need you to make a long haul for me."

"Indeed. To where, sir?"

"Graniteville. I know it's a distance, but Jack must be here to tend the store should the need arise. It's a good order for the dry goods."

"That's fine, sir. When will I go?"

"Well, tomorrow would be best, if you can."

Charles was happy to oblige Mr. Hutchins. *It will be a solitary few days. I will have extensive time to think without the day to day charade to contend with.* She saw an enjoyable respite in this trip.

"Thank you, Charles, it's unusual for us to deliver so far away, but this came up suddenly today, and it's for a friend of mine."

"Yes, sir." *It will give Jack time to think, and he will notice how empty the day is without me!* Charles rechecked the harnesses and smiled at the thought. A flash electrified her brain and made her entire body droop when she realized: *Jack will have plenty of time to spend with Elizabeth.*

"You're a good worker, Charles, and you will have earned a bonus from your continued service."

I earn nothing but grief and loneliness. If I possessed anything, I have just cast it to the wind. What have I done? Charles's stomach dropped in rancor at the realization. *I have created my own undoing. My love is free to woo my childhood friend, and I am powerless to intervene.* Charles held on to Mi'kmaq as the explosion of truth bathed her with remorse. She pushed the dizzying thoughts back enough to carry on, but the sense of hopelessness enveloped her and clung to her depths. Strange Providence kept the nauseating color of Charles's face hidden from Mr. Hutchins.

"Come inside, and I can give you the details of the trip."

If I could do anything, it would be done in vain. Once I am discovered, I will be admitted to an asylum.

Charles followed Mr. Hutchins into the shop to learn the specifics of the journey. When Charles returned to the yard, Jack and Miss Pomery were still together on the far side of the tack house, sitting on a bale of hay.

"Hey, Charles, I'm sorry you got stuck with this long trip. Hutchins will make it right for you. He is fair and just. Well, Miss Elizabeth, I better be gettin' back to work, and, Charles, you better go pack."

Charles nodded and bolted into the stable.

"Wow! I wonder what that was for. He's real uneasy with women, though. Maybe you scared him."

"I've never had that effect on a man," she said matter-of-factly. "Maybe he's eager to get started on his trip. I'll walk with you over to the shop on my way out."

Chapter 70

Charles wept as she lay on her bed. She had tried to calm herself, put reason into her head, and not carry on in this puerile manner. Jack entered Charles's stable house gingerly. He didn't wish to startle his friend, but he had to announce himself to belay thoughts of deceit.

"Charles? Hey, ho! What's going on? You afraid of a long trip?"

Charles shook her head and stifled the sobbing.

"What is it then, Charles? Have I forgotten something? Is it Miss Pomery? I've only just met her. She's new to town…"

Charles froze to hear every word that Jack uttered.

"Charles, she's nice. I like her. I like her more than any girl I've dated in a long time. But you don't have anything to worry about. I'm still here." Jack helped Charles sit up. He seemed to have a grip on his blubbering. Jack offered him a handkerchief. Charles wiped his face and looked at Jack.

Jack could not understand Charles's expression, and his behavior was unlike anything Jack had seen. He looked into Charles's eyes and tried to find the cause. The moist, chestnut windows that were beautiful, large eyes reflected nothing back to Jack, yet, at the same time, they lured him like the song of a siren. Charles's eyes held deep mysteries. The secrets interested but eluded Jack. Jack had known this from the day Mr. Hutchins introduced the two able hands. Jack never thought about the grief and sorrow that was most assuredly cloistered there. Until now. Now it enveloped Jack and raised him to a new level of understanding. In that moment, Jack wished to purge Charles of all anguish and desired to swaddle the younger man in his strong arms and make his life cloudless and joyful.

A few minutes elapsed in silence. Jack jolted himself out of his thoughts— his perverse and immoral thoughts. "You're the damnedest puzzle, Charles." He paddled himself to the closest shore of safety. "Hardest worker I've ever seen, but show him a pretty girl, and he falls apart."

Jack's comment landed brazenly on Charles's ears, returning her to sobbing and rooting into her bedding.

"Hey, come on, now. Come on, you're acting all girly, crying like this. Heck, you even sound like a girl."

The piercing, discordant javelin of words made Charles stop weeping.

"That's more like it. Buck up." Jack wetted a handkerchief in the basin and handed it to Charles. "Jehosephat! I never saw such carrying on."

Chapter 71

Jack arrived at the school room in the late afternoon to meet Miss Pomery. She had cleaned up for the day and was ready to step out with Jack. School was back in session with the shortening of the days. "Jack, it is nice that you came to meet me."

"Anything for a pretty lady." They left the building and begin walking across the school yard. "Hello, pretty little lady," Jack added as a little girl wandered up to them.

"Why, Charlotte! Why aren't you home? Your mother will be worried sick!"

"Hello, Miss Pomery, hello, sir. I found a baby squirrel on the way home. It was lost."

"*Lost?*"

"It didn't seem to know where it was, so I brought it to the big tree with the knot hole in it." Miss Pomery stared at the child. The silence offered the little girl a chance to elaborate further. "I think there's a squirrel's nest in it. It probably lives there with a big family, full of brothers and sisters and aunts and uncles—"

Miss Pomery halted the girl's meandering nonsense. "That was kind of you." Miss Pomery was hypnotized by the little girl and she stood and studied her.

Jack hadn't noticed any mystery and would like to continue to his date.

"Jack, we need to walk Charlotte home. It will just be a tiny detour—you know where the Spruce's home is. Charlotte, please don't *ever* pick up squirrels!" Elizabeth lashed out, surprising herself with her own voice. She softened a bit. "They are soft and sweet, but they could bite you. Now, young lady, let's get you to your mother."

Elizabeth could see that Jack saw this interruption as a crucial problem with obtaining his evening meal. "Jack, maybe we could do something extra tonight. We could go to your favorite tavern. I know that I have kept you from your usual haunts for the past few months."

This placated Jack as they took the child home.

When the couple started for the tavern, Jack had a nicer spring in his step. "What got into you, Elizabeth? I thought you were going to whip that girl all the way home. I had no idea you were so stern and had such a keen hatred of squirrels."

"Jack, I just lost my head. I don't hate squirrels. Something about Charlotte gave me a strange feeling, and when she said that about the squirrel, well, I over reacted. I snapped at her, it was too harsh."

"I think you were just being a good, caring teacher." Jack was impressed. "Gone doodle! You have the energy of a kite in a storm, Elizabeth!"

"Thank you," she replied bashfully.

"Maybe her class of folk don't see the value of common knowledge. That little girl hasn't strayed five yards from her own front porch. She probably don't know what lives in our woods, nor what critters are harmful."

Chapter 72

Another summer waned, and the autumn began its hold on New England. Charles directed Sophie and Mi'kmaq back to Concord. She delivered a load over to Louden and was bumping along on the return trip. This wagon road was well worn and had ruts enough to shake your teeth loose. Charles traveled without noticing her surroundings. She had become very depressed over the summer and had kept to herself. Not even the rough traveling jarred her from deep meditation. She spent her time praying and thinking. She prayed for her soul, for the copious sins she was guilty of. She thought of how she tangled herself up in a web of deceit, and how she could untangle it without being committed for mental lapse.

Molly Pitcher. This legendary fighter with the Continental Army was still the subject of awe and patriotism. She was lauded for her actions of taking water to the troops and carrying on with firing the canon when the men had fallen. "She didn't pretend to be something else," Charles mused. "She never gave the pretenses of being a man who could own property and vote. I have voted and, for better or for worse, I am a man. What punishment shall I have earned for those two sins alone? Yea, and what of the sins of my youth?"

Tears ran down her cheeks briefly, and she swiftly tucked the memories back into the dark trove of unspeakable transactions within the yawning abyss of her mind. She recalled several Bible verses that made her stop feeling sorry for herself.

Cause me to hear thy loving
kindness in the morning;
for in thee do I trust:
cause me to know the way wherein
I should walk; for I lift up my soul unto thee.

The structure of religion was willingly grasped and would allow the brain respite. It was this familiar routine that assuaged Charles' mind. Piety redirected the path in which guilt was piloted. Although culpability was still with him. Without mitigation, she could feel at ease, knowing she did not carry the burden alone.

The cool air blew her hair about her face and pulled her from her reverie. She looked at the mountains and forest, enjoying the beauty and inhaling the clean air. Charles watched the team and saw strength in their backs, comparable to the granite that was this land. "All of these things are strong and they go through the ages, just so."

She pushed thoughts of 'fairness' of an individual's life far away. It was, as in her own thoughts, "just so" and did not warrant need or dissection.

The darkness that lurked within could illustrate exactly the power those hooves hold. Thoughts surfaced and showed Charles a plausible and compassionate end to her wearisome life. Strength in those wild limbs, the percussive pounding and *clop clop*: trampling and kicking, they could snap a body like a twig. This could effectively remove all thoughts as the brain softly yielded to the unforgiving force.

A shiver ran through Charles. "Spread sin upon sin. No," she said aloud to pull her mind from those murky depths. "No. This misery may be my destiny, but I am not alone." She tried to think about happy things—nature, horses, love. She thought of Pearl Ann and her enduring strength through any trial. She thought of Jack. She tried not to, but it was no use. She thought of the sylvan memories of running across grass fields and inspecting insects. Miss Pomery. Miss Pomery and Jack. Rachael and Jack. Pearl Ann and Jack. Jealousy infused and irked her. Sweat trickled from her head in the cool air. It was all becoming too much.

She grasped at what would stave her thoughts and was relieved that home was a few hundred yards more. Charles returned to the dry goods yard and dutifully cared for the mares and the equipment. She ran now for safety, her body shaking uncontrollably, as if that which had become habit was unavailable. She dove into the womb of the tack house and paged directly to Philippians 2:3. Frantically she read out loud, "'And through covetousness shall thy with feigned words make merchandise of you: whose judgment now of a long time lingereth not, and their damnation slumbereth not.'"

This verse did not seem to help as much as others. *Is it wrong to love a man? Do I not have the same right as any? If I wish for a suitor to accept me, is this covetous?* No. But the answer still hid tangled within the conundrum of lies in which she lived.

Charles was hungry after such a lengthy journey and miffed at herself for bungling the scriptures. She decided to pay a visit to Jack's favorite tavern. She ordered food and drink—that which she never partook of, rum. She ate her plate of food and drank her beverage. She had Artie refill her tankard with more rum. She drank that and had it refilled a third time. Charles felt raucous but still not happy.

James entered with Dusty. They saw Charles and walked over to join him at his table.

"Evening, Charles. Nice surprise to find you here," James said as they approached his table.

Charles waved an animated hand over her head at the men.

Dusty picked up the sticky tankard and sniffed. "Are you alone tonight?" Dusty and James exchanged seasoned looks of understanding and began to pull up chairs for themselves. "Charles, how about, how about if James and I join you?"

"That would be just finey-winey, Dusty-Wusty. Jamey-Wamey."

James and Dusty decided it would be good to take their young friend home first and then grab food. Charles being three sheets to the wind was as shocking a sight as watching a preacher tipple the sacramental wine.

The boys helped Charles home and into the stable house. She vomited several times *en route*. James decided Dusty could handle the situation better than he and left to find Jack.

Dusty encouraged Charles to get into bed. "No, no, no, Dusty. I have to be in my nighty shirt for bed and then say prayers!"

Dusty helped Charles into his nightclothes with difficulty since Charles was like a squirming Chinese noodle. "Charles. Charles!"

"Yes, my good fellow?" Charles sat up straight as an arrow as his shirt was removed and beamed at Dusty with as much dignity as she could muster.

Dusty saw, but kept mum. Nothing was uttered, Dusty kept to his task.

Charles knew Dusty's friendship was *nonpareil* and knew he would not comment. Dusty, in his silence, still couldn't prevent his mind from guilt, however, and what his wife might say.

"Shhhh, Dusty. It's *our* secret, okay? Nobody need know. Least of all *J-u-l-i-a*!"

Dusty was worried. "Oh, Charles. You need, you need to go to bed. Where is, is James? Why isn't he here, here with Jack?"

"Well, that's just it. Where *is* Jack? Jack doesn't *need* me." The depressive nature of rum hit her, and tears gushed forth in torrents. "Jack is about the most self-absorbed person in the whole, uh, whole, that thing! Dusty, you are such a good friend," Charles pawed at him wildly. "Please give—" Charles pointed across the room to finish his thought. "—bucket."

Dusty complied, and Charles continued heaving for over an hour. At one point, Dusty thought Charles mumbled something. "What, what, Charles? Come again?"

"Merchandise." Charles finished this bout with the bucket. She was exhausted and felt awful but managed, "*I* was merchandise, but I am *not* covetous. Yes."

"Do you need something?" Dusty asked, hoping for a reprieve to a more comfortable setting, even though he knew he would stay rooted to aid his friend. Charles finally managed to sleep. James did not return with Jack, so Dusty shouldered the daunting evening alone. He felt so helpless and wished he could mend little Charles's problems. Wild horses would never make him divulge Charles's secret: not for drinking too much for the first time, nor for whatever he was hiding from. Charles was living in a way that indicated extreme desperation. Dusty could not imagine what events Charles lived through to precipitate this fate. Still, he would never ask Charles about this night. In fact, he felt guilty just venturing into thinking of another soul's background.

Chapter 73

Miss Pomery was in the Hughlett's mercantile chatting with the missus. Pearl Ann had been shopping and noted the fabrics that had arrived.

"Why, Mrs. Hughlett, why didn't you tell me you got this dreamy bolt in?"

"Just got it today, dear. Come up from Manchester by wagon. Isn't it lovely?"

"I'll say! Miss Pomery, how do you like it?"

"It is beautiful, but a little too rich for a school teacher."

"Mrs. Hughlett, I'll take four yards of this fabric."

"What are you going to make out of it, Pearl Ann?"

"Don't know, but it's a must. Maybe some new dresses for the girls."

"I didn't know you had children!" Elizabeth said with amazement.

"Oh, I don't, love. Justice and I tried and tried. Just wasn't meant to be. No, I'd be making it for the lassies at the institution."

"Begging your pardon, Pearl Ann, what institution is that? Is it here, in town?"

"There is a lovely school run by Anglican sisters

about seven miles from here. Most of the girls are or-phans, but they get a few little ones from families down on their luck."

"*Minnie Pearl*! I thought you looked familiar! What a small world. How silly of me not to recognize you."

"Miss Pomery, my manners have taken flight, for which I deeply apologize. You must have supper with me tonight! I won't take no for an answer."

"I would love to—Oh, I have already made plans with Jack."

"Bring him. That man. I've been trying to get him and Charles over for a coon's age. I know Charles is out of town, but I'll see you and Jack at six pm, sharp. How grand!"

Elizabeth looked at a few items on display and Pearl Ann paid and left with her bundle. Once she was gone, Mrs. Hughlett apologized to Elizabeth, "Sorry about that, Elizabeth, Pearl Ann has a way of stopping everything. Let's get your things rung up."

"I know, she is quite a character. And I'm glad she came in. I enjoy doing things with Jack, but—"

"Oh?"

"Maybe I' just don't have the patience for men to-day. Jack and I have had some lovely times, but he's not the best at courting and making a woman feel...womanly? Pearl Ann will break up the monoto-ny."

"Oh, dear. Monotony."

"Maybe that is too strong a word. I think the world of him, really I do, but he just seems, sort of—"

"Boring?"

"No, no, not at all. More...more brotherly. Like he is just going through the motions."

Mrs. Hughlett closed the register and tidied the

package. "He has been quite the confirmed bachelor, Elizabeth. He's courted a lot of girls, but I don't think I can remember anything too serious." She handed the package to Elizabeth and trailed on. "Of course, Rachael and Prudence have been trying to get their hooks into him for years."

"How wicked of you to say."

"It's Liza Rutledge's own doing. She interferes with her daughters far too much, and now they are practically spinsters," Mrs. Hewlett spit succinctly. "Jack is a good man. There would be no harm come of a woman who marries him."

"Well, thank you, Mrs. Hughlett, for your help and conversation. I will remember your advice."

Chapter 74

The dining room in the Georgian manor was set with precision. Fine bone china, antique silverware, and beautiful long tapers set a tone that neither Jack nor Elizabeth were used to. Jack wore breeches, Wellington boots, and an ascot. His long-sleeved shirt, under the waistcoat and vest, was graciously cut and had ruffles at the cuffs. His boots had been newly polished, and had a bright shine. He had made an effort in his dress, as he used to when he would court many of the fine, young maidens about town.

Elizabeth wore her finest dress. It was *a la mode de Paris*, sporting short sleeves and the bodice cut fairly low, so as to show more skin. The fabric was finely woven cotton in white with pastel lilac. Silk ribbon accents were meticulously stitched on the sleeve cuffs, and bordering the neckline, and along the bottom hem. More of the ribbon wrapped around the waist and tied in a bow in the front. She wore long, white cotton gloves upon arrival, but removed them while dining. Her shoes were soft, white slippers with white satin ribbons that crisscrossed up and over the ankle to secure them in place.

Without any attempt to impress or humble her guests, Pearl Ann's elegance could not be concealed. She wore a simple gown of subdued gold silk. The bodice in the new, simple style, that gathered around the breast gently, was set apart from the skirt by a slim, black brocade ribbon of leaves and vines. The bottom hem sported brocade gold triangles that arose like the Alps from the base. Between each triangular alp was a floral motif, embroidered in gold thread. Pearl Ann's hair was gathered on top of her head and stayed in place with tortoise-shell combs. Each comb had a small inlaid scene of a bluebird singing on a tree branch. Her signature piece hung over her delicate collar bones on a black silk ribbon: displayed was the beautiful gold broach with an intricate gold filigree design. The brilliant, China-blue hue of the inlay trumpeted the exquisite art.

They had finished four courses and were waiting for the fifth. Elizabeth felt more at ease at this point of the evening, the formality of the event lessening with each glass of wine. "Pearl Ann, this evening with you is divine! Do you entertain often?"

"Not as often as we used to—Justice and me, that is."

"Elizabeth, Pearl Ann and Justice used to have the finest parties around. Folks would talk about what a wonderful time they had for months."

"You went to them, Jack?"

"Well, some. Many were formal affairs with founding leaders, war heroes, and dignitaries. I wouldn't have been comfortable in their surroundings if I had been invited to that kind of evening. If you will pardon me," Jack reached for the wine bottle and filled his glass, "would either of you care for more wine?"

"Yes, not a full glass, please, Jack. You know you

are the most gracious of men." Pearl Ann thought highly of Jack and did not care for him deriding his own background. "You would have done just fine in that crowd."

Elizabeth looked at them both with an expression that begged for more telling information.

"Elizabeth, you are too polite to ask, so I will tell you. *No.* Simply, no. Jack and I are just old friends. Nothing else."

Jack looked at both women with slight confusion. "Pearl Ann, of course, we are." To him, that statement came from out of the blue. "Why, what do you—oh! Elizabeth, no, I mean, yes. That's it exactly, we are just old friends!"

"Good old Jack! For such a smart man, a talented man, he's just plumb dim when it comes to women. Right, Jack?"

"Well, I don't think I'd say clueless, Pearl Ann. I've had my share of courting. Many a time I've had young ladies telling me—"

"That's okay, Jackie." Pearl Ann patted his hand and nodded at Elizabeth with a cunning grin. "You are simply delightful, dear, don't ever change. Elizabeth, keep your eye on this man, he can surprise you."

"I think you are right. For the record, Jack, I hope you stay friends with Pearl Ann for eons. She is a remarkable woman." Pearl Ann and Elizabeth clinked wine glasses.

"Why, thank you, dear. How kind of you."

Elizabeth had tried to navigate the conversation in a way that illuminated a little more background on Jack and Pearl Ann, but it was difficult without being blunt. Fortunately for her, Pearl Ann can sniff out and predict what anyone is thinking. Her grin seemed to say a lot. But did Elizabeth read it correctly? She wasn't sure, but she thought listening carefully was key. Pearl Ann did not mince words, nor did she throw out idle comments.

"You two women act as though you haven't recently met."

"Ah, see what I mean, Elizabeth? He does notice and deduce the proper conclusions! Good job, Jackie!"

Jack was delighted by the compliment but asked suspiciously, "Why do you say?"

"Because you hit the bull's eye. I've known Elizabeth since she was about nine years of age. Let's just say our paths did cross in a mutual setting."

The service brought the final courses of the meal, which everyone enjoyed. Pearl Ann was an exceptional hostess and relayed elaborate and interesting stories. The evening was long but felt entirely too short for Pearl Ann's guests.

"...so, we knew he was going to give us trouble. Justice pushed his chair back and stood up— all six foot three of him—he said, ever so sweetly, '*Excusez-moi, mais etre vous la Roger Killington célèbre qui a perfectionné la technique de la distillation de lait de sow pour une meilleure absorption des vitamines chez les porcelets?*' Excuse me, but aren't you the famous Roger Killington who perfected the technique of distilling sow's milk for higher absorption of vitamins in piglets?"

Elizabeth and Pearl Ann laughed and laughed at the story, but Jack did not speak French and so feigned a small laugh to try to keep with the women and the joke.

"Justice's comment came from so far south, it threw the man for a loop. He was delighted by the compliment even though he didn't understand a word of it. But it did make him back off from telling Justice he was mistaken. That just goes to show you, you can catch more flies with honey than with vinegar."

"How true that is! Do you still travel abroad much?"

"Can't say that I have. It's just not the same. Besides, I'd have to face my relatives without Justice there to buffer the difficult moments. No, I have plenty to do here in our own town, and that keeps me going."

"Do you have family here?"

"I had an aunt here, in New England. More accurately, down in Virginia. That is what made it possible for me to be raised here instead of in France." The two guests held still hoping for a little more of her interesting story, but Pearl Ann sat quietly. Politely, they waited, and she tossed out, "I write often to my relatives, you know. Family is important, of course. How else does one know one's history?" Pearl Ann touched her broach and sipped from her glass with a sly, knowing look on her face. She looked up again, smiled and said jovially, "This is my home. I have no need for the 'old country.'"

"We are so lucky. Not only do we get Pearl Ann, but we don't have to put up with those extremely rude distilled porkie-lets. I bet they taste just awful."

"Elizabeth, raise your glass in a toast, to Jack and the porkie-lets!"

Chapter 75

In the cold late night hours, two young girls were bundled warmly for an unexpected excursion through the dark, cobbled streets of Concord. They cut across corners and through front yards to speed transit. Finally reaching their destination, they scrambled up the large steps of the Georgian home and banged frantically on the massive front door. They entered the residence for just a few minutes. Emerging from the warmth of the home, the two girls began wending their way back to their origin but this time a third person, Pearl Ann, ran with them.

The trio arrived at the girls' home, entered, and removed their coats. In the dim lighting and warm room, the girls stood leaning over, trying to catch their breath. It was an exhilarating mission, and their haste with the skill of Nike brought Pearl Ann to help their mother. Blood chilling screams came from a back bedroom, and Pearl Ann went straight to Julia to help her.

"You girls need to go on back to bed, to bed. Pearl Ann has everything under control." Dusty was rattled and unnerved from the cacophony but managed to maintain his household.

"Pa, we wish to help!" Louisa Johansson said excitedly to her father.

"Yes, Papa, we are big now, and can do lots for Mama," her twin, Phoebe, added to her plea.

"You two, you two are very big—too, too big! But Mama will need you to get all the sleep you can, so that you can help with your baby brother tomorrow."

"Is it a brother or a sister? Is it here, yet?" Louisa was the leader of the two.

"Oh, I hope it's a girl, girl, girl!" Phoebe said with fervor, but she really didn't care what the baby was.

"No, not yet which means it's still a surprise for all of us. Now, skedaddle back to your bed!"

The twins went to their room as instructed, but it was far too exciting a night to sleep.

"Dusty, come in here. I need you to hold this while I get this little one free," Pearl Ann shouted from the other room.

Dusty hesitated but gathered the courage to go into the room, and see up close, the horrors of childbirth.

Chapter 76

Several days had passed since Charles came back from Graniteville. Her head hurt the first day back, and her feelings were bruised from her behavior. She slept long that first morning and was ill from the indiscretions of the previous evening. Jack and Mr. Hutchins didn't bother her and let her sleep. Charles hadn't had a sick day in eight years.

Later that morning, Jack and Charles were in the yard working together. Charles had seen very little of Jack since her return from the long Graniteville trip. She was happy to work with Jack again.

"It gets a little lonely, but it's not too bad. Mr. Hutchins can't afford to send us both on long journeys," Charles said.

Jack continued his work but did not reply to Charles.

"Did you get all the regular stuff delivered okay? I'm sorry I wasn't here to help." Charles stopped working and watched Jack puttering away in his own world. A few short steps brought her close to Jack. She reached out and touched the set chin with her gloved hand, directing it around so that she could look at it closely.

Jack made no counter-motion but answered the question, "Oh, sure. No problems at all."

"Looks like your face healed just fine where you got whipped by that rope. I can hardly see a bruise."

Both of their faces came close enough to feel the other's breath. Charles felt her heart inching its way skyward, backed up and suggested, "Do you want to go fishing this afternoon?"

Jack mirrored Charles's steps to maintain their proximity. "Nah, I can't." He looked up and wondered what strange, tugging force made him want to stay close to Charles. It made him exhilarated with a feeling he had never experienced. He pulled himself away and managed to derail the moment with, "Hey, Dusty's wife had twins the other night!"

Charles was happy for Dusty and Julia, but the wilted expression on her face did not reflect the feeling. "Are the babies healthy? Is Julia okay?"

"Oh, sure. Fat, healthy little things. Julia is already worried Dusty isn't getting enough to eat. She'll be up and cooking to fill him up before long. He always gets a little chunky when she's expecting, anyway. You'd think he was going to have the baby."

Charles was relieved by the report. "Twins again! What are their names?"

"Uh, S...S...B...B...Heck, I don't know. But Pearl Ann delivered them early, early in the morning."

Charles didn't really care about minor details, but spending time with Jack was paramount. "Oh. Well, we could do something else later tonight," she persisted.

Jack reacted strongly to the suggestion and almost yelled his response. "Not tonight! Elizabeth and I have something planned, Charles."

Charles was openly hurt and walked away from Jack. She went into the stable house.

Jack was mad at himself for his response and his behavior of pushing Charles aside and not spending time with him. He trailed Charles into the tack house.

Charles lay on his bunk, face down. He was not crying or whimpering.

"Look, Charles, I've been seeing this girl pretty steady. I made plans with her for this evening."

Charles did not move.

"I'm sorry if I made you angry. I didn't mean to yell. We could go fishing or something, tomo—no, I can't tomorrow. How about the day after tomorrow?"

"Fine."

"Great! And you can tell me the high points of your trip. You really haven't said much about it. Everything went fine, right?"

"Yes. Everything went fine. Leave me alone."

Chapter 77

The tall steeple jutted through the forested north-west part of town, and its bells chimed announcing the end of the evening service. The venerable church was a stately, French-Georgian design. The large double doors had columns on either side of them, rising to a pediment that crowned the main entry. Casement windows were along each wall, and three gables were on each side of the ridged roof. The wise architect kept the ceiling low for that of a public house so heat would stay to warm the congregation. This allowed for an upper floor for use as seen fit by the rector. Many people attended the early vespers service, not as many as its counterpart on Sunday, but it was still a crowd Father Hezekiah was proud of. While the bells still pealed, the good people began leaving the sanctuary.

"Jack, it's good to see you this evening," Mr. Hutchins noted.

"Yes, sir."

"I told Jack it wouldn't kill him to attend." Miss Pomery had an air of accomplishment in her voice. "Did you survive, Jack? Hearing the Word should motivate even you, Jack Harrison."

"Ah, it was fine. Words everyone should recall to keep 'em going."

"Were is our young Charles tonight? Is he still ailing?"

"Charles? I think he is okay." Jack had to consider his response after he answered Mr. Hutchins. Guilt laid heavily on his mind. "Why?"

"Charles hasn't missed a Wednesday service in, I don't know how long. I thought you knew, Jack."

"No, sir, I didn't. I'll be."

"You work side-by-side every day. How could you not know? Why is it so surprising to you?"

"I guess I don't know how he spends *all* of his spare time. I guess that's why he never went to the tavern with us on those nights." Jack was embarrassed from his ignorance of such common knowledge about his best friend. He mulled over the information as Charlotte Spruce approached Miss Pomery.

"Miss Pomery, Mother wants to invite you to tea tomorrow after school. She said I have to be the hostess."

"Of course, Charlotte, that will be nice. I'll come directly after I clean up the school room."

Charlotte hopped back to her mother.

"Jack, that's a terrible way to be a best friend. Don't you take any interest in Charles?" Elizabeth motioned for him to lean close to her so that she could whisper to him. "Jack, *I* think Charles is pretty special, don't you?"

Jack replied curtly, but in the same soft voice, "I don't think he's your type, Elizabeth."

"Oh, what 'type' suits Charles?"

"Well, not that I can judge for another, but I'd say someone with strong moral fiber, a good sense of humor, and outgoing, but not overshadowing. Pearl Ann, for example, is too loud for Charles."

"Why, Jack, I think you just described *me* to the letter!"

"No, I don't think so."

Elizabeth pointed out a family leaving the building. "Jack, look, over there." She nodded her head in the direction of the lingering Rutledge family.

"Yeah, so?"

"I heard you have spent a lot of time with Rachael and Prudence. Are *they* the right type for Charles?"

"No." His patience began to wear thin. "I think I need to excuse myself and see if Charles is sick." Jack was having a terrible night. Elizabeth regretted her evil taunting and saw that he was downcast.

"I'm sorry, Jack. I just heard—"

"What have you heard? No, no don't tell me. I don't want to know. Why do you ask me these personal questions? It's not proper!"

"Oh, Jack! You are right that it is none of my business who you have or have not courted, I'm sorry I brought it up." Elizabeth felt bad for needling Jack.

Pearl Ann caught her eye across the yard and started toward them. As she walked up, Elizabeth looked straight at the approaching woman. "I think I got the information I was looking for, though," she said coyly and looked back at Jack.

"Evening, you two. Will you be bringing Jack with you to have cakes?"

"Good evening, Pearl Ann. Lovely idea."

Jack squirmed a bit. "I need to check on Charles, Pearl Ann. I think he's coming down with something. He hasn't been quite himself lately."

"Suit yourself, but you can't dodge me forever. Elizabeth, ten minutes or so?" Elizabeth nodded, and

Pearl Ann began to leave. After about half a block, she turned around and yelled back to Jack, "Charles isn't sick, Jack! But you *should* go check on him." She continued for a few more steps, turned, and added, "It would be best to take Miss Pomery with you."

"What did she mean by that, Elizabeth? If he's not sick—how would Pearl Ann know if he is or isn't sick? Why would I need your help to check on my best friend? Elizabeth, I think this has been the most confusing night of my life. I knew I stayed away from church for a reason."

Chapter 78

Twilight approached, and the temperature would drop quickly once the sun had gone down. It was a time when having a lantern in reach was a wise plan. Although it was an early hour in the evening, Charles was fast asleep on her bed. Her sleep was stormy and did not offer her restful escape.

Jack really did want to check on Charles after the service. He didn't take the advice, but walked Elizabeth the short distance to Pearl Ann's, then headed in the direction of the dry goods store, alone, toward Charles's stable house.

The quiet, cool evening was enjoyable. Jack didn't spend much of his leisure time in solitude. He preferred being with others, so when he was alone, the experience left an impression on him. While he walked along the boardwalk, he listened to his feet land on the hollow wood planks. The deep sound was pleasing and familiar, yet at the same time lonely. It reminded him that he was alone in the streets of this large town. He didn't regret this thought, but it steered his mind toward philosophical thoughts of existence and what was to become of any of us.

The affinity of others might present itself *because*

of these thoughts. They were deep, conundrums that men had considered through the ages, but had failed to provide answers for in as many years. Thinking in this way usually just made his head hurt. Jack had no doubts that he was a good American with exemplary work ethics. He enjoyed life and felt that all of the riches one discovered on the path through life was the bounteous fruit that had been made available because one had lived by strong moral and ethical tenets.

His wandering thoughts sped his walk through town and brought him quickly to the livery yard and Charles's home. It was a relief to him now that his thoughts centered only on Charles. The horses smelled a person approach, recognized Jack's scent, and greeted him with optimistic snorts and stamps, in hopes that he might offer them a treat. He said nothing to them and continued to Charles's door.

Jack entered the tack house. The room was pitch black when the door shut, so Jack stumbled around to find a candle. Charles lay undisturbed from Jack's noisy clatter. Jack tried to rouse him by shaking him. Charles awakened with a start and was fearful of the ominous shadow looming over him in the flickering, dim candlelight.

"Easy, easy, Charles. It's just me, Jack." Jack picked up the blanket at the end of the bed and unfurled it. "Here, you need this. It is cold in this room. Are you feeling all right? You didn't go to church like you usually do."

Charles was dumbfounded and stared at Jack.

"Yes. I know you usually go to the vesper service midweek."

"How—how did you find out?"

"Well, it's not a secret, is it? I mean, it's a public place and all."

"I thought you would think I was 'girly' going to another service each week."

"You're right, I haven't had much need for prayer and stuff. Makes no difference to me if you go. Fact is, I probably wouldn't have gone if Elizabeth hadn't made me."

"Elizabeth."

"Yeah, don't you like her? You're my best friend, I want you to like her. She's kind of special to me."

"You saw a lot of her when I was gone on the long hauls?"

"Well, yes. My best friend wasn't around. I walked her home tonight, in fact. Hey, you're not jealous are you?" Elizabeth's comments landed on him like a cannon ball. "You haven't taken a fancy to her, have you?"

Charles was silent and rolled so that she was facing the wall.

"Come on, Charles, don't do this to me." Jack bent over Charles and pulled on him. "A woman is no excuse for two good friends, like us...."

The two wrestled until they faced each other. Jack saw streaks glistening down Charles's face. "Oh, come on now. Come on, sit up. What is this?" He pulled Charles to a sitting position and held him up. Charles burrowed his face into Jack's shoulder, and Jack wrapped his arms tightly around him, holding him securely. The flickering candle reflected upon Jack's tanned face. It showed worry with a perplexed expression. He caressed Charles' back and ran his hands through his soft, brunette hair.

Chapter 79

Entertainment, fellowship, as well as food and drink, were all enjoyed at the local tavern. Jack, Dusty, Mr. Hutchins, Mr. Hughlett, and James sat at a large table in the local tavern and chatted. Sheriff Simon Bernard approached.

"Afternoon, gents."

Mr. Hutchins waved. "Simon! Quick boys, get him a seat."

The men pulled a chair over and adjusted their own seats to accommodate him.

"You boys heard of the big doin's tomorrow night?"

"You mean about the match?" James said in anticipation.

"That's the one. Any of you plan on partaking?"

"Yes, I think I might have a round with The 'Vice,' The 'Vice.'"

"If anyone has a chance, it's Dusty."

All the men concurred.

"Well, I'm pretty strong, pretty strong—"

"Pretty strong? Strongest man in Concord. Lifting that granite every day, I'd say that gives you an advantage."

"For strength, yes. But the 'Vice' is a professional: he has strategy none of us has."

"I think my money is on Dusty. Imagine having the purse of ten real silver dollars."

"Thanks, James. But, Simon is right. I have no training, no training."

"What training do you need? Just sit on him."

"He can duck out of the way faster than I can blink, can blink. I'm not too wiry. Besides, Julia doesn't want her husband to come home all bloody. She has enough to, enough to clean up with a second set of twins."

"Maybe I'll try. I am wiry and fast." Jack was in earnest, but everyone knew he was not a fighter.

"And one punch, one punch from the 'Vice' and it's lights out."

"So, I won't give him the chance to catch me."

Sheriff Bernard watched over his community like a mother duck, and he didn't like any of his flock to stray into the wolf's mouth. "Well, I don't condone any of it. These shows that come through here are good, but not when they are going to make mincemeat of my towns-folk and friends. Silver dollars or not."

Artie, the barkeep, approached the table and set a drink down for Sheriff Bernard. "Ye will try to milk a pigeon, lads. Aye, a pigeon. These traveling men go through towns and perform every night. Not only do they have the strength and bulk to take on ten goodly sized men, they have savvy. Aye!" Artie didn't feel his words had the right punch. He thought his advice fell on deaf ears and tried to be more inspiring. "Ye'll not take them down, men. They are snakes lying in the grass, peaceful as the mornin' dew, and when the chal-lenger steps in with all of the confidence of a new lamb frolicking in the warm sun abeaming on the fresh meadow hay, he readies you for an eternity box. Aye! A good run is better than a good stand. That's what I say."

Mr. Hutchins nodded. "Artie's advice is sage. To wit, one good punch will mean I'm out of a hand for a few days while he heals. Stay out of it, Jack. Not your league." He did not want to see anyone hurt, but his slant from a business perspective might offer a more absorbable reason for Jack not to fight.

All the men enjoyed good entertainment, but the elder gents saw the impending slaughter of one of these strong, local boys in a futile attempt for glory.

Chapter 80

The shining sun immersed the earth with golden rays, making it irresistible not to walk the longest route on your path. Jack walked with Miss Pomery through the Commons on such a day, enjoying their time together.

Jack looked at Elizabeth's beautiful auburn hair sparkling in the sunlight. He took her hand that was elegantly holding onto his arm and traced her fingers with his. He stopped walking and put his face up to hers. Elizabeth's heart pounded. They kissed slowly and enjoyed the pleasure. Elizabeth's eyes closed to a sliver and drank in the moment. Jack reached up to her face with a more determined grip, and she pushed him with the slightest amount of force. He understood, relaxed, and looked at her with a question.

"Jack, I want to tell you a bit about me." She paused to make sure Jack was listening. "I was raised in an orphanage. My parents died when I was very young."

"I'm sorry to hear that." He took her hand and held it tightly, bringing it to his lips, and brushed it with a gentle kiss.

"When I was about six or seven, I can't remember

what age I was, a girl was brought in to live with us. She became my best friend and confidant. I loved her very much." Jack was listening carefully to the story. Elizabeth continued, "Something terrible happened to her, and she ran away. The sisters in charge never found her,.I haven't seen her since. I miss her. My friend wrote to me after a few weeks of leaving the orphanage, and she told me she was fine but never told me where she was. Letters came for about six months, then they stopped. Life moved on, I was trained, and then I left the orphanage to become a teacher."

"Very sad. So, what do you think has happened to her? Do you think she popped a spring or something? I mean, whatever horrible thing happened to her could have made her...you know, maybe *distracted*."

"I don't know. The letters came from Concord, so when the school here became available, I applied."

Jack was half listening and half ogling his beautiful girlfriend. She removed his exploring hand.

"So you think she's here, in Concord," he asked.

"I thought so. I was offered the Concord school as I wished." She paused a moment, leaving Jack hanging.

"So, Elizabeth? You can't stop the story there. You are here now—" He would have liked to take her into the woods, but could see that he was not going to have success prising her mind from her quest.

"I'm sorry, I have felt like my search has been in vain." She paused a moment and fought back a tear. "It has been so long now. People move to other towns for other opportunities. It seems incredible that I could hope to find her. She may not even be alive." Tears pushed their way down Elizabeth's cheeks. She had been so strong, and in a few simple words, her pride had melted publicly. She turned away from Jack and dabbed her face with a neat, embroidered handkerchief.

"What's your friend's name?" Jack tried to sound confident. Crying women made him uncomfortable.

"I'm sure she took an alias when she ran away. She did not wish to be discovered."

"This is a big town, Elizabeth. She could still be here. Maybe your paths will never cross." They sat together on a park bench. "What's her name? I know a fair few women in the area." Jack looked away from Elizabeth and rolled his eyes. *God help me! I am such an idiot! Did she notice?* Jack continued, using his most comforting voice. "Maybe I have crossed paths with her. I deliver all over the county."

"Well, I *had* given up on her. So many years have passed, she might not even be living now. But then I met your driver."

"Charles?"

"Yes. He looked familiar, but I just thought I'd seen him drop off goods, or maybe I'd seen him around town."

"What about him? What does he have to do with your friend?" Jack was agitated with her comment. Charles seemed to always pop up in Elizabeth's conversations with no logical reason other than to badger him.

She saw his dander rise, took his hand, and caressed it. "It wasn't until you picked me up from school that one day that I connected things."

"What things? What does Charles have to do with anything?" Frustration rose, and Elizabeth was afraid Jack would get up and walk away. "Charles is…Charles is just Charles!" he demanded.

"That little girl we walked home…"

Jack's nerves were becoming raw from the way she meted information, and it seemed that confusion always resulted when Elizabeth was with him.

"The Spruce girl? Elizabeth you have lost me completely." Jack was at the end of his rope. He nearly yelled at her, "I wish you would just explain in plain English!"

"Yes. This is plain. Jack, that little girl was adopted."

"Yes, she was. I remember the celebration. No offense, but I think she's a little too young to be your friend."

"Not my friend, silly, her daughter!"

"Her daughter? I think you have been working too much. Women are supposed to keep house and raise children. This job is a strain on you." Elizabeth stared at Jack with an icy beam. Her frigid message melted through him. "Okay, Elizabeth, just how could she be your friend's daughter?"

Elizabeth stood. "Never mind, Jack." She started walking away.

"Elizabeth, please don't go. Come back and explain it to me. I'm sorry my head is so thick."

She turned toward Jack with her arms crossed. "I miss my friend. I just want to find her." She wiped an eye with her handkerchief. Jack went to her and led her back to the bench. They sat silently for a few minutes until Elizabeth composed herself.

"I didn't understand why she ran away. I was so saddened by it. I was sure it was my fault, even though she wrote to me." A few sobs eked out, but she maintained her demeanor. "But as I grew older and wiser to the ways of the world, the pieces started to fall into place."

"So, why do you think Charlotte Spruce could be her daughter? How would that happen?"

Wiping her eyes again, she chuckled. "You think your head is thick, Jack!" Jack remained silent. A deep breath helped her elaborate. "I can only imagine what happened to her. But before she ran away, she was extremely tired and not her usual cheery self. She got fat, too. I have no idea how...or why...but she was with child."

"Oh. But I still don't see the connection, why Char—"

"Jack, my best friend's name was Charlotte LeSage. Charlotte Spruce looks just like her at that age."

"Wow. I don't see it. Oh, but I don't know what your girlfriend looked like for compar..." Jack was flustered and could hardly put a complete sentence together. "What about Charles—he's not a piece of your puzzle. He's a darn good hand, that's all."

"What is Charles's full name?"

"Charles John Livery."

"Charlotte's dad's name was John. Do you see how the names fit?"

"No, there is no connection. These are just the wiles of a woman."

Elizabeth sighed at Jack's narrow mind. She handed him the letters she had in her bag.

"These are the letters she wrote to me, and, no, she doesn't sound raving mad." Elizabeth waited patiently for Jack to read through the papers. She sighed. She felt so close to achieving her goal, but it seemed like such a steep price as it revealed the depth of Jack's personality.

"I have been working with Charles longer than the Spruce girl has been in Concord. Charles is a great worker. And strong. Never complains. He would never shirk responsibility. I can't agree with your theory."

They sit in silence for a few minutes. Jack's perfect afternoon has eroded completely.

"But why?" Jack was agitated. "Why would he live like that? So near the child? He is kind of small…Maybe, it's just a coincidence. Ah! I bet Charles could be a brother or a cousin—a distant cousin. Elizabeth, I think you are reaching a little too far. I know you want to find her and—I know my best friend. He's a great hand. Normal folk just don't do that kind of thing, Elizabeth. It's not a respectable way to live."

"Charles wouldn't be a brother. Charlotte didn't have any siblings, and she would live to survive because she didn't have any other choice."

Chapter 81

Charles was at Jack's house helping fix a coop. They were running out of daylight, but the repairs were nearly complete.

"Hand me one more peg. That'll fix it. Now, let's go get those planks." Jack and Charles brought some planks from the front of the house. They affixed the crude boards to reinforce the coop. "That oughta do it. Those birds are livin' in style now. You're a great carpenter, Charles."

"Hopefully the wolves and fox can't get to them now."

"Much obliged for your help tonight, Charles. Couldn't have done it by myself. Can I offer you something to eat?"

They walked into the small, one-room home together.

"I can make us something if you're hungry. Do you have anything?"

"Oh, I think there's some hard cooked eggs and some rye bread. But you're helping me, Charles, let me fix it." Jack fixed some food. They sat at the small table and ate together. "It's good to have you back, Charles. Mr. Hutchins has sent you on too many long trips. We should go out tonight and celebrate your return."

Charles sat quietly, as usual.

Jack grinned. "They say it is worth ten silver dollars to the guy that can go five rounds with the 'Vice' later tonight. I bet I could do it."

"If you don't wish to use teeth anymore," Charles commented succinctly.

"Naa, you just gotta be faster than them. You know, duck and jump around. Be wiry."

"Uh, uh."

"I've eaten enough. You ready to go?"

"You're not *really* going against him, are you? The 'Vice'?"

"Sure! It's easy money! Besides, I have plans for that purse. I'll be okay. I'm quick. Come on, let's go."

ॐॐ

The boxing ring has been set up on a dirt lot, away from the center of town. There was a large showing of citizens gathered to watch the fight. Jack was in the ring about to go against the Vice. Jack had his eyes set on his opponent and showed no fear of battle. Men cheered him on.

The Vice strutted around, showing off his muscles and fearless expression. Charles turned away and did not cheer. The official hit a small bell he carried with a metal hammer. The crowd cheered and sighed with the regularity of a pendulum on a short chain. The entire match lasted nearly one full minute. The standing man was declared the winner.

Charles, Pearl Ann, and Elizabeth Pomery helped Jack into his kitchen. Elizabeth retrieved the kettle to fill. "I'll put some water on. Do you have any tincture?"

"In the—*ouch*—cupboard. There should be a clean

rag in there, too. Dang! I coulda had him."

"If you had had him any better, there wouldn't have been much of you to bring back home." Charles was glad it was over and that it was a quick end.

"Well, you are some kind of fool, Jack Harrington, that's all I have to say." Pearl Ann felt the need to add a little salt to his injuries. "Just what was going through your head when you decided a thorough pummeling would do you good?"

"I thought I could do it, and I did. I got a few good punches in." He shifted positions in his seat and moaned from pain. "But you know, sometimes you just have to do things."

"Staying conscious would have been beneficial, and a nice touch," Elizabeth noted as she cleaned the blood from his face.

Pearl Ann whispered to Charles, "I think it's time you tell him, Charlotte. Don't you?"

Charles looked at Pearl Ann with eyes open as big as silver dollars. It was Minnie Pearl who knew best. Charles was relieved that she held Pearl Ann in her confidence, but was still afraid.

Jack was too busy nursing his pride and open wounds to notice this other conversation and continued his defense. "Thank you, Miss Pomery, for your vote of confidence! I don't know why we men do stuff like that. Just makes you feel like a man, I guess. You know what I mean don't you, Charles?"

"No, I guess I don't."

"Come on, you know what I mean—sometimes you just gotta get some dirt under your nails, rub some blisters. Makes you feel like you're alive and part of the living."

"I guess," Charles said without conviction. Pearl Ann handed him a clean, damp cloth and put her hand out to take Elizabeth's blood-soaked one. Charles looked at the cloth and Pearl Ann said to him softly, "You know the rewards of hard work and being true, Charles. I know you do. *Think*."

"Don't you ever feel that way?" Jack rattled on. "You must! Of course, you do. As hard as you work each day, you know what I mean. You torment me, and I deserve the bitter quaff, I know, my friend."

Charles wasn't sure what Pearl Ann was trying to say, but she removed her thick work gloves, picked up the clean cloth, and took a deep breath. Pearl Ann smiled at Elizabeth and nodded her head. Charles stepped very close to Jack. She began dabbing at Jack's facial wounds. She spoke to him in the low, soft voice she used to comfort animals, "No, I don't think so. I don't like to see any kind of pain or suffering."

A moment of silence was filled with a chair sliding and then banging on the wooden floor. Pearl Ann shifted her skirt and plopped down on the chair.

Jack was vexed by Charles's behavior. "You are a kind soul, Charles. I guess you *wouldn't* like anything like that. You are a strong, young man that is unusually…gentle."

Elizabeth followed suit, a little quieter, by sitting down in another chair.

"Zut, alors! Soyez courageux!" Pearl Ann was about to jump out of her skin in anticipation. Charles looked at her with a glare of frustration that Pearl Ann translated as, "I know! I will, Pearl Ann."

Charles helped Jack off with his shirt, and pants while Elizabeth and Pearl Ann looked away. Charles helped him into bed and dabbed his wounds a little more. Jack winced from the sting of the tincture that had been soaked onto the cloth.

"That should do you until morning. The bleeding

has stopped. I'll clean—*you* should clean up again, using this medicine in the morning." Charles faltered. "*Wow, vous l'êtes certainement demain va en souffrir.* Wow, are you going to hurt tomorrow."

"My head hurts so much, it sounds like someone is speaking French. Pearl Ann, you know I can't understand that language. Hey, Charles, will you get me that bottle of whisky from off that shelf?"

Pearl Ann retrieved the bottle of whisky.

"*Whiskey, il sera plus facile, mais il vaut mieux lui dire avant qu'il ne boit trop,*" Pearl Ann warned Charles as she handed him the bottle.

Elizabeth looked at him slyly and raised her eyebrow, "Jack that means, 'Whiskey will make it easier, but you better tell him before he drinks too much.'"

"Oh. Thank you. Elizabeth, I suppose you speak French, too?"

Charles handed him the bottle before Elizabeth could answer. "Pearl Ann is right, of course. I don't think this will heal you, but I suppose you might feel a bit better from it," she said while making a face at the thought of drinking the vile liquid.

Elizabeth jumped in with her answer. "No, Jack, I only know a few phrases from what fur traders and trappers would use."

Jack hurt, and he was tired. He took a long draught of whiskey. It was obvious that the drink began calming and numbing him immediately. "Pour yourself a glass, everyone, enjoy a dram… Oh, that's right, Charles, you don't partake in the rye." He belched loudly and hiccupped. "How come?"

Charles thought of that night she drank too much rum. The unpleasant night was branded into her memory. She made an ugly face. "I don't know, Jack. I guess I just don't like it."

The world was looking blurry to Jack as he imbibed half of the bottle of whiskey. Pearl Ann, Elizabeth, and Charles sat at Jack's table and talked. They all felt better staying with Jack tonight. His lapse of judgement was already on another ill-thought-out fight—this time it was going to be with spirits.

"I want to thank you. Ahem! I said, I want to thank you."

"Whom do you wish to thank, Jackie?" Pearl Ann threw her question across the room to the man lying on his bed that was now gloriously besotted.

"Charles! Come over here, my bosom buddy!"

Charles arose from his seat and walked across the room.

"You don't need to thank me. Please, don't thank me. That liquor should be making you feel less now. Let me have the bottle."

"Yep. I'm feeling a lot better now." Jack tried to sit up and then stand. He slipped, defeated, back onto the bed.

"Stay down, slugger."

"Don't go away, Charles!" Jack juggled the air to bring Charles to him. "The night is young. We have a lot to discuss, you and I. You know, Charles…"

"What is it, Jack?"

"You are so kind to me. Cleaning up my bloody face, bringing me home—if you weren't a man, I think I'd be in love with you."

"Okay, I think you are done for the night, Jack." Fear trickled through Charles. She stepped away from the bed. "I better go home now."

Pearl Ann glared at Charles and swore something under her breath. "Did you hear what Jack said, Charles? Everything is okay," she said, pushing at Charles a little more.

"Honestly, Pearl Ann, Jack is impossible!" Elizabeth stated exasperatedly.

"No, no! Don't take it the wrong way! Charles, I—I just haven't had anyone take care of me like this in a long time. You know, Dusty and James—they're the best mates a man ever had. But they're not like you. You...well, I feel like I can tell you anything and you wouldn't ever laugh at me, or judge me or nothin'. I guess I just trust you. That's it! Trust. I guess you're about the best friend a man ever had. Come and give me a hug, pal!"

Charles stooped over and hugged Jack, who immediately pulled Charles onto the bed and started crying over him. "Yes, sir, you are the best friend a guy ever had. Yep, nobody ever had as good a friend."

"Jack, really—" Jack and Charles struggled and ended up face to face, looking into each other's eyes. "Trust."

Charles had tears streaming down her face. She looked up at the women at the table. They both nodded to encourage her.

"Yeah." Jack was sloshed.

Charles tried to stand, but Jack held onto her. "Let me go, Jack."

"Stay with me awhile longer, please, Charles?"

Charles readjusted the way she was sitting so it was more comfortable.

"Have you ever had a woman?" Jack continued

"What? How do you mean, Jack? Pearl Ann, Elizabeth!" Charles desperately pointed to the two women at the table, as if she were identifying criminals and redirecting blame.

"You know—*courted* a girl."

All formal rules of etiquette floated away with the pint of whiskey.

"I'm not—well—"

Jack interrupted before Charles could relay a proper answer. "I know you're not comfortable. You're just too shy. See, too shy!" Jack reiterated toward Elizabeth just to make sure she heard. He turned back to Charles and continued. "I guess I am too. In all the courtin' I've done, I can say no one has really grabbed hold of me, you know, so that I felt connected to them in some way."

Elizabeth turned to them with a hurt look. "That's pretty philosophical from a man who's had his brains bashed around and is now working on pickling them."

"Crazy. Plumb crazy."

"Yes. You have not made honorable choices today."

"All of it! It just don't make no sense."

"Well, *you* are not making sense. I think you've had enough whisky, Jack," Elizabeth said hotly. Her ego was bruised from Jack's words. She looked at Charles, small and scared like a trapped animal, and it helped her keep perspective.

Jack began singing. "Oh, the whisky speaks, and we all go to drink…Ugh, my head is really throbbing."

"Jack, do you *really* trust me?" Charles attempted.

"Yup. Loyal as the day is long. Charles, I'd trust you with my best horse—oh! That's right," Jack was giggly and amused with himself, "I do!"

"Pearl Ann, take this bottle. He's pickled." Charles grabbed the bottle from Jack, who didn't fight the assault. Charles looked at the glass bottle before handing it to Pearl Ann.

Bouteille. Charles thought. The bottle was familiar. She gave Pearl Ann a confused look and felt the curves of the whiskey bottle.

"Vous vous souvenez, quand vous étiez une petite

fille. Je sais que votre père vous a raconté des histoires. Il aimait à leur dire à moi, aussi! You remember, when you were a little girl. I know your father told you stories. He loved to tell them to me, too." Pearl Ann could only guess at what was going through Charles's mind, but she knew Charles remembered something that had been dredged up tonight. She smiled.

Jack had been still and oblivious to this moment of revelation. He popped like a cork and shouted startlingly, "Where are you from, Charles?"

"Virginia."

"That's right, Virginia. That's pretty far south of these parts. How'd you end up in New Hampshire?" He offers his own answer, "It was a girl, I bet. No, no—family. Pass me a drink."

Pearl Ann handed a shot to Charles and the empty bottle back to Jack.

"Definitely not family, well, not really." Charles considered the small glass, sniffed the foul smell, then shot it back.

Jack tried to get another drop from the empty bottle. He looked around the room and then yelled, "Then it was a woman! I knew it! Always a woman!"

"No. Not a woman."

"What do you mean, not family really? You got any family? Brothers, sisters?"

"I guess you could say I had a sister."

"Ah! I knew it! I knew you had a sister. What's her name?"

"Elizabeth."

"Elizabeth—that's just beautiful. Hey, that's your name, too!" Jack pointed to Elizabeth. "Very English. Genteel. Younger or older?"

"We're the same age."

"Wow! Twins! That is fantastic! Just like Dusty's kids."

"No. Not twins."

"Oh…" Mockingly, Jack mumbled, "Doesn't have a sister or a brother but now—I said—I—give me another drink!"

Elizabeth handed Jack a cup of water.

"She's right, drink the water. Not only are you going to hurt all over tomorrow, but you're going to make yourself sick, to boot."

"So, where is she?"

"Who? Elizabeth?"

"Yes."

"I hadn't seen her in a long time—"

"Can't she write? Or can't you read? Oh, my gosh! She died in some tragic event. Oh, Elizabeth, Elizabeth!" Jack roared, lamenting the thought.

"Quiet down, you ninny. Listen," Pearl Ann sais. She had waited for this testimony and didn't want to miss a word.

Charles continued. "She's still living and quite well. I used to write to her, but I never let her know my whereabouts so she could never write back." Elizabeth and Charles looked at each other across the room. "I regret that, and I'm sorry."

"Well, I'll be. Ain't that the darnedest thing?" Jack was looking through Charles, but not at him. "If I look at you like this, I can see three of you, and your hair is really big!"

Charles had had enough of this stressful evening. She set her glass on the table, picked up Jack's clothes, and laid them on the back of a chair.

Pearl Ann was disgusted with Jack. "Jack, sometimes I wonder just how hard a head you have on your shoulders."

"Oh, yeah but you know what I mean…Sometimes you just gotta get some dirt under your nails, rub some blisters. Makes you feel like you're alive and part of the living."

"You're starting to repeat yourself, Jack, and I don't think having your head split open, by choice, is what Pearl Ann meant. It is, however, a good point," Elizabeth did not have firsthand experience with someone who had become so drunk.

"Charles understands, don't you, Charles?"

"I guess. If—if you are hiding something."

"Don't you ever feel that way? You must. As hard as you work each day—"

"I don't like to see any kind of pain or suffering, remember, Jack?" Charles looked at Pearl Ann and Elizabeth. The whiskey, as bad as it tasted, ran through her. Its sedative effect was making her tired and had relaxed her. She closed her eyes and listened as Jack's speech tumbled around in his head.

"I had some plans for those ten coins."

"You didn't fight for the money, Jack."

"Oh, sure I did, Elizabeth! It would have made a great start to married life."

"I agree, but I think you fought because you are lost, Jack. You know the way *now*."

Pearl Ann tossed into the ring with excitement, "Yes, finally! Elizabeth, good. She needs your help."

Charles got up quickly, as if the two women poked her and stood by the scuttled Jack.

"You have a great start anyway: you are strong, loving, a good worker."

"I wanted to give my wife more—"

"Yes, I understand, but what you still don't understand is that your *wife* is what you are lost about. But you are going to be fine, you have more than enough to offer. She will be more than comfortable. She loves you deeply."

"What do you mean, *she*? What wife? But, I was going to…I haven't asked for a wife. Who loves me deeply? Hey, whoa! I didn't get married! Are you tippling, Elizabeth, a little?"

"You were going to ask me. I know, and I'm flattered, but I don't love you—not as a wife, more like a sister."

"Beat up, bleeding, and now rejected—and in front of all of you."

"Buck up, lad, it's not as bad as it seems. Pete's sake, man, open those swollen eyes of yourn!" Pearl Ann looked straight at Charles. "*Gwennagwir,* my dear. *Gwennagwir.*"

Charles bent down to look into Jack's blackened eyes. She reached for his face, gently directed it to her, and kissed him. Jack kissed back and raised his hands slowly into the air. He put his hands on the soft, smooth hands that gripped his face and sat back. "It is okay, Jack," Charles said. "I love you."

Jack continued his light grip and looked at Elizabeth and Pearl Ann. They smiled back. Charles's tear streaked face smiled, and she began to laugh.

Elizabeth chuckled and with tears streaming down her face said, "Jack, my best friend that I lost so long ago, Charlotte—"

"Charlotte?" Jack looked into Charles's eyes, caressed her face, and kissed her again.

"*Oui, Jaques. Ce moi.*"

"Jack, you've known all along. Admit it," Pearl Ann said. "You've played this silly life for over eight long years. And sweet Charlotte—"

"I guess I couldn't admit it. I was so afraid. Afraid. If Pearl Ann and Elizabeth hadn't been here and nudged me into admitting everything, I would have run. Again. I have been so scared. Oh, Elizabeth!" The two girls embraced with tears of joy.

Elizabeth's face shined with the spray of her own tears of joy. "It's over, now, Charlotte. We are all safe and can stop living in lies. You are safe. *Safe*."

"Jack, I love you so much! *Je t'aime beaucoup!*"

"You were really jealous of Elizabeth, weren't you?"

"No, just the idea. Besides, nothing good would have come from scratching my oldest friend's eyes out."

All four laughed.

The tension in the room had dissipated. The three women cooed and congratulated each other and Jack, pleased with the night, in spite of the fog of pain and liquor, managed to lobby, "The boys are never going to let this roll off."

"No, no, Jack. They won't tear you down. They think you're the greatest. So do I." Charlotte and Jack became lost, looking into each other's eyes. Eyes that had faithfully done the hard work of surviving and were now rewarded with a love that glowed beyond the mortal realm.

"Miss Pomery, I think you and I need to go home. Jack has Charlotte to look after him, and you and I have things to do."

"What things, Pearl Ann? I haven't any plans, I just lost my boyfriend."

Pearl Ann smiled at Jack and Charlotte with a huge grin. "Why, planning the best wedding of the century, what else?"

Notes

Fluyt: a Dutch-made vessel from the Golden Age of Sail, with multiple decks and usually three square-rigged masts, usually used for merchant purposes. It had a pear shape and shallow draft which allowed the vessel to bring cargo in and out of ports and down rivers that other vessels could not reach

Mishupeshu: Algonquin word for water panther

Georges's lament, page 128: written in French but should be in Breton. "Oh, I should be with little John! What if he is killed? Anne will not cope with death."

Rose Bertin: the first "fashion designer" to become a celebrity in her own right. She is widely credited with having brought fashion and haute couture to the forefront of popular culture. Notable clients: queens of Spain, Sweden and Portugal, Grand-Duchess Maria-Fёdorovna of Russia and, most famously, Marie Antoinette.

Squamsauke (also Squamscot): a spirited young horse Jack works with when Charles is introduced to him. The word is a tribe of the Pennacook Confederacy, which inhabited the Merrimack River valley of southern and central New Hampshire

Mi'kmaq: one of the horses pulling Charles's wagon on his first solo trip. The term refers to a First Nations people indigenous to Canada's Maritime Provinces and the Gaspé Peninsula of Quebec. (*First Nations* in Canada is the same as *Native American* to the US).

China blue or Jingtai blue: Pearl Ann's broach is cloisonné or glass enamel. The color was developed during the Ming Dynasty.

About the Author

K K Willey lives in the Southern San Joaquin Valley of California. Two daughters and one son are her *raison d'être*, but cats, gardening and music add to the balance of her universe. When she is not daydreaming about how life may have been during some other colorful era, she is focused on spreading the love of music as a junior high school band director.

www.ingramcontent.com/pod-product-compliance
Lightning Source LLC
Chambersburg PA
CBHW070220260626
47160CB00002B/619